the daughters

the daughters

JOANNA PHILBIN

poppy

LITTLE, BROWN AND COMPANY
New York   Boston

Poppy

Hachette Book Group
237 Park Avenue, New York, NY 10017
For more of your favorite series, go to www.pickapoppy.com

Poppy is an imprint of Little, Brown and Company.
The Poppy name and logo are trademarks of Hachette Book Group, Inc.

First Edition: May 2010

Library of Congress Cataloging-in-Publication Data

Philbin, Joanna.
    The daughters / by Joanna Philbin. — 1st ed.
        p. cm.
    "Poppy."
    Summary: In New York City, three fourteen-year-old best friends who are all daughters of celebrities watch out for each other as they try to strike a balance between ordinary high school events, such as finding a date for the homecoming dance, and family functions like walking the red carpet with their famous parents.
    ISBN 978-0-316-04900-9
    [1. Fame—Fiction.   2. Wealth—Fiction.   3. Friendship—Fiction.
4. Models (Persons)—Fiction.   5. High schools—Fiction.   6. Schools—
Fiction.   7. New York (N.Y.)—Fiction.]   I. Title.
    PZ7.P515Dau 2010
    [Fic]—dc22

                                                                    2009045621

10 9 8 7 6 5 4 3

RRD-C

Book design by Tracy Shaw

Printed in the United States of America

To my parents

For everything

We,
the daughters,

have formed the following rules and guidelines for optimum happiness and drama-free living:

1. Never read tabloids or surf the celebrity gossip sites. But if you have to, try not to look at the stuff about your parents.

2. All friends are good, but only another Daughter knows what your life is really like. Bond with as many as possible.

3. Friends are always more important than guys. *Always.*

4. Be nice to everyone, and if people *still* say you're conceited, then just let it go.

5. If you need to discuss parental drama, only do so with another Daughter. (See rule #2.)

6. Never talk to the press about your parents. Especially when they're hanging out in front of your house and yelling at you to say stuff.

7. Always date a guy at least a month before taking him to a red-carpet event. Same goes for taking him on your plane, bringing him on tour, etc.

8. If you see a Daughter being criticized on a blog, always write a post sticking up for her, even if you don't know her.

9. When meeting new people, only give them one name—your first one.

10. You are not your parents, and your parents aren't you. No matter how well-known—or mortifying—they are.

chapter 1

"Katia!"

"Katia!"

"Over here!"

"Over here!"

Lizzie Summers stood where she usually did when she was out with her mother — off to the side, hidden in the crowd, safely out of frame — and watched the world's most famous supermodel drive the paparazzi crazy.

"Katia!"

"Over here!"

With her shoulders thrown back, her back slightly arched, and one manicured hand placed jauntily on her hip, Lizzie's mother pivoted left and right, her multimillion-dollar smile so bright it could blind people. Today it was even brighter than usual, because *Plenty* magazine had decided to kick off Fall Fashion Week with a luncheon in her honor. But like most Fashion Week events, there were about fifteen minutes of frantic picture-taking before anything really got started.

"Katia!" someone yelled.

"You're *beautiful*!" someone screamed.

Lizzie looked out the window of the Mandarin Oriental's private dining room, down at the green domes of trees in Central Park and beyond, at the elegant and crowded skyline of Fifth Avenue, and sighed. *Um, yeah*, she thought. *She's beautiful. Understatement of the century*.

Her mother, Katia Summers, wasn't just beautiful. One fashion designer (Galliano? Gaultier? Lizzie couldn't remember) had called Katia "walking proof of God." And if her mother's twenty-year career as a supermodel was any indication, everyone else thought so, too.

As Katia's only child, Lizzie had logged more hours of her life looking at her mother in person than just about anyone, and even she had to agree: her mom was Seriously, Jaw-Droppingly, Is-That-Humanly-Possible Gorgeous. Day or night. Made-up or fresh-faced. Bedhead or updo. No matter how few hours of sleep she'd had or how annoyed Lizzie was with her, Katia Summers was never *not* breathtaking. And if beauty was really the sum of a person's parts, then each of Katia's parts was almost perfect. There were the eyes that famously changed color, from turquoise to green to an exotic indigo-purple, depending on her mood; the glacial cheekbones that made the lower half of her face a perfect V; her naturally pillowy lips and the trademark pout, caused by a small overbite her parents had never fixed. There was the thick, extension-free blond hair that fell in waves to the middle of her back, and her lean but voluptuous body. *Yes*, Lizzie would think, as she looked at her mom across the breakfast table or in the elevator — *perfect*.

Katia was so perfect that at thirty-seven, when most other models had already hung up their Manolos, she was still in peak demand. She starred in the ad campaigns of at least one A-list designer each season, did spreads in the biggest issues of *Harper's Bazaar*, *W*, and every country's edition of *Vogue*, served as the face of L'Ete cosmetics, and once a year graced the cover of *GQ* or *Details*, covered by nothing but a macramé bikini bottom and her own strategically placed hands. And now she was about to make the career leap that only a precious few supermodels could even attempt, let alone pull off. She would go from supermodel to super-mogul. Clothes, perfume, housewares — Katia would design it all. Katia Coquette — a "French-inspired" (read: extra-sexy) lingerie line — was just the beginning. And from the sight of the press clamoring to take her photo and the fashionistas watching Katia with approval, Katia Coquette looked like it was going to be a huge hit.

Checking her watch, Lizzie walked over to the open bar.

It was already past noon, and she'd told her best friends, Carina and Hudson, that she'd meet them by one. School started tomorrow, which meant that today they would grab something from Pinkberry, stroll through the West Village, and catch up on their summers — their last-day-of-summer ritual. Since nursery school, Hudson and Carina had been her best friends. Lizzie thought of them as the Brita filters for her life. If something happened to her, good or bad, she passed it through them, and when it came out the other side, she would almost always feel better. Lizzie thought it was because the three of them had one huge thing in common: they each knew what it was like to have a life divided up into two parts: public, and private. They'd even made up their own rules for how to deal with it.

She leaned on the edge of the bar and slipped one throbbing foot out of her mom's four-inch Christian Louboutin gold peep-toes. She knew that Louboutins were supposedly the best shoes in the world, but they pinched her feet and crunched her toes. She much preferred her thick-soled, extremely-comfortable, eighty-five-dollar Steve Madden platforms, but Katia had vetoed them for these kinds of events.

"Ahhh," she said, stretching her toes. Nearby a bartender sliced lemons on a cutting board.

"Feet hurt?" he asked. He looked like he was in his early twenties, and had one of those little patches of hair on his chin.

"I don't know how people wear these things," she said.

The bartender nodded but his gaze traveled over to where Katia was still surrounded by cameras.

"She's gorgeous," he said, almost slicing off a finger. "She's even hotter in person."

Lizzie looked over at her mom, still posing. She couldn't resist. "That's my mom," she said.

The bartender's mouth opened as he looked back. "That's your *mom*?" he asked in disbelief.

Lizzie smiled. Nobody ever believed her. "Yep," she said.

"Really?" the bartender asked. "It's just you guys don't really look anything…"

Before he could finish his sentence, Lizzie heard her mother's voice calling from across the room.

"Lizzie! Honey! Come take a picture!"

Lizzie turned around. Her mother was waving one golden, perfectly toned arm in what looked to be her direction.

"Come on!" Katia yelled. "Take a picture!"

Here we go again, Lizzie thought. Every time she went to an official function with her mom, she wound up getting roped into a photo session. Couldn't Katia have mercy on her, just once?

"Come on, Lizzie!" Katia mouthed over the din of the clicking cameras. "Just a couple!"

The crowd of skinny, pale fashion editors craned their heads to get a look at Lizzie. There was no getting out of this. She slipped her foot back in the shoe and hobbled over to her mom, wishing that her father, Bernard, could have been Katia's date to this instead. But somehow he always seemed to be on deadline for his column for the *New York Times*. It was kind of annoying.

When she reached her, Katia draped her slender arm around Lizzie's waist, and pulled her in tight. "My daughter!" she announced to the crowd.

Lizzie faced the collection of black, vacant cameras lenses in front of her. For a long few seconds, nothing happened. Finally, there was one weak flash. Then another. And then another.

And then…

"Can we have just a few more with you, Katia?" someone yelled. "*Just* you?"

"Yes, Katia, just you!"

"Hey, Mom," Lizzie whispered into her mother's ear. "Can I go meet my friends now?"

Katia squeezed Lizzie's waist and removed her arm. "Of course," she whispered.

"Congratulations," Lizzie whispered back.

Her mom patted her on the back and turned back to the cameras. Lizzie was free.

As she walked out of the room, she felt her shoulders relax and her breath come back. Being at these kinds of things always made her tense. In a few minutes, she'd be on the subway, hurtling downtown toward her friends, and she could forget all of this. But the same question gnawed at her, for what was probably the billionth time, as her heels clicked on the smooth marble floor of the hotel lobby and the mortification of the photo op slowly wore off: Did her mom *really* not know what her own daughter looked like?

There was a time when the paparazzi had wanted to take Lizzie's picture, back when she and her mother had been the Sexy Supermodel and her Adorable Kid. When Lizzie was little, the photographers had followed her and her mom everywhere: to nursery school, to the park, to FAO Schwarz.

But then Lizzie got older. And Lizzie changed from the Adorable Kid to the Awkward Teenager. While Katia stayed the Sexy Supermodel.

Actually, awkward was putting it kindly. She was Different. Unusual. Odd.

Or, as Hudson and Carina liked to put it: *striking.*

"Like what Uma Thurman probably looked like, until she got pretty," Hudson would say.

But Uma Thurman didn't have hazel eyes that were so enormous they seemed to bug out of her face. Or a long, meandering nose that faked left and went right. Or straight, thick eyebrows that were as flat and furry as a Sesame Street character's, even when they were plucked. And Uma Thurman certainly didn't have bright, curly red hair that was the texture of Brillo and turned into a bush anytime the temperature went above eighty degrees.

And most importantly, Uma Thurman had not been *expected* to be beautiful. Who expected the daughters of Buddhism professors to turn into Hollywood actresses? But the only daughter of Katia Summers, otherwise known as "Walking Proof of God," was expected to at least be cute. And that wasn't quite what had happened.

Lizzie liked to think that her weird looks meant she could avoid the paparazzi. If she were out with her mom, and they got surrounded coming out of a café or Starbucks, clearly she could stay on the sidelines and none of the photographers would mind. But that wasn't how Katia saw it. Every chance she got, she wanted Lizzie in the photo. Lizzie figured that she was either oblivious to the fact she had a weird-looking kid or trying to prove a point. But how could a supermodel think that looks didn't matter? As she walked down into the stifling heat of the subway station, Lizzie decided that maybe her mom *was* just oblivious. Which was worse.

Lizzie swiped her MetroCard in the turnstile and dashed down the steps to the waiting train. As the doors closed, she found a seat and pulled *The Great Gatsby* from her bag. She wanted to finish it before tomorrow, even though *Gatsby* was summer reading for the tenth grade, not the ninth, at the Chadwick School. But her taste in books had always been a little advanced. She'd learned to read at three, tackled the first two Harry Potters by six, and begun writing stories at eight. She'd been writing ever since and this summer she'd attended the exclusive Barnstable Writer's Workshop out on Cape Cod for six weeks. There a writer had kept talking about Fitzgerald, and Lizzie had been embarrassed that she'd never read him before. Now she didn't want the book to end. There were paragraphs that were so beautiful that she read them over and over. One day, she hoped, she would be able to write a quarter as good as Fitzgerald. Or maybe a tenth.

At Bleecker Street, she got off the subway and limped up the steps to the sidewalk. Her aching feet wobbled in the Louboutins, and it was all she could do not to fall on her face as she walked past sienna-colored brownstones with flowerboxes in the windows, and plate-glass storefronts of bakeries and coffee shops. She loved the West Village — it always reminded her of an earlier New York, when the city was filled with artists and writers and before that, horses and carriages. Now the streets were dotted with fancy clothing boutiques and sushi joints, and filled with NYU students back from summer break, carrying shopping bags from Bed, Bath & Beyond. One day, when she was a famous writer she'd live down here, she thought, just as she turned the corner and saw the blue and green facade of the Promised Land. Otherwise known as Pinkberry.

She threw the glass door open and rushed inside, toward the table in the corner where two girls, one petite and blond, one taller and black-haired, sat waiting for her.

"Lizzie!" shrieked the blond girl as she leaped out of her chair. Carina Jurgensen threw her tan arms around Lizzie as if she hadn't seen her in years. "Oh my God, *hi!*" she said, jumping up and down on her flip-flops, as her blond ponytail swung back and forth. "I missed you, Lizbutt!"

"I missed you, too, C," she said, returning Carina's frantic hug as best she could. "And you're so tan."

"And you're so *tall*," Carina said admiringly, letting her go. "Pretty soon I'm gonna feel like a midget around you, I swear." Her cocoa-brown eyes were wide and electrically alive. Sometimes Lizzie thought Carina was more alive than anyone she'd ever met.

"Oh my God, that dress is to die for," said Lizzie's other best friend, Hudson Jones, as she stood up and hugged her, too. Wavy black curls framed her heart-shaped face, and her green eyes sparkled. "Is that Margiela?" she asked in her soft, gentle voice, looking at Lizzie's dress.

"It's my mom's," Lizzie said. "And it barely fits."

"Then have some Pinkberry," Carina said as they sat down. She pushed a tub of pomegranate yogurt with mochi across the table. "Here, got you your favorite."

Carina Jurgensen had lived her entire life in New York, but at first glance she looked like a surfer girl from the north shore of Oahu. Petite but athletic, with sunstreaked hair that never faded and a sprinkling of freckles on her button nose, Carina actually did surf, and snowboard, and climb mountains, and anything else that allowed her to be outdoors. She was fearless. Ever since they'd been little, Carina had been the first of them to do anything scary — whether it was Rollerblading straight down a hill in Central Park on a crowded Sunday, or flirting with the guys at St. Brendan's. Because she was unable to sit still for longer than a few minutes, Carina didn't like to spend a lot of time in front of the mirror, and she was so pretty she didn't need to. Her favorite season was summer, and her favorite summer look was what she wore today: shorts, a T-shirt with cut-off sleeves, and camouflage-patterned flip-flops. Guys tended to find Carina Jurgensen completely adorable, though she usually didn't notice.

"I so need this," Lizzie said, digging into her yogurt. "It's a gazillion degrees outside."

"Yeah, but Hudson's still cold," Carina joked, nodding at their friend.

"No I'm not," Hudson argued, pulling her deconstructed fringed wrap closer around herself. "I'm just being sun-savvy."

If Carina was the beach-blond surfer girl, then Hudson Jones was the sophisticated urban hippie-chick. She was beautiful, with French toast–colored skin and dazzling green eyes, courtesy of her mom's Afro-Caribbean heritage and her dad's French-Irish background, and she had the slender build and perfect posture of a girl who'd studied dance all of her life. Hudson was also incredibly stylish. Under her wrap, she wore a silk coral-colored tunic dotted with sequins, gladiator sandals with crisscross straps that traveled up to her knees, gigantic silver hoops, and a one-of-a-kind multicolored woven bag that she'd picked up in Buenos Aires. On Hudson, it all managed to look perfect.

"How was your mom's thing?" Hudson asked, taking a small bite of her green tea yogurt with blueberries. Hudson was always going for the healthy option.

"Good, but she roped me into a photo op again. When is she gonna get that nobody — *nobody* — wants to take my picture?"

"Lizzie, stop," Hudson said in a cautious voice. Lizzie's looks were well-covered territory among the three of them and she knew that her friends were tired of talking about it.

"No, you guys know I don't care, I just wish *she* saw it," Lizzie said. "Anyway, Carina. How was Outward Bound?"

"So, so, *so* incredible," Carina said, shaking her head as she wolfed down her yogurt. "Colorado is the most perfect place on earth. But I didn't take a shower for almost a month. You guys shoulda seen me. I was covered in dirt. It was awesome."

"What'd your dad say when he saw you covered in dirt?" Hudson asked.

Carina grinned. "That I'd wasted a summer. What'd you think?"

Carina's father, Karl Jurgensen, was a workaholic. He was also one of the richest men in the world. Metronome Media, his empire of fat glossy lifestyle and fashion magazines, newspapers, cable news channels, and social-networking sites spanned continents and employed thousands of people. He was building what he hoped would be the biggest streamed-entertainment site in the world, with every television series, reality show, or movie available on one user-friendly website. Karl had so much money that he'd also become one of the country's biggest philanthropists, donating millions to fight poverty and world hunger. With his charismatic personality and dashing looks, Karl was one of the most eligible bachelors in New York, if not the world. He'd divorced Carina's mother when Carina was in the fifth grade and since then Carina had lived alone with him in a palatial penthouse on Fifty-Seventh Street.

Most of the time the two of them managed to get along. But Karl's impatience with his free-spirited daughter could set off a violent explosion between the two of them, and by the end of the school year, Carina and the Jurg, as she called her dad, usually weren't speaking. Which was why she spent every summer as far from him and New York as possible, climbing mountains in Colorado or learning how to scuba dive.

"How was your dad's party this year?" Hudson asked.

Carina shrugged. "Pretty good, I guess," she said. "He thinks he raised two million." Every year around Labor Day, Karl, or the Jurg, turned his Montauk estate into an amusement park to raise money for charity. There were roller coasters, spinning teacups, fireworks displays, and even an underwater submarine ride in one of his lakes. A ticket to "Jurgensenland" cost a thousand dollars and a dinner table for the ball at the end of the evening cost ten thousand.

"And how was the end of the tour?" Lizzie asked Hudson.

"Crazy," Hudson sighed. "Thirty cities in forty-five days. I don't know how my mom does it. By the ninth day I was exhausted."

"Any Holla drama?" Carina asked, getting right to the point.

Hudson rolled her eyes. "There was this guy from *Rolling Stone* on the tour with us, doing the usual article on 'Holla Jones and her Unstoppable Career,' and he asked me how old my mom was. I was so jet-lagged, I told him the truth: thirty-seven. And when it got back to my mom, she *freaked* out. As if three extra years were that big a deal." Hudson stood up and placed her half-empty carton into the trash can. "Moral of the story? Don't ever talk to the press. Even when they're, like, living with you day and night."

Hudson's mother, Holla Jones, was a pop star. Her multi-octave voice and radio-friendly hits had made her a star at nineteen, and now she was an icon. Year after year, through a combination of touring, cutting-edge album production, and an iron will, she reached the top of the Billboard charts. But the iron will had lately become a problem. It related to everything: her daily, three-hour workouts with a personal trainer; her strictly organic vegetarian diet; and her relationships, which were usually over before they began. Hudson's dad was a case in point. He'd been a backup dancer on one of Holla's first tours — and then promptly disappeared the moment the tour ended, scared off by Holla's fearsome discipline.

Hudson and Holla's bond was fierce, almost sisterly, and Lizzie often admired it. But it also made her a little nervous. Hudson had inherited her mother's voice, her looks, and her presence, and now was about to record her own album. But where Holla was all fast beats, flashy costumes, and high-energy pop, Hudson was soulful, slow, and a smoky torch. Unfortunately, Holla wasn't so aware of the distinction.

"Any cute dancers?" Carina asked as they walked out onto the street.

"Uh, no," Hudson said. "They were all on the other team."

"Too bad," Carina said, making a beeline for a jewelry stand set up on the street. "I was too stinky to even think of hooking up with anyone on that mountain, even though this one guy was really hot," she said, holding up a pair of dangly coin earrings to her ears. "What do you guys think? Cheap or cool?"

"Cheap," Lizzie said.

"And do you really need them?" asked Hudson.

"Whatever, they're ten bucks," Carina said, producing a bill from the back pocket of her shorts and handing it to the man in the

Rastafarian cap behind the table. Despite her granola tendencies, Carina liked to spend money. And her dad gave her plenty.

"Speaking of hot guys," Hudson murmured, staring at something up the street. "Look at him."

Lizzie turned and followed Hudson's gaze. Walking out of the southern end of Washington Square Park, fists in the pockets of his jeans, white iPod wires trailing from his ears, was a very hot guy. An *alarmingly* hot guy. He was so cute that Lizzie could only look at him in small, bite-sized glimpses. Large blue eyes. Chiseled face. Straight brown hair that was a little shaggy over his forehead. Full, pink lips.

"Wow," Carina muttered. "Now *that* is a hot college guy."

But Lizzie could tell he was younger than that. And then she realized there was something familiar about his walk. It was a loping, easy stroll, as if he was totally in his own world and in absolutely no hurry. "Oh my God," Lizzie said when it hit her. "That's Todd Piedmont."

"What?" Carina asked, awestruck. "The guy from your building?"

"Didn't he move to London?" Hudson asked. "Like, three years ago?"

"Maybe he's back for a visit," Lizzie replied.

"Is that what happens when people move to London?" Carina wondered. "They become total hotties?"

"Go say hi." Hudson grabbed Lizzie's arm and gave her a nudge.

"Yeah," Carina seconded. "Before he gets back on a plane and never comes back."

"Wait — by myself?"

"You guys were BFF," Hudson pointed out.

"Yeah, when we were *six*."

As she watched her old neighbor reach the curb, she tried to wrap her brain around the fact that this was the same boy she'd bossed around, played with, and once made cry. But whoever it was, she was just happy to be wearing a pretty dress and peep-toe heels, even if they did kill her feet.

As two kids the same age living three floors apart, she and Todd Piedmont had trick-or-treated together, sledded in Central Park, ran around the lobby on rainy days, or just rode the elevators for hours, pushing buttons for their tolerant neighbors. Todd's parents, Jack and Julia, were almost as glamorous as her parents. Jack was the head of an investment bank and did triathlons on the weekends, and had a rugged self-confidence that made women giggly and other men very quiet. Julia was an elegant, dark-haired beauty who worked as a contributing editor at *Vogue*. They seemed completely in love.

But Todd could be a little moody. Sometimes he'd disappear into his room with a book for hours, even when Lizzie was at his house. He could also get his feelings hurt easily, like when Lizzie poured his favorite kind of grape juice down the garbage disposal and he burst into tears. (It didn't help that she was at least half a foot taller than him.) In fifth grade Todd went to an all-boys school, St. Brendan's, and started hanging out more with the boys in his class. And when he did see her, Todd acted weird. He'd ignore her in the lobby, or barely mumble a hello if she ran into him on the street.

"Todd!" his mother would say, in front of Lizzie and her mom. "What's happened to your manners?" "Hi," he'd sullenly say, and then make a beeline for the elevator.

15

The next year, when Lizzie and Todd were almost twelve, his family decided to move to London. Lizzie was relieved. No more awkward moments in the elevator. No more Todd weirdness.

But then Todd did something *really* strange.

It was at the Piedmonts' going-away party. Todd and Lizzie were hanging out by themselves, as usual, in the kitchen, while the grown-ups mingled in the living room. They stood in the kitchen in awkward silence, eating red velvet cupcakes. Suddenly Todd grabbed her by the shoulders and pulled her to him. She felt his damp lips press against her mouth for an instant, and when it was over, her cupcake was on the tile floor, frosting-side down. Then her parents came in to say they were leaving, and that was the last time she ever saw him. His parting gift to her had been that quick, sloppy first kiss.

Now as she watched Todd come toward her, she wondered if that kiss had been so sloppy after all.

"Come on, you're gonna miss him!" Hudson said, giving her a slight push. "Go!"

Lizzie took a wobbly step forward on her Louboutins. The good thing about looking like a Sesame Street character, she thought, was that people usually remembered you. She limped toward him, and was just a few feet away when Todd yanked the iPod wires out of his ears.

"Lizzie?" he asked, a smile curling around the edges of his mouth. "Lizzie Summers?"

She took a step and wobbled on a crack in the pavement. "Oh!" she cried, and before she knew it, tumbled right into his chest.

"Whoa, you okay?" he asked, catching her in his arms. With her nose pressed into his T-shirt, she got a whiff of Downy, Ivory soap, and boy-sweat. His arms felt strong around her, as if they had finally developed real muscles. "Here you go," he said, propping her back on her feet. "You all right?"

"So, um, what's up?" she asked breezily, trying to pretend that she had not just tripped and almost fallen on her face.

"Not much, how are you?" he asked, a faint English accent tweaking his *r*'s. He was taller than her now, and standing this close to him she was eye-level with his lips. They were definitely on the full side — had he had these before?

"Um, what are you doing here?" Her right leg started to shake like it did whenever she was nervous. "I thought you were in London."

"We moved back," he said. "Just a couple weeks ago."

"You moved *back*?" she practically yelled.

"Yeah. My dad wanted to. And then my brother got into NYU," he said, gesturing behind him toward the park, "so it seemed like the right time. And we're actually back in the old building. You guys moved away, right?"

Lizzie had sensed a year ago that moving had been a terrible idea. Now she knew why. "Yeah, last year. To the west side. I think the building got annoyed, you know, with all the photographers."

Todd smiled. "I'm sure I'll still see you, though. Every day, probably."

"You will?"

He flicked a piece of hair out of his eyes. "I'm going to Chadwick."

Lizzie blinked. For a moment, she thought she might lose her balance again. Todd Piedmont was going to go to her school? He'd been gone for three years, become alarmingly hot, and now she was going to be seeing him again every day — all day long?

"That's great," she said casually, hoping that her pounding chest wasn't a dead giveaway.

"Hey, you guys," Todd said to her friends. Lizzie had been too distracted to notice that they had come to stand on either side of her.

"How's merry old England?" Carina asked playfully.

"And how long are you here?" inquired Hudson.

"Todd's moved back," Lizzie announced. "And he's going to Chadwick." She looked over her shoulder to see their reaction. Carina looked flabbergasted, and Hudson was blushing.

"Actually, I gotta go," he said to Lizzie, oblivious to her friends' reactions. "I'm meeting my brother at his dorm. But maybe you can be my tour guide tomorrow?" he asked, smiling, as he stepped past her.

Lizzie nodded dumbly. "Sure."

"Well, see ya." He waved to Carina and Hudson, stuck the wires back in his ears, and set off down the street.

All three of them stared after him in silence.

"Holy mother of God," Carina breathed when he was halfway down the block.

"He's going to our *school*?" Hudson sputtered.

"Apparently."

"You guys are gonna fall in love," Hudson blurted.

"What?"

"He asked you to be his *tour guide*," Hudson said meaningfully.

"Because he doesn't know anyone else."

"Still. There were sparks. C, did you see the sparks?" Hudson asked.

"I almost caught on fire," Carina said.

"This is fate," Hudson announced.

"Oh my God, *stop*," Lizzie groaned.

"It *is*," Hudson argued. "Don't you think, C? Don't you think this is fate?" Hudson was way into astrology and destiny stuff. *Way* into it.

"Okay, let's break it down," Carina said, turning to face Lizzie. "He was your first kiss, he's hotter than Christian Bale, *and* he's going to school with you," she said, counting out her points on her slender fingers. "Yep. I'd say a higher power could be involved."

As Lizzie watched Todd turn the corner, she wondered whether Hudson was right. Unlike her best friend, she didn't breathlessly check her horoscope every day, or take quiz after quiz on the Internet to learn the name of her soul mate, but maybe this was all happening for a reason. It all seemed too weird. Too...well...destined.

"When's his birthday?" Hudson asked.

"November."

"Hmmm," Hudson said, nodding. "Scorpio. That's good with Taurus. A little intense, though. You might want to be careful."

"You guys, nothing has even happened yet," she reminded them.

"Oh, but it will," Carina said knowingly as she slipped on a pair of silver Oakleys. "It totally will." Then she led the way down the street.

chapter 2

"His name's Todd Piedmont. He starts today. He just transferred from London. He's tall with brown hair. *Really* blue eyes. "

Mr. Barlow leaned back in his swivel chair, studying her, and cradled his white-haired head in his hands. "And what did he have for breakfast?" he asked dryly.

"He asked me to show him around," Lizzie pointed out, trying not to blush. "I'm just trying to be helpful. Isn't that the Chadwick way?" She knew she was being totally obvious, but she couldn't even pretend to be casual about this.

"Is there any chance your interest in Mr. Piedmont is of the less... *altruistic* variety?" Mr. Barlow asked, raising one white eyebrow. Thirty years as the head of the Upper School had made him a little skeptical of teenage Good Samaritans. And his five years as a Marine before that made him a little scary.

"No...," Lizzie hedged.

"Then far be it from me to deny your need to help people,"

Mr. Barlow said, snapping forward in his chair and reaching for the cabinet below his desk. He pulled out two folders and dropped them on his desk. "All right, Miss Summers. Let's see if your schedules match up."

As he bent his lanky frame over the files, Lizzie took a moment to glance around his office. Nothing had changed over the summer. The mantel above the fireplace was still crammed with old Christmas cards and photos from students who'd graduated, and the taupe chenille couch was still worn at the arms. The acid green carpet from the eighties still hadn't been replaced. Chadwick was one of the most expensive schools on the Upper East Side, but clearly none of the tuition was going toward Mr. B's office, she thought.

"You both have the same homeroom, same English, same world history..." Mr. Barlow said, slapping the file closed. "He's all yours."

"Thanks, Mr. Barlow," she said, about to leave.

"Hold on there, Summers."

Slowly, Lizzie turned around.

"I heard very impressive things from the director at Barnstable," he said, taking a sip from a cup of takeout coffee. "He said that you won a special prize."

"Just for being the youngest one there."

"For Most Promising," he said with a smile. "And for that reason I hope you'll submit something to the fiction contest this year. I think you've got a good shot at winning, Lizzie. Even as a freshman. You're one of the best writers we have here." He smiled gently. "No pressure, of course."

Of all the teachers at Chadwick, Mr. Barlow was her most fervent supporter, ever since her eighth-grade English teacher,

Miss Hardwick, had shown him a story Lizzie had written for the literary magazine. This year, Mr. Barlow would also be her English teacher. Lizzie wasn't sure if that was going to be good or bad.

"I can show you something this week if you want," she offered. "Maybe get your feedback?"

Mr. Barlow nodded. "I look forward to it. Now go show the illustrious Mr. Piedmont around."

As she stepped out of his office into the crowded hall, her heart pounded, but whether it was from Mr. Barlow's pep talk about the fiction contest or Todd Piedmont's imminent appearance, she wasn't sure. Sometimes it was hard to believe that someone like Mr. Barlow, who had actually known real writers, and some famous ones, thought that she really had talent. Maybe she should submit something to the contest.

In the hall, people waved hello and stopped her for first-day welcome-back hugs. But she tried to keep moving. She'd gotten up an hour early to straighten her hair with her mother's state-of-the art ionic blow dryer, and she had only a small window of time until her long, straight, red locks sprang back into a Ronald McDonald–worthy 'fro.

She checked the ninth-grade homeroom: no sign of Todd. He wasn't in the lounge. She was on her way to check the lockers when she saw a guy standing in front of the main bulletin board, scanning the schedules. Over one shoulder he wore a schoolbag with some weird, vaguely European insignia she didn't recognize. His uniform pants were that new-looking, inky black. His white oxford shirt still had crinkles in it from being folded. His hair was shaggy over his collar. It was him.

She tapped him on the shoulder. "Hey there."

When he turned around, any and all composure she had managed to achieve instantly melted. "Hey, tour guide," he said, a smile lighting up his face. His eyes seemed even larger and bluer than they'd looked the day before. "How are you?"

"You got your wish," she teased.

"I just hope you're not a bad influence," he said, grinning. "Like before." She felt the blood rise to her cheeks, and her stomach churn. She prayed that she didn't throw up.

"What do you mean, before?" she asked, trying not to stare at his perfect white teeth.

"You were always the one who wanted to throw water balloons onto Park Avenue," he said. "You practically got my family thrown out of the building after we hit the doorman."

"But you loved it," she countered. "I was just trying to keep you happy."

"You *made* me," he pretended to argue. Then he looked her up and down as if he were seeing her for the first time. "But now I'm finally taller than you so you can't boss me around anymore."

"Don't be so sure of that," she said. She cast her gaze down to his schoolbag. She needed a break from those piercing blue eyes. "Let me see your schedule."

She watched him open the flaps of his bookbag and reach inside for his schedule. A familiar-looking blue paperback peeked out amid folders and papers.

"Wait," she said. "Is that *The Great Gatsby*?"

He paused and then looked up at her with surprise. "Yeah."

"That's so funny," she said. "I'm reading it right now. I'm kind of obsessed with it."

"Me, too." He pulled the book out of his bag. His copy was even more wrinkled and battered than hers.

"I finished it a while ago, but I like to carry it around with me," he said, flipping through the pages. "Kind of like a rabbit's foot or something." He gave a sheepish shrug. "I want to be a writer."

"So do I," she said.

"You do?" he asked, peering into her eyes. Her heart lurched into a rapid-fire sprint just as she felt someone walk up behind her.

"Todd? Oh my God!"

Ava Elting neatly stepped her Pilates-toned body past Lizzie as if she weren't even there and threw her arms around Todd's neck. "I *heard* you moved back," she cooed, her voice rising and falling as she hugged him. "It's *soooo* good to see you."

As usual, Ava looked like she'd spent hours getting ready for school. Her perfectly-shaped auburn ringlets were pulled back with a jeweled barrette, her brows were plucked into neat tadpoles, and her fingernails were French manicured. Just looking at her could be exhausting. It had probably taken her all weekend to get that groomed. But Lizzie secretly wished she could be the same way.

"Hey, Ava," Todd said, pleasant but cautious, returning the hug. "Good to see you."

"So you had enough of stuffy old England," she said, tipping her head and batting her saucer-shaped brown eyes. "What happened?

Did you miss being around girls with good teeth?" She giggled and swung her Hervé Chapelier shoulder bag up her arm.

"Well, um, my dad made us move," he said. "But yeah, I guess you could say the girls here have, uh, better teeth," he said in a resigned voice. "Or whatever."

"Of *course* they do!" Ava said, playing with the diamond A that she always wore around her neck. "I'm sure they're going to miss you."

Todd just blushed and looked down at the floor.

There was something else Ava excelled at besides grooming, and that was talking to guys. And anyone else, really. Ava Elting was probably the most confident girl Lizzie had ever seen. She had been that way since the third grade, and her constant socializing — and flirting — had propelled her to the top of the New York City private school food chain. There wasn't a charity committee she didn't oversee, a party she didn't get invited to, or a guy she couldn't talk up — usually to stunning results. True, she was pretty, with her toned runner's legs and carefully styled hair, but it was the force of her personality — and her shameless flirting — that usually got her any guy she wanted.

"Oh, hey!" Ava exclaimed, turning around and suddenly acknowledging Lizzie's presence. "I'm so rude! How was your summer, Lizzie?"

"Great," Lizzie said through a gritted smile. "How was yours?"

"Oh, you know, it was the usual — tennis camp in Florida, and then riding camp in Bedford, and then just lying out in Southampton…wait!" She looked back at Todd. "We should all have lunch today. When's your lunch period?"

"I don't know, is it down there?" Todd asked Lizzie.

Lizzie wanted to mention that it had been years since she and Ava had eaten lunch together, but she just looked back down at his schedule. "Eleven forty-five," she said.

"Oh, I'm twelve thirty," Ava said disappointedly, tossing one of her curls. "Whatever. You'll just have to come over after school sometime this week so we can catch up."

"Sure," Todd said with an appreciative smile. "That'd be great."

Lizzie felt her stomach sink. She knew for a fact that Ava had barely even known Todd before he moved away — he definitely hadn't been one of the popular guys at St. Brendan's. Now, just because he was cute, she was going to pretend they were old buddies. And flirt with him. Yuck.

The bell rang, signaling the five minutes until homeroom.

"Oh, hey, guys," Ava said as her three best friends — Ilona Peterson, Cici Marcus, and Kate Pinsky — came to stand in their usual protective circle around her. "Say hi to Todd Piedmont."

Ilona, Cici, and Kate each gave Todd a deliberately thin smile. Ilona was the prettiest of the three, with her three-hundred-dollar, butter-colored highlights and long, curled eyelashes. She also had the biggest chest at Chadwick. Cici was Ava's second in command, with freckles and heavy brows and a permanent scowl. Kate was the quiet one, with bright blue eyes and chemically straightened black hair. Using the first letter of their first names, Carina, Hudson, and Lizzie called them the Icks. Around Ava, the Icks were generally harmless. But as soon as their leader was gone, they could be — and usually were — ruthlessly mean. Nothing and nobody was safe. Their preferred weapon was the collective snicker followed by a piercing deathstare, and their preferred target was usually Lizzie, or Carina, or Hudson.

The three weren't sure how they'd become the Icks' Number One Enemy, but the only thing they could come up with was their parents. Like some of the girls in their class, the Icks seemed to assume that Lizzie and her friends were wildly conceited — no matter how hard they tried to prove otherwise. The nicer they acted toward the Icks, the meaner the Icks were in return. Lizzie sometimes thought that if her mother had been a murderer instead of a model, the Icks would have probably been kinder to her. Only Carina sometimes escaped their wrath. Her dad's extreme wealth, and his fondness for the New York social circuit, meant that Carina had one foot in Ava's world of invitation-only charity dances and Hamptons polo matches. If Carina had really cared to, she could have been even more popular than Ava.

"Hey guys," Todd said, greeting each of them. "You all know Lizzie, right?"

The Icks glanced at Lizzie with distaste. "Hi," Ilona said listlessly, flicking her eyes over Lizzie's pale legs. "Nice tan." Kate and Cici giggled.

"Hey, Ilona," Lizzie said curtly. She looked over at Todd to see if he'd picked up on their laugh, but his eyes were on Ava and her unbuttoned-just-a-bit-too-low oxford shirt.

"Well, I gotta go," Ava said. "I'll text you later and I mean it, let's totally hang, okay?" she said, putting a hand on Todd's arm. "Oh, and Lizzie, good to see you!"

With a quick wave at Lizzie, Ava turned to go, leading the way for her posse down the hall. Todd stared at the back of Ava's rolled-up kilt, swinging from side to side, until it disappeared around the corner. "She's nice," Lizzie said as vaguely as possible.

"Yeah," Todd answered, turning toward her. His face looked a little vacant, as if his mind was still somewhere else. "She's a cool girl."

Did Todd really think a cool girl was someone who knew the entire city and threw parties? Or a girl who loved *The Great Gatsby* and wanted to be a writer?

She led him down the hall toward the open homeroom door. "We're right in here," she said, leading the way inside.

As they walked in together, twenty pairs of eyes watched them weave their way through the desks. *Yes*, Lizzie thought. *Todd Piedmont is going to be a very big deal at the Chadwick School.* Even Hudson and Carina were staring.

"Want to sit here?" Todd asked, pointing to two empty desks. As she nodded and sat down beside him, she caught a glimpse of her friends' excited smiles.

Lizzie rolled her eyes back at them, hoping they'd get the message to stop gawking at them. But she felt a telltale blush creep across her face. From the butterflies dancing around her stomach and the way she almost felt dizzy, she knew that she'd already reached the Crush Point of No Return.

He leaned over toward her, so close she could smell his mint toothpaste. "You're with me all day, right?" he asked.

Lizzie gulped. "Uh-huh," she said.

Oh my God, she thought, looking down at her desk. There was no way she was going to make it to three thirty.

chapter 3

Tut-tut-tut-tut-tut-tut.

The last page came rolling out of the printer into the tray, and Lizzie scooped up all twelve pages in her hands. She still didn't have a title, and she wasn't sure of the ending, but she was proud of her story. Maybe this would be the one she'd submit to the fiction contest. She hoped Mr. Barlow would think so, too.

The main characters were a little familiar: a gawky teenage girl in the shadow of her beautiful actress-mother decides to get her hair cut just like her, with disastrous results. The girl then ends up realizing she actually likes her hair, and wishes she hadn't done it. Anyone who read the story, and knew who'd written it, would know exactly what — and who — it was really about. But Lizzie's real self, complete with her secret thoughts and feelings, always crept into her stories. She couldn't help it. Mr. Barlow was always telling her that the best writing came from personal experience, anyway. "Only by being yourself can you be *more* than yourself," he liked to say whenever he read her drafts. Still, it was a little embarrassing to be exposed like that. Even though there was a certain relief when her characters dealt with something that bothered her. It was almost as if she'd dealt with it, too.

As she walked back to her spot in the computer lab, she heard Ilona, Cici, and Kate start giggling across the aisle. *Whatever*, Lizzie thought as she sat down and opened her Gmail. They'd been doing this all day, and she knew why. Todd was still hanging around her, three days later, even after it was clear he didn't need a tour guide anymore. Carina and Hudson, naturally, were convinced that Todd had an insane crush on her. Lizzie didn't know, but the idea that Todd might actually be into her was way too exciting, and possibly a jinx. Things like that just didn't happen to her. As for the Icks, Todd's attention just seemed to be another reason to send some obnoxiousness in Lizzie's direction. Why she needed to feel self-conscious about a good-looking guy following her around, Lizzie wasn't sure, but to the Icks, any chance to make her feel self-conscious was apparently worth it.

As she read her e-mail, the giggles got louder. She was just about to say something when she heard someone say, "Hey, Lizzie."

Lizzie looked up. Hillary Crumple, who was in the eighth grade but dressed like she was in the fourth, stood beside her in the aisle, her gigantic backpack strapped to both shoulders, and the loose hair from her ponytail standing on end around her face. As usual, her heart-shaped face was just a little too shiny and her yellow-green eyes didn't blink.

"Hey, Hillary," Lizzie said, fighting the urge to run to the door. "How was your summer?"

"So I saw Hudson on *E!* last week," Hillary replied, launching right into her favorite subject. "They were doing this thing on celebrity children style. How does she dress like that? Does she have a stylist? Or does she just find all those things herself? What do you think? Do you know?"

Hillary's rapid-fire questioning left Lizzie speechless as usual. "Um, I'm not sure," Lizzie mumbled.

"I saw her mom this summer," Hillary went on, undeterred. "In concert. Oh my God, she was so amazing. They said that Hudson's making her own album. Is she? Do you think she'd let me hear a song? What's her music like? Is she gonna be on *American Idol*?"

She stepped closer. Lizzie prayed for a stun gun.

"Um, I don't know," said Lizzie, turning back to her computer and starting to type a little. "Actually, she's pretty private about that stuff." *Help*, she thought.

"Do you think she'd ever take me shopping?" Hillary persisted, stepping even closer. "She has such great style —"

"Hey? Is this seat taken?"

Lizzie almost cried out with joy when she saw Todd walk up behind Hillary. "Nope!" she chirped, pulling her bookbag off the chair next to her.

"I'm Todd," he told Hillary as he moved past her.

"This is Hillary Crumple," Lizzie said. "She's in the eighth grade."

"Hey," he said.

After three days, Todd now looked like a typical Chadwick guy. He'd learned to let the knot of his tie hang just a few inches down from his collar and had traded his European bookbag for an

L.L. Bean. As he sat down next to her, Lizzie felt her stomach turn into a Slinky.

"Well, just tell Hudson I said hi," Hillary said, clearly petrified by Todd, before walking back to her computer.

"What was that all about?" Todd asked as he logged on to his e-mail.

"Oh, she's Hudson's stalker."

"What?" he asked, staring at her.

"She's tries to be her friend. In a huge way," Lizzie explained. "Hudson's so nice to her. But it kind of creeps me out." Lizzie felt guilty even explaining it.

"Well, you seemed like you were being really nice to her," he said reassuringly. "That's the only thing you can do."

As he typed in his password, Lizzie snuck a sideways glance at him. Todd was so different from the other guys in their class. While Eli Blackman and Ken Clayman constantly drew attention to themselves in class with pranks and jokes, Todd had a calmness to him that made him even more attractive. Somehow that quiet, sensitive kid who'd followed her around their old building had turned into a smart, funny, humble, and down-to-earth guy. Who also happened to be gorgeous.

"Hey, what's that?" he asked, pointing to the story she'd turned upside-down.

"Oh, just something I wrote."

Todd picked it up and turned it around. "Can I read it?"

Lizzie paused. She'd never given a guy — much less a guy she liked — one of her stories. But right now his interest was so exciting she couldn't think of a reason not to give it to him. "On one condition," she said. "You give me one of yours."

"Only after I read this," Todd countered with a smile. "Just so I know what I'm up against."

Across the aisle Lizzie could see the Icks' eyes fixed on the two of them hungrily. She looked back at him quickly. "Sure," she said, even more nervous now that she knew they were being watched.

"Oh, let me ask you something," he said, leaning closer to her so that their elbows bumped. Her heart did a somersault. "If I had a party Saturday night, do you think people would come?"

Lizzie blinked. "Uh, yeah. I think so," she said, pretending that she wasn't sure.

"Good, because I'll have the place to myself," he said. "My dad'll be in Southampton and my mom...is still in London." He gave her a cautious look.

"Really? She's not here yet?" Lizzie asked.

His jaw muscle popped up and down. "She's not coming. My dad met someone back here...that's why we moved. They're splitting up."

Lizzie felt herself blush as she stared at the computer mouse. She felt bad that this was the first she was hearing this. She should have asked about his parents before. "And you decided to move with your dad?" she finally asked.

"He wanted me to," Todd said. The muscle in his jaw popped again. "Maybe it wasn't the right thing. I don't know. I think my mom's pretty hurt."

She felt an overwhelming urge to cover his hand with her own.

"And keep this between us if that's okay," he said. "You're like Nick Carraway in *The Great Gatsby*. The guy everyone tells all their secrets to." He grinned at her, showing her his perfect white teeth. "So...maybe you can come over early and help me set up?"

Her heart felt like it might leap out of her chest. "I'd love to," she said.

"Cool." He stood up and slung his backpack over his shoulder.

He wanted her to come over *early*. Her mind reeled.

He leaned down and grabbed her story. "Don't worry. For my eyes only."

"It better be," she managed to say, just as Ava Elting glided through the doors of the computer lab. Her auburn curls bounced on her shoulders, and her diamond A necklace glinted in the fluorescent light like a weapon. "I just heard about the party — I'm so psyched! I would have had one but my parents aren't going to the country this weekend. So annoying." She wrinkled her nose and pulled her vanilla-colored handbag further up her arm. "Can I do anything? Bring over some music? I just made the most amazing playlist."

Todd took a step backward toward the door. "No, I think I'm all set. Just bring your people."

"Oh, no worries. I will," she said emphatically.

Todd looked at Lizzie and waved just before he ambled slowly out of the lab.

Ava turned around. "Oh, hey, Lizzie," she said, with much less enthusiasm. "You going to Todd's?" She sat down in Todd's vacated seat. Across the aisle, Lizzie could feel the Icks watching them.

"Yep," she said, standing up and packing her bag. "Todd and I go way back, actually. We've been good friends since we were kids."

Ava was too busy logging on to her e-mail to get the dig. "Oh, right," she said distractedly. "See you later."

As Lizzie walked to the door, she almost had to pinch herself. He'd invited her over to his house. Before everyone else. He'd confided in her about his parents. He'd taken her story to read. *And he'd invited her over to his house. Before everyone else.*

Could this really be happening? Was this what she thought it might be? Could she and Todd really be, well...a thing?

She couldn't wait to tell Carina and Hudson. With just a few minutes left before the bell, she raced down the hall. They'd know what this meant.

chapter 4

Lizzie was still thinking about Todd the following night, as her town car inched its way down Forty-Second Street. Even in the gathering dusk, she could make out the edge of the massive white tent in the middle of Bryant Park, lined by tall skinny plane trees. While a million fourteen-year-old girls would probably kill to be going to see a show at Fashion Week — on a school night, no less — walking into the tents with her mom always made Lizzie a little nervous. And tonight would be even crazier than usual. This would be the fashion world's first glimpse of Katia Coquette, and her mom had made sure to amass an especially high-profile crowd for the runway show.

But for right now, she still had a few extra minutes to think about Todd's party. It was still two nights away. Carina and Hudson were convinced that it was a date. "I called it!" Carina cried when she heard the news.

Hudson immediately went online to check the astrological

prediction for Saturday night. "Mars is in Cancer!" she gasped. "That means you're totally gonna hook up!"

Lizzie wasn't sure about that, but her friends' excitement only added to her own.

"Okay, we're pulling up right now," her mother said beside her, into her slim black phone. "Wish me luck, honey. See you soon." Katia slipped her phone back into her tiny silk clutch. "Your father said he's going to try to make it to the after-party," she said to Lizzie. "But he's running late with his deadline."

Tonight her mother looked even more breathtaking than usual in a clingy purple halter dress that showed off her cleavage and toned shoulders. Her blond hair had been artfully piled into a messy, chic knot, and her expertly applied fake eyelashes looked like delicate black spiders clinging to her lids. *How on earth am I related to this person?* Lizzie thought.

Katia patted Lizzie's hand. "You look great, honey."

"Thanks," Lizzie fibbed. She didn't feel great. Her strapless Trina Turk dress pulled tightly across the hips, while the straps of her mom's spike-heeled Manolos dug into the flesh of her toes. Plus, her updo felt more like a beehive. As the car traveled another few feet in traffic, she decided to finally ask the question she'd wanted to ask for weeks. "So, Mom...you're not gonna make me pose with you, right?"

Katia gave her a quizzical look as she pulled out a jeweled compact. "Well, you're my date, aren't you?" she asked, popping it open and checking her lipstick.

"I just would rather that I was in the background for this. Maybe I can just meet you inside at the seats?"

"But how'll you find me?" Katia frowned slightly as she squeezed a pin-sized drop of Chanel lip gloss onto her finger and patted it on her lips. "You used to love Fashion Week."

"I know," Lizzie said. "It's just so intense."

The car came to a stop. "This is as far as I can go," announced the driver.

"Okay. We'll get out here," Katia said.

"Mom? Is that cool?" Lizzie pressed.

"Fine, Lizzie," Katia said hastily as she opened the door.

Katia got out of the car, and Lizzie followed her out into the steamy September twilight. It was so humid that her strapless dress stuck to her back. For a few minutes they walked unnoticed past the crowds lining the steps into the tent. Assistants wearing black SEVENTH ON SIXTH T-shirts and IDs around their necks scurried back and forth. Up ahead, just inside the doors, Lizzie could see flashes from the paparazzi's cameras like lightning. Suddenly she wanted to be back in her room, lying on her bed and videochatting with Carina and Hudson.

Suddenly a young blond guy wearing a black SEVENTH ON SIXTH T-shirt, an ID, and a hassled expression rushed up to them.

"Katia? I'm Phil, I'll be escorting you inside," he said, waving them past the first round of security guards in front of the steps.

They followed him up the steps and into the main lobby of the tent. A frigid blast of air-conditioning sent goose bumps along Lizzie's skin. Ahead of her, she could see the snaking lines of people — noncelebrities — waiting to get into the two different runway rooms. Several leggy girls hawked free copies of *Women's Wear Daily* and booths set up around the room advertised different sponsors — bottled water, sunglasses, watches. The noise inside was deafening. It reminded her of the time her dad took her to see a Giants game — the tangle of people all trying to squeeze into one line at their section of seats. At least she had finally gotten up the nerve to ask her mom to let her sit this all out.

She was about to ask Phil to lead her to their seats when a flash of light popped in their faces.

"Katia!" someone screamed. A moment later, they were surrounded. A fleet of paparazzi closed in around them, screaming at them, snapping their pictures. *Clickety-clickety-click. Clickety-click-click. Clickety-click-click.*

"Katia! Who are you wearing?"

"Katia! Why lingerie?"

"Katia! Will you be modeling it?"

"Katia! Over here, *over here!*"

"KATIA!"

The cameras were so close that Katia and Lizzie couldn't move. Phil tried to clear a path through the cameras but it was impossible. Lizzie tried to remember to breathe.

"Katia! Katia! Katia!" they yelled.

Lizzie teetered on her heels while in front of her, Katia struck her favorite pose — shoulders thrown back, hand on hip, brilliant smile. The crush of cameras and the din of the screams could have sent anyone in their right mind running back out to Bryant Park, but Katia was used to this. This, in fact, was why they were here.

Lizzie reached into her bag and let her fingers close around her phone. She had a desperate urge to text C and H, and have them take her mind off this ambush.

39

And then her mother turned around. "Honey!" she called out with the same fake smile on her face. "Come here!"

Lizzie watched, dumbfounded, as Katia held out her arm and waved to her, just like she had a few days ago. "Come up here! Take a picture with me!"

Lizzie froze. Why was her mother doing this? Hadn't she just said Lizzie could skip this?

"Honey!" Katia yelled. "Come *on*!"

Lizzie gulped. Had her mom already forgotten what they'd talked about in the car? She stepped forward as Katia reached for her and pulled her in closer, until she had her arm around her.

The flashes were blinding. Lizzie tried to smile, but her jaw was locked so tight it felt like a grimace.

"Smile," Katia whispered. Lizzie wanted to shove her away, but she couldn't. It was official, she thought. Her mother wasn't oblivious. She was selfish. She'd decided to ignore everything Lizzie had said.

"Thank you," Katia said into the stream of flashes. "Thank you." That was what you said when you wanted the paparazzi to stop taking your picture, as if they'd been doing you a favor.

"Katia, we have some reporters waiting," Phil yelled into Katia's ear, taking her by the elbow. She nodded, and he led her over to the press area, where several television crews waited to interview her.

"Congratulations on your new line!" said a reporter, aiming his tape recorder at Katia's mouth. "What made you decide on lingerie?"

Her mother pointed to her ample chest. "What do *you* think?" she asked in her sultriest voice.

Lizzie grabbed a free bottle of Voss water from a nearby booth and tried to think past her anger. Why had her mom done that to her?

She sipped some water and moved out of the way of another frigid stream of air from one of the vents. The pack of photographers at the doors had moved on to someone else now, a starlet known for losing a dress size every season. Lizzie watched her try to keep her cool as the paparazzi engulfed her tiny frame.

At last they were on the move again. Phil began walking them toward the main exhibition space. "Katia incoming," he said into his mouthpiece, in a deadly serious voice. "Katia incoming."

Then a small, muscular man with a platinum buzzcut and large, liquid brown eyes stepped out of the chaos. He wore torn black jeans and a T-shirt with an image of an American flag pocked with bullet marks, and his eyes had a wired and jittery look to them. "Katia *darling*!" he cried, flinging his arms around her mother as if she had just survived an earthquake.

It was Martin Meloy. As he and Katia embraced, paparazzi shoved each other to capture the moment. A shot of the world's most famous supermodel hugging the world's most successful fashion designer was worth a lot of money.

"Martin!" Katia said, kissing him on both cheeks. "Thank you for coming. I know you have your show tomorrow so I appreciate this."

"Not a word, darling," he replied, grasping her hand in his. "I don't sleep starting in July, so I've got it all under control," he said, winking.

Lizzie stared at him, starstruck despite her anger. Martin Meloy wasn't just a designer — he was THE designer. A Martin Meloy dress, or more importantly, a Martin Meloy quilted leather bag with real silver hardware and a special pocket for your iPhone, was the holy grail of fashion. His ad campaigns were deliberately edgy, with a simple photo of a girl sitting against a wall, wearing one of his items or accessories, hardly showing them off. But the girl was never just a girl. She was a mysterious combination of cool and beautiful and the Martin Meloy state of mind — which seemed to involve being effortlessly chic and rebellious at the same time. Martin Meloy supposedly handpicked her himself each year, and then designed his collection around her.

Katia and Martin had worked together once or twice, but were mostly just good friends.

"Darling, just go in there and *kill*," Martin advised. "You'll be divine."

"Thanks, love," her mom said. "And you remember my daughter, Lizzie."

Martin's restless eyes traveled over Lizzie's face but only touched down for an instant. "Of course," he said, leaning in to give Lizzie a perfunctory kiss on the cheek.

"Hi," she said, smiling politely. He never really remembered her.

"Thanks for coming again," Katia said.

"Love love," Martin said, the same way someone else might say "Bye bye." And then he was gone.

"Mom," she started, wanting to ask her mom if she could wait to sit down, but there was a push of the crowd behind them, and before Lizzie knew it, they were both inside the main exhibition space. The plastic-covered runway seemed to stretch a mile down the center of the room. The air smelled spicy and sweet from all the perfumes. Hundreds of editors, writers, photographers, actresses, celebrities, and rock stars socialized from their seats, filling the usual half-hour of waiting time. As the assistant led the way toward the front row, Lizzie could see heads all across the room turn to gawk at them.

"Um, Mom," Lizzie began, but Katia was already chatting with a dreadlocked singer who'd written a song about her once. Lizzie had no choice but to shimmy sideways to the two empty gold chairs at the far end of the front row.

She dropped into her seat. Now she was trapped. And she knew what was coming.

"Couldn't I have just skipped this?" she asked her mom when she finally sat down.

Katia gazed at her questioningly, her greenish-blue eyes brilliant in the light. "Oh, honey. It won't be too bad. I think it's going well." Even this close, her mother's skin didn't have a pore. She patted Lizzie's knee. "Just don't forget to smile."

And then, as if on cue, they were surrounded again. The photographers hovered like locusts, flashing and clicking, their lenses just inches away from them, screaming more questions at her mom.

"How do you stay in such great shape?"

"How do you juggle career with family?"

"What was the inspiration for your design?"

Calmly, Katia began to answer the questions. But Lizzie felt the onset of a full-blown anxiety attack. With her head bent, she fumbled in her bag for her phone. Now she really needed to text Carina and Hudson...

"Hey!" a voice said.

She looked up to see the foam-covered dome of a microphone in her face. On the other side of it was a man wearing pancake makeup and eyeliner. An entertainment reporter. Behind him another man stood with a video camera on his shoulder.

"Are you the daughter?" the reporter asked.

Lizzie nodded dumbly.

"So what's it like having the hottest woman in the world as your mom?" he asked breathlessly. He thrust the mic back at her face.

Lizzie stared at it. She couldn't think all of a sudden.

"Is it fun having a mom who's a supermodel?" he asked in the same hyper-enthusiastic tone. "And what do you think of her clothes?"

Lizzie thought for a moment, staring at the microphone. She knew what she was supposed to say. *It's fun! It's cool! Her clothes are great!*

But was this really fun? Fun was walking through the Village with Carina and Hudson. Fun was wearing her favorite pair of ripped-up corduroy shorts and Old Navy flip-flops, and lying on her back in the Meadow, watching the kites dance in the sky while she sipped a Frappuccino. Fun was writing in her journal, or sitting at her computer, lost in thought, writing a story. Fun was petting her white Persian cat, Sid Vicious, while lying on her bed.

Fun was *not* squeezing into a dress that was a size too small and wearing heels that gave her blisters, and standing, frozen smile plastered on her face, next to the hottest woman in the world. Or having a gazillion cameras in her face for minutes on end.

Or being ambushed by a man wearing more makeup than half the women in the room and his annoying questions.

"Actually, it kind of sucks," she blurted into the mic. "And I think her clothes are a little slutty."

The reporter's mouth dropped open. Far back in his mouth, Lizzie could see a gold filling. Seconds ticked by.

"I mean...it's cool," she corrected herself. "It's great! I was just kidding."

He just gaped at her. Clearly, it was too late to correct herself. Finally he tipped the mic back to his face. "What's your name again?" he asked.

She swallowed. This wasn't good. "Lizzie."

"Lizzie. Well, thanks for sharing." He turned to the cameraman. "I think we're done here," he muttered.

The camera. She had almost forgotten. This had all been recorded.

"Wait a minute —" Lizzie said.

Before she could finish, the reporter and the cameraman had stepped away, back into the swirling mass of people. A moment later, they were gone.

Lizzie sat, paralyzed. Briefly, she thought of running after them, but she knew it was pointless. They were gone for good. And she had no idea who they were.

"Thank you," she heard Katia say on her left to the photographers. "Thank you very much."

Had her mother heard what she'd said? And had she really just said that?

As the cameras finally stopped, Katia squeezed Lizzie's arm. "Let's get this show on the road, huh?" she asked, grinning.

"Yeah," Lizzie said faintly, trying to breathe. Miraculously it looked like she hadn't heard a thing.

A pounding remix of one of her favorite songs suddenly filled the space and the lights dimmed. More assistants appeared and pulled off the plastic from the runway. Anticipation crackled in the air. The moments before a show began usually gave Lizzie chills, but this time she was too panicked to pay attention. All she could hear was what she'd said to the reporter.

Katia squeezed Lizzie's hand in anticipation. "Here we go," she whispered.

Lizzie tried to squeeze back. She had broken the golden rule, the First Commandment. Well, actually, it was rule number six of being a Daughter, but it was still a big rule. It should have been number one.

She had put down her mother.

In public.

To a reporter.

On video.

Now Lizzie was *really* never coming to Fashion Week again.

chapter 5

"Fuzz? That you? Dinner's here!" her father called from the kitchen.

"Be right there!" she called back, as she walked into the apartment with her heart in her mouth.

She was still in shock. After the show, she'd told her mom that she had homework to finish and run out of the tent, leaving her backstage surrounded by more reporters and a flock of fashionista friends. The twelve-minute show had passed by in a blur. Her answer to the reporter pounded inside her head, blocking out the DJ's music. Instead of the models coming down the runway, all she could see was the reporter's open mouth and his gold filling. Now her Trina Turk dress was soaked from sweat, and she wished she could just take a shower, go to bed, and pretend this had never happened.

But she couldn't. There was *tape* of her saying what she'd said. It was out there, loose in the world. Even though Katia hadn't heard her, it was just a matter of time until she did, which meant she was going to have to tell her. Lizzie's throat knotted up just at the thought of it.

She opened the door to her room, and felt the knot relax slightly. Her room always calmed her. She called it the Cloud because every color was either blue or white. The walls were painted the color of the sky, and the carpet was a luxurious white shag. Her desk was white, her MacBook was white, and even Sid Vicious looked like a big fluffy snowball curled on her white and blue tufted bedspread.

"Hi, Sid," she said, sitting on the edge of the bed and unbuckling her sandals.

Sid raised his head and blinked sleepily. A lone tooth stuck out of his mouth and almost up his nose, giving him a surly, defiant air. She'd given him his name because of it. Lizzie liked to imagine that he was the preeminent punk rock star of the cat world.

Sid went back to sleep, and she took out her iPhone. All the way home in the town car, she had been too panicked to text her friends. Now she thought she might call one of them.

"Fuzz?" she heard her dad yell. "Food's getting cold!"

She put down the phone. She'd wait until after dinner. She changed into a T-shirt, shorts, and Havaianas, and when she walked out to the kitchen her dad was doing a last polish on his column with a red pencil. Takeout containers of steaming Thai food were spread out on the table in front of him.

"Got pad thai and duck skewers," he said, looking up. "And spring rolls. Nice and healthy," he said, chuckling.

From the time she was born, it had been obvious to everyone who Lizzie actually did look like: her father. She and Bernard

Summers had the same buggy eyes and the same confused nose, and even though his hair wasn't red, it was the same frizzy, gravity-defying texture. They both had thick eyebrows (though his were furrier), full lips, and broad knuckles that they cracked when they were nervous. When he married Katia, the press had dubbed them "Beauty and the Beast." But despite his odd looks, Bernard Summers had enjoyed a very successful life. He was a brilliant journalist, and had twice been a finalist for the Pulitzer Prize. Plus, he'd married the most beautiful woman in the world (who happened to appreciate good writing). Lizzie liked to think that she'd inherited some of her dad's writing talent along with his looks. But she didn't expect to marry someone gorgeous. Weird-looking girls usually didn't score the Brad Pitt look-alikes of the world.

"So, how was the show?" her father asked as she sat down.

"Great," she said, trying to sound upbeat. "Mom did an amazing job."

"I would have been there, but this column's not even close," he said, shaking his head. "And we have to leave for Paris in the morning. Those L'Ete people wouldn't budge. There's so much red tape at that company it's like talking to the Pentagon."

L'Ete, a French cosmetics company, was one of Katia's biggest and best modeling contracts. Three times a year her mother flew to Paris to stand in an evening dress and heels in front of obvious landmarks like the Arc de Triomphe and the Eiffel Tower. As if wearing a certain kind of blush would transport you to Paris.

"Would you rather I stayed home with you?" he asked. "Instead of Irlene? I don't *have* to go."

"I'll be fine, Dad. Go. It'll be okay." Lizzie chewed her duck. If Katia had heard what she'd said to the reporter, maybe a nice long trip was exactly what they needed.

Suddenly Lizzie heard the front door burst open. "I'm home!" her mother called from the hall, and Lizzie felt her stomach tighten again. *You're going to have to tell her,* she thought. *Tonight — before they leave.*

"We're in here!" Bernard called out as Katia burst through the swinging door.

"Guess what?" she asked, her aquamarine eyes shining like an excited child's. In her dress and heels, she looked way too stunning to be standing in their kitchen. "Saks, Nordstrom, and Neiman Marcus all placed orders. Isn't that *incredible*?" She stomped her feet on the ground. "And Bergdorf's, too. I can't believe it! I can't believe it!"

Katia never got this excited about a modeling assignment. It was almost sweet.

"Fantastic!" Bernard crowed. He stood up and gave his wife a vaguely paternal hug and kiss. The fifteen-year age difference between them came out whenever Bernard was proud of her. "I knew you could do it. Lizzie said it was a great show."

Katia kicked off her heels and sat down at the table. "The Paris stores are interested, too," she said. "I'll be meeting with them after the shoot with L'Ete. Of course, that means we might end up staying a bit longer than a week." She said this last part to Lizzie as she spooned a small heap of pad thai on her plate. Instead of following a certain diet, her mother simply ate three-quarters less than everyone else.

"That's okay," Lizzie said, straining to be nice. Seeing her mom was starting to make her angry again. "It really was a great show. Congratulations."

Katia ate a small nibble of food. "Martin Meloy was there," she said to Bernard. "He said some kind things."

Lizzie mowed her fork over her rice. "Mom?" she began, still looking at her plate. "There's something I need to tell you."

She felt Katia's eyes on her, waiting.

"When we sat down, and the paparazzi came up to us, this guy, a reporter, kind of ambushed me, and he started asking me questions, and I think I said some stuff that came out wrong."

Katia didn't say anything. Still looking down, she waited.

"It wasn't anything too bad, but I still thought I should —"

"I heard what you said, Lizzie," her mother said. "I heard the whole thing."

Lizzie looked up. Her mother was staring at her plate, dragging a piece of tofu around with her fork.

Bernard looked up from his reading. "Heard what?" he asked absently.

"Lizzie spoke to a reporter," her mother said in a low voice. Lizzie felt her heart skip a beat. "About me."

Her father put down his work. "What?" he asked.

"It just slipped out. I didn't mean it."

"*What* slipped out?" Bernard wanted to know.

Lizzie paused. *Please Mom*, she thought. *Don't tell him.*

"She said she was sick of me," Katia murmured. "And some other things." In an even lower voice she added, "On videotape."

"*What?*" Bernard sputtered. "This was *filmed*?"

51

Katia held up a cautionary hand. "I already spoke to Natasha. It was a couple of guys from an English news channel, nothing big. She's taking care of it." Katia turned her stony glare back at Lizzie. Her eyes had turned into a deep, furious purple. "I'm just sorry that's how you feel, Lizzie. I would never have asked you to come if I'd known. And from now on, you don't have to come."

"Mom, I didn't do it on purpose," she argued, starting to get panicked. "And I did ask you before we got there —"

"You're *fourteen years old*," her father broke in, his voice perilously close to a shout.

"Dad —"

"You should know better than that," he yelled, cutting her off. "She's your mother!"

"Don't you think I *know* that?" Lizzie shot back. "Don't you think I deal with that *every single day*?"

Katia and Bernard looked at her, startled.

"Do you think that's fun for me?" she went on. "Getting my picture taken with you? Being *compared* to you?"

Katia stared at her, aghast. Lizzie was startled, too, but she couldn't take the two of them judging her. Not when they so clearly didn't care about her feelings.

"I asked you tonight in the car if I could just meet you inside!" she yelled. "Remember? And you totally blew me off!"

"Lizzie, don't be so dramatic —" Katia said.

"Look at me! Do you think it's easy going to things like that with you? Why don't you get it? Or do you just want to show everyone how great you look for having a fourteen-year-old daughter?"

Katia's face went pale. Bernard rose to his feet. "Go to your room," he ordered. "Now!"

"Is that what it is, Mom? Am I just there to make you look good?" The words were bubbling up from within her, from places she didn't even know existed.

"Well, I'm sorry, Lizzie," Katia said coolly. "I'm sorry that I've given you a good school and a beautiful apartment. I'm sorry I'm such a terrible mother."

"That's not what I'm saying. I'm just telling you it's hard! It's hard being around you!"

Katia took a deep breath. "Maybe if you were just more comfortable with yourself," she said. "If you didn't compare yourself... if you just accepted the fact —" Katia stopped herself, as if she realized what she was about to say.

"That I'm ugly?" Lizzie asked, her voice trembling.

"Oh, Lizzie," Katia sighed, looking down at her lap. She was either unwilling or unable to look Lizzie in the eye. And that was as good an answer as any.

Lizzie's face was so hot it felt like her skin might sizzle off the bones.

She stood up, letting the legs of her chair screech painfully against the tile.

"Lizzie," her dad said in a warning voice.

She ignored him.

She ran straight out of the room, into the hall. In one swift motion she pulled open the front door and slammed it behind her so hard the walls shook.

She bypassed the elevator and dashed into the stairwell. Flight after flight, she ran down the stairs, the sound of her steps echoing against the walls. At last, when she felt like she might throw up, she stopped and leaned against the cool wall. The first sob came, and then she couldn't stop. She sat down on a step and threw her arms around her bare, stubbly knees, and feeling as sad and alone as if she'd never had parents at all, she cried.

chapter 6

After she collected herself, she took the elevator to the lobby and went to the Barnes & Noble on the corner. She read *The Great Gatsby*, sitting cross-legged on the floor of the fiction section, until she finished it. At ten o'clock she tiptoed back into the apartment, on alert for a run-in, but her parents' bedroom door was closed. When she awoke the next morning they were gone.

Now as she climbed the limestone steps of her school's main staircase, she felt unsettled and uneasy, as if she'd had a bad dream. She'd never screamed like that at her parents before — she'd never even come close. But even worse was what her mother had said. Every time she remembered Katia's words — and the subtext underneath them — she felt a sharp pain in her chest. So her mother hadn't been oblivious after all.

It was all so painful and embarrassing that she wasn't even sure what to say about this to Carina and Hudson. At least being here at school, she could try to push last night out of her mind.

When she walked into homeroom, Hudson and Carina were sitting in their usual spot, in the desks by the blackboard, but both of them looked upset. Carina had her tin of Carmex out, and was rubbing it onto her lips, which was always a sign that she was stressed about something.

"You guys okay?" she asked, looking around quickly for Todd.

Carina's suntanned face looked a little pale. "Something just happened," she muttered. Lizzie could see that she was holding her iPhone.

"What?"

"Not here," Hudson said, shaking her head. They pointed to the door, and Lizzie, puzzled, followed them back out into the crowded hallway, and then into the ladies' room.

"What happened, you guys?" she asked, more seriously.

Carina and Hudson squeezed themselves into a single stall like they did whenever there was a crisis, pulled her inside, and shut the door. This was definitely not good.

"Will you guys just tell me?" she asked.

Carina handed her the iPhone. "Look at this," she said.

Lizzie looked down at the screen. It was a video clip on YouTube. On it she could see her mother, sitting in a folding chair, in her purple halter dress, fielding questions from the press. It was the fashion show.

And then she saw herself. Sitting next to her mother. Wearing the strapless Trina Turk dress. And talking into a microphone. Lizzie turned up the volume, just as she heard herself say the words she couldn't get out of her head: *Actually, it kind of sucks…And I think her clothes are a little slutty.*

She watched it three times until Hudson gently pulled the iPhone out of Lizzie's hands. "You okay?" Hudson asked, slipping the iPhone back into her cotton tote, silkscreened with a picture of her French bulldog.

There had been 12,378 hits already. In two hours it would be double that. Every fashion and celebrity gossip blog would have a link to it by the afternoon. And underneath the clip a post had said:

She's just jealous cuz her mom is hot. And she got hit with the ugly stick.

"Lizzie, talk," Carina said, her brown eyes filled with worry.

"Does your mom know?" Hudson asked calmly. She smelled like Kate Spade's orange blossom–scented perfume.

Lizzie nodded. "I told her last night. And then we had a huge fight. Now she's on a plane to Paris. But the publicist was supposed to take care of it."

"Well, obviously that publicist's doing a crappy job," Carina said. "I say you call her up and complain."

"Or go down there and talk to her about it," Hudson suggested, her green eyes sparkling. "Ask her if there's anything you can do. She won't be mad."

"Uh, right," Lizzie said, staring at some graffiti of a broken heart that some nameless girl had scratched into the wall. "You guys haven't met Natasha. She's paid to get mad." She touched the wall of the stall to keep herself steady. "Oh my God, you guys. I called my mom a slut."

"You called *her clothes* a slut," Carina corrected her.

"Why'd you do it?" Hudson asked patiently.

Lizzie shrugged, feeling tears come to her eyes. "I asked her before we got there if I could skip the photo craziness and it was like she didn't even hear me. And lately, the cameras and the pictures, the posing with her...it's just kind of hellish."

From deep inside her bookbag, her iPhone dinged with a text. Her first thought was that it was her mother. She pulled out the phone and checked the screen. "It's Natasha," she announced to her friends.

She clicked on the message and read it aloud. *"We need to talk. Call me at the office. ASAP. N."* Lizzie put down the phone. "Great. She wants to kill me."

"She probably just wants to help you," Hudson said, twisting her black hair up into a makeshift bun and securing it with a pencil. "This is not the end of the world, okay?"

Lizzie nodded. Her friends were right: this wasn't the end of the world. Even if twelve thousand people had already watched this.

She wrote Natasha a quick reply, saying that she would be able to stop by after school, and then walked back into homeroom, where Todd waited for her near their usual cluster of desks, looking adorable as usual. "Hey," he said, grinning. "Everything okay?"

"Sure, everything's fine," she said, even though she wanted to cry.

The rest of the day was torture. During each class, she pretended to listen and take notes, while in her mind a deep male voice announced YOU ARE A TERRIBLE DAUGHTER, over and over and over.

When the bell rang after their last class, Lizzie, Hudson, and Carina walked straight to the corner of Fifth Avenue, hailed a cab, and jumped in.

When they got to Natasha's office building in midtown, Lizzie paid the driver and stepped out of the cab.

"Are you sure this is a good idea?" Hudson asked, looking up at the tall, foreboding skyscraper. It was one of hundreds that lined the cool canyon of Third Avenue but this one looked especially scary.

"I think so," Lizzie said. She looked enviously at the people walking past, their faces free and innocent of wrongdoing. Chances were that none of them had ever insulted their mothers on YouTube. "Okay, let's go, you guys," she said.

She swung her bookbag to the other shoulder and led the way through the revolving doors, into a soaring atrium-style lobby.

After a swift, silent elevator ride, they walked out into a sterile-looking reception area done in a depressing burgundy color scheme. She'd been here only once before, with her mom.

"You want us to go with you?" Hudson asked, biting her pouty lower lip with concern.

"No, that's okay. You guys wait out here." Lizzie gestured toward the two couches.

"Just don't forget, *she* works for *you*," Carina said, bossily pointing an index finger in her face.

"Right."

Lizzie headed toward the frizzy-haired receptionist. The phones were ringing off the hook.

"You can go right in," the girl said, pointing down the hall. "Last office on the left. Natasha's expecting you." Apparently, she'd seen the YouTube clip, too.

Lizzie turned and padded down the soft-carpeted hallway, her bookbag sliding onto her arm. *Relax*, she told herself, tying her hair into the best version of a ponytail she could. One ten-second clip wasn't the end of the world. It wasn't like she'd done anything illegal. Natasha was used to DUI arrests and panty-less crotch shots. Surely she'd be able to put this in some kind of perspective for her. Even if she was a tad uptight, from what Lizzie remembered.

Toward the end of the hall, she heard a familiar, withering English accent.

"She's a *teenager*!" the voice said. "You know how *bloody* disagreeable they are, they say *whatever* comes out of their mouths. It's not like it *means* anything!"

It was coming from the last door on the left. *Maybe Natasha won't be able to put this in perspective*, Lizzie thought.

"No, Katia *doesn't* have a comment, and there are *no* problems at home," the voice went on. "And my God, there is *real* news out there. Haven't you ever heard of Darfur?"

It was too late to turn back. With a gulp, Lizzie stepped through the doorway.

Natasha sat behind a desk piled so high with trades and magazines and newspapers that at first Lizzie could barely see her. She was tinier than Carina, and always looked like she was playing dress-up in her uniform of sharp, pinstriped suit and lace-trimmed camisole. She wore her usual accessories — a thick silver cuff bracelet and a silver Cartier tank watch, and a razored fringe of black bangs ended just above her tiny, raccoon-lined eyes.

Those eyes darted in Lizzie's direction, like a cobra's, as she said, "Look darling, I have a meeting. Another crisis, you know. Yes, lunch would be fab. Talk soon." She pulled off her Bluetooth and tossed it in between a stack of newspapers and a thick September *Vogue*. "Well, hello, Lizzie," she said. "Speak of the bloody devil."

Lizzie sat down in a Lucite chair in front of her desk. This had almost definitely been a mistake.

"I just wanted to say I'm so sorry about what happened," she started. "This was all a big mistake. And if there's anything I can do —"

"Do you have *any* idea what kind of a day I've had?" Natasha demanded, in a tone that suggested she was about to answer her own question. "*Do* you?"

"Um, actually, uh . . . ," Lizzie began.

"On an average day, I get a *hundred* phone calls — a hundred and *ten*, tops," she said, gesturing to the sky. "But today, I've had one hundred and *seventy-five* phone calls, all because of you, Lizzie, and it's not even four o'clock!"

As if on cue, her six-line phone began to ring. Natasha inhaled deeply and pressed her index finger against the inner corner of her eye, as if she was trying to prevent a total nervous breakdown. "Amanda!" she hollered toward the door. "Can you get that, please?" Natasha removed her finger from her eye and took another deep breath.

"You've had a hundred and seventy-five phone calls?" Lizzie asked.

"I have had calls from *Star*, from *Us Weekly*, from TMZ, from the *Daily Mail* in London, from Paris, from Tokyo," she continued, lifting each of her black-polished fingers. "All of them wanting to know why Katia's daughter said such horrible things about her mother."

"But my mom said you were taking care of it —" Lizzie said.

"It's the bloody Internet, for God's sakes!" Natasha snapped. "Now, I've done what I can, but listen to me, Lizzie, listen to me very carefully," Natasha said, placing a hand on her heaving chest. "I don't know how you behave at home, but you can't just go shooting your mouth off when you're in public. And especially not in front of a *camera crew*. This is the twenty-first century, Lizzie. Privacy doesn't exist anymore. Do you understand that?" Natasha shook her head as if privacy was too absurd for even her to contemplate. "And at Fashion Week? My God, you've been there enough times, you know how things get. If this were your first time I would have understood, but my *God*..." She let her voice trail off with outrage. "You have to be smart, Lizzie. You have to *think*," she said, vigorously tapping the side of her head. "You *have* to be more careful about what you say. To call your mother's designs slutty, Lizzie, I mean, honestly. You have to *protect* your mother. We *all* have to."

"I was just surrounded," Lizzie stammered. "I got freaked out, the guy ambushed me —"

"You say to them everything's fine, everything's good, and that your mother's an *inspiration to women everywhere*," she emphasized. Natasha's phone rang again. "Amanda?" Natasha yelled toward the open door.

"Have you heard from my mom?" Lizzie asked tentatively.

"Not yet. But I'm sure I will. It's causing quite a stir."

"Oh," Lizzie mumbled.

Natasha turned around to face her computer monitor. "Let's see," she said, reading from the screen. "The *Post* wanted it to be the lead story for their Entertainment section this weekend. Famous mother and daughter catfights through history, or something like that. *Star* wants to put you and Katia on the cover for next week. Oh, and Tyra wants to do an intervention-type show with you and Katia. *When Your Mom Is Hot, and You're Not.* We're *obviously* not returning that call."

A tall, twenty-something girl in skinny jeans and with a hang-dog expression knocked on the door. Lizzie could only guess it was the long-suffering Amanda.

"Yes?" Natasha asked.

Amanda trudged into Natasha's office. "That photographer called again for Katia's kid. About the ugly modeling?" she announced, placing the slip on her desk. "Don't worry, I got rid of her."

There was a long silence. Lizzie pretended to become very interested in the box of Kleenex on Natasha's desk.

"Amanda?" Natasha said sweetly. "This is Lizzie Summers. Katia's daughter."

Amanda went pale as she stared at Lizzie. "Oh," she said. "Hi. Sorry."

"You can go now," Natasha commanded.

Without a word, Amanda walked out. Natasha turned toward Lizzie and gamely attempted a smile. "I was going to tell you about that," she said. "A photographer saw you on the clip. She thought you had a *unique look*," she said, hooking her fingers into air quotes around the words.

"It was for ugly modeling?" Lizzie asked. Maybe it was time she finally embraced this.

"That's just the slang term for it," Natasha said. "It's *real-person* modeling. Using people who aren't *traditionally* beautiful to sell products. It's starting to get some attention here and there in the ad world. But speaking as *your* publicist, too, it's out of the question," she said, crumpling the message slip. "I want you to stay away from anything and any*one* with a camera. The longer you make yourself scarce, the sooner this circus will go away. And really, Lizzie...would you want your mother to think that you turned this into a career opportunity?"

She tossed the slip toward the trash can at the side of her desk just as the phone rang again.

"Oh God, hold on," she said, glancing at the screen. She clipped on her Bluetooth. "Hello?" she whined. "Yes, hi. Yes, I know it looks bad. But my God. *Slutty* isn't the f-word," she said, swiveling to the side.

Lizzie looked back at the trash can. There, on the carpet, just inches from Lizzie's feet, was the slip. Natasha had missed the can. The crinkled piece of paper lay just inches from her foot, begging to be picked up. Suddenly she wanted to see the words in writing: "ugly modeling." Maybe it would help her finally accept it.

In one seamless motion, she leaned down, snatched up the slip, and stuffed it into the front pocket of her bookbag.

"Yes, I know it's Katia, but I don't understand why this is news," Natasha said, still looking out the window. "Haven't you ever heard of the Sudan?"

Lizzie got to her feet. This seemed the right time to make her exit. She waved at Natasha, who still hadn't seen her get up.

"She's a teenager!" Natasha screamed. Lizzie took off down the hall.

When she reached the lobby, Carina and Hudson had their noses buried in issues of *InStyle*.

"Let's go, you guys," Lizzie said hurriedly, as the receptionist watched her closely.

Hudson and Carina joined her at the elevator bank. "So what happened?" Hudson whispered.

"Natasha says she's finally taken care of it," she said.

The elevator doors opened with a whoosh.

"But have either of you guys ever heard of ugly modeling?" she asked. She didn't know why, but saying "ugly modeling" filled her with a sense of defiance, even purpose. So the whole world thought she was ugly. There was actually a certain relief in it.

The doors closed. "You mean, people so weird-looking they're hot?" Carina asked.

Hudson nudged Carina hard in the arm. "People who are different-looking. It's the new thing."

Lizzie felt for the slip in the pocket of her bag. "Some photographer called Natasha about me and said I had a unique look," she said. She pulled out the slip and smoothed it open. "I just can't tell who it is," she said, trying to read Amanda's scribbling.

Carina grabbed the slip. Her dad was constantly leaving notes for her in his barely legible handwriting. "That says Andrea Sidwell," she said, reading. "One fifty Crosby Street."

"Oh my God, Lizzie," Hudson said dreamily, placing a hand on Lizzie's wrist. "She wants you to be a *model*?"

"Well, a *weird* model, apparently."

"You have to do it," Hudson said, shaking her head. "This is fate. You have to."

"No way," Lizzie said, pressing the lobby button over and over.

"Why not?" Hudson asked.

"Because Natasha said it was a bad idea. And it probably is, with the whole YouTube thing happening. And, come on. An ugly model? Is that something I want to be?"

"Look at all those people who model for American Apparel," Carina reasoned. "They're weird-looking. And hot."

"That's because they're in their underwear," Lizzie reminded them. "No, I'm not doing it."

The elevator doors opened, and they walked through the lobby.

Outside, the streets were crowded with the start of rush hour. A red double-decker bus filled with smiling tourists lumbered by. Despite Natasha's tirade, Lizzie felt better. Calmer. She'd move on from this. And, she was even a little bit flattered. A photographer wanted her to be a model. Even if it was ugly modeling, nobody had ever asked her to do that before.

"If you don't want to do it," Carina said, "then why'd you save that slip?"

Lizzie put the slip back in her bookbag without saying anything. Carina had a habit of making points that were impossible to debate. And then she heard her iPhone chime. She pulled it out. It was a Facebook friend request and a message from Todd.

You ran out before I could remind you about tomorrow night. You're still coming over right? 7 o'clock.

66

"Oh my God, you guys," Lizzie said. "Todd just texted me. To remind me about tomorrow night."

She showed her friends the message. "I knew it!" Carina cried. "He *wants* you."

"Are you gonna friend him? You have to friend him!" Hudson squealed.

Lizzie pressed the Confirm button. She and Todd Piedmont were now officially friends. But maybe, just maybe, Lizzie thought, they were on their way to being more.

chapter 7

"Here, Lizzie, try this one," Hudson said the next afternoon, as she plucked a lace-trimmed lavender camisole from the pile on the shelf.

"It looks a little low-cut," Lizzie said doubtfully.

"That's the whole *point*," Carina cut in, as she swiped the cami from Hudson and added it to the top of the stack of tops in Lizzie's arms. "And *please* tell me you're gonna flirt with him tonight."

"Yes, it helps if he knows you like him," Hudson teased, her gigantic silver hoops dangling merrily on either side of her heart-shaped face.

Lizzie felt her stomach turn over. In exactly seven hours, she would be walking into a possible date with Todd, or at least a Planned Hang-out Alone in His House, and she was woefully unprepared. She'd corralled her friends for an emergency trip to Big Drop in SoHo, except now they were making her even more nervous, and so was the store. A teenage girl slammed into her as she rifled through the racks with her mom.

"What if this isn't a date?" Lizzie said, fingering a stretch jersey top. "Then it'll be a little ridiculous for me to be flirting with him."

"Right, this isn't a date," Carina muttered. "Because he *really* needs you to help him put out Doritos." She pulled a long black dress with spaghetti straps off the hanger and held it up to herself. "Do you guys like this?"

Hudson frowned. "Do you really need that?"

"For the school dance in a couple weeks," Carina said with a shrug as she slipped it off the hanger. "Whatever."

"Here, Lizzie, try this one, too," Hudson said, tossing her a sparkly top with crisscross straps.

"All right, I'll be right back," Lizzie said. She needed to go before Hudson picked out any more clothing she didn't have the courage to wear.

She yanked the curtain shut and looked in the mirror. Her eyes bugged out, her nose looked like the Leaning Tower of Pisa, and her hair, thanks to the muggy weather, was starting to look like the Bride of Frankenstein. Maybe a sexy top couldn't hurt.

The lavender cami was the first one she tried. It gapped a little in the chest area, unsurprisingly, but as she twisted this way and that in the mirror, it didn't look bad. In fact, it was kind of pretty. The color set off her hair and warmed up her pale skin. As usual, Hudson's style sense had been right.

"What do you guys think?" she said, sticking her upper body through the curtain.

Hudson pulled Lizzie all the way out of the room and looked her up and down. "*Big* thumbs-up. C?"

Carina looked her over with the black dress still in her arms. "Yep. Totally hot."

Lizzie turned to look in the store mirror. It *did* look good on her...but would Todd think so? She tried to see herself through his eyes. Was her skin too white? Maybe she should have dug out the Jergens self-tanning lotion from the back of her bathroom cabinet. And her upper arms...why did they have to be so thick and shapeless? She turned around. She'd almost forgotten about the weird cluster of moles on her back in the shape of the Little Dipper. And then what would Todd think if she showed up in this? They'd been childhood buddies, for God's sake. She'd never worn anything fancier than a pair of jean cut-offs and a T-shirt in front of him.

"I don't think it's me," she decided.

"What?" Hudson blinked her green cat eyes. "It's perfect on you."

"It's kind of..."

"Sexy?" Carina said. "That's a *good* thing."

"I don't think so, guys," she said, and scurried back into the fitting room. She could feel her friends giving each other looks on the other side of the curtain. But it was her body, wasn't it? It was up to her if she didn't want to go over to Todd's house looking like Ilona Peterson.

She tried on the rest of the tops, but none of them fit or worked. After they waited for Carina to buy her dress, they walked out into the stream of tourists on Broadway.

"Okay, that was lame," Carina finally said.

"You're the one who just bought something without even trying it on," Lizzie pointed out.

"But you looked so beautiful in that color," Hudson said. "Why didn't you like it?"

"It just wasn't me," Lizzie said, hoping that might kill the subject.

"But it was!" Carina argued, almost colliding with a man walking out of Dean & Deluca with an iced coffee.

"You don't see yourself the way we do," Hudson said diplomatically.

They turned east onto Spring Street and walked toward NoLIta. Lizzie loved SoHo — the cobblestone streets, the ancient warehouse buildings, the mixture of tourists and artists and models. A man stepped out of Balthazar Bakery with a loaf of French bread and pedaled away on a bicycle, as if this was Paris.

"Well, maybe I don't see myself the same way, but my eyes are my eyes," Lizzie said. "I don't know how to change that."

"I do," Carina said, unwrapping a LUNA Bar she'd pulled out of her bag. "Call that photographer."

"What photographer?"

"The one from yesterday, from your meeting with Natasha," Hudson chimed in.

"No, wait," Carina said, stopping dead in her Jack Rogers flip-flops. She pointed straight ahead of her. "We're in her neighborhood. She was on Crosby Street, right? One fifty Crosby Street."

Carina had a photographic memory. Sometimes it was a little scary.

Carina walked closer to the corner. "That building says one-oh-five —"

"We're gonna *go* there?" Lizzie asked with alarm. *"Now?"*

Carina shrugged, her shoulders grazing the tips of her blond hair. "Why not?"

"Because I don't even know if I want to do this," Lizzie said. "I haven't decided."

Carina headed down the block. "Don't think about stuff so hard," she said.

Lizzie could feel herself getting sucked into the C Cyclone, as she and Hudson called it, but there was little she could do about it.

"Here it is," Carina said, coming to a stop in front of an ordinary glass door. "Andrea Sidwell," she read off the list of residents tacked next to the front door. "Fifth floor." Calmly she rang the buzzer.

"Carina!" Hudson said. "Stop!"

Carina dismissed them with a wave of her hand. "We'll tell her it's you. She'll be psyched."

"But I don't know what to say!" Lizzie argued.

Hudson took Lizzie by the hand. "I'll try and help," she said calmly.

Through the intercom there came a crackle of static and then the sound of a long, steady buzz. Carina grabbed the door handle and pulled it right open. "We're in," she said, her eyes bright with adventure. Carina lived for stuff like this.

"Oh God, help me," Lizzie whispered.

On the fifth floor they walked out of the elevator into a long, curving hallway. A door at the end was marked A. SIDWELL. STUDIO. "This is such a bad idea it's not even funny," Lizzie said.

"It'll be fine," Carina whispered. She pressed the doorbell.

A few seconds later the door opened, and a woman with friendly blue eyes, ripped biceps, and a messy blond ponytail stood on the threshold. In baggy workout pants, bare feet, and a black T-shirt that said SILVERSUN PICKUPS, she looked like a college student, though Lizzie figured that she was in her early thirties.

"Well, hello," she said happily, looking down at them without a shred of surprise. "So I guess you're *not* the delivery guy from Dean & Deluca."

"Are you Andrea Sidwell?" Carina asked in her most direct and adult voice.

"I *am*," she said in a mock-serious tone.

Carina nudged Lizzie forward. "*This* is Lizzie Summers," she announced.

Andrea stared at Lizzie for a brief, amused moment, as if she was pretty sure this was a joke, and then she blinked. "Hey, Lizzie." She stuck out her hand and grasped Lizzie's. "I'm Andrea Sidwell," she said with a radiant smile. "What an awesome surprise. Come on in, you guys."

Andrea turned to walk down a narrow entry hall, and the three of them followed. "Sorry about the mess, guys," Andrea said over her shoulder. "I wasn't expecting guests. But I know you can deal."

The hallway opened into a spacious, high-ceilinged loft flooded with sunlight from large casement windows that faced the street. An M.I.A. song played on the sound system, just loud enough for the beats to pack a wallop, while a few fat votive candles lit in the corner gave off a fresh piney scent. A makeshift set had been set up in the center of the room, complete with light stands, tripods, a fan, and a giant roll of white paper that served as a backdrop. Framed black-and-white portraits hung on the brick walls.

"Can I get you guys something to drink?" Andrea padded over to the small kitchenette. "Vitamin Water? Green tea? Cold bottled chai-whatever?"

"Vitamin Water would be great," Hudson replied for the group, as Lizzie walked over to check out the portraits.

They were mostly of people's faces in various levels of close-up, just like the ones she'd seen once in a Richard Avedon exhibit at the Whitney. Except these weren't of old movie stars like Marilyn Monroe and Cary Grant. They were of ordinary people. Some were teenagers. Some were middle-aged. Some were elderly, with wrinkles and age spots. And all of them had obvious flaws: big teeth, big noses, untweezed eyebrows, jutting chins, deep wrinkles that made their faces look like creased roadmaps. But you couldn't take your eyes off them. In the shadows made by the camera, they were mesmerizing. They were, weirdly, beautiful.

"So I'm shocked they gave you my message," Andrea said to Lizzie, handing each of them a bottle of orange Vitamin Water. "The girl I spoke to didn't exactly fill me with confidence. So were you totally weirded out?"

Lizzie twisted off her cap and glanced at her friends. "A little," she admitted. "What is it you do exactly?"

"I mostly shoot for magazines and ad campaigns, and I use 'regular' models, too," she said, hooking her fingers into quotes. "But this kind of work," she said, walking toward the wall of photos, "*this* is much more my thing. Real people. Like her." She pointed to a photo of an elderly woman with long gray hair that flowed past her shoulders. "I saw her on the 6 train. She's seventy-eight, a great-grandmother, and when I told her that I thought she could be a model, she thought I was on drugs. But she turned out to be a natural. I shot her for a shampoo ad. She's been working ever since."

Andrea walked over to a photo of a stocky bald man with startled, childlike eyes. "I met him in line at Gray's Papaya on Seventy-Second and Broadway. Look at those eyes. Amazing, huh? I shot him for a Toyota ad. They *loved* him," Andrea said, shaking her head. "All of these people had something worth looking at. Something beautiful. And most of the time, I wasn't the only person who thought so."

"They are beautiful," Lizzie agreed.

"Of course the other kind of beauty is still going strong — the kind we see in *Vogue* or *InStyle*," Andrea went on. "But there's something else happening now." She folded her toned arms and smiled. "Something I call the New Pretty. Like Selina." She pointed to a portrait of a teenage girl. She was tall and what some might call big-boned, with tiny shell-like eyes, long, stringy blond hair, and full cheeks. She wasn't anything close to what the boys in her school might have called hot, but she was so unusual-looking that she commanded attention.

"I found her in Albuquerque," Andrea went on. "She's done three layouts for me, and the European magazines went nuts for her. She just signed with a modeling agency."

"So then why is it called *ugly* modeling?" Lizzie asked.

Andrea rolled her eyes. "Ugly, right," she said with a rueful chuckle. "If we use a girl who's not six feet tall and ninety pounds and drop-dead gorgeous, people call it ugly modeling! A better word for it is *unique*. And that's you, Lizzie." Andrea stepped back from the picture and turned to face her. "None of these people thought they could model. None of them thought anyone would want to see them. But people do. And I think they'd want to see you, too. You have that *thing*, Lizzie — that kind of face that makes you pay attention. You have the New Pretty."

Lizzie stared at her. This woman, who seemed incredibly cool, successful, and with excellent taste in music, thought she was beautiful? And wanted to photograph her?

Carina, as usual, broke the awkward pause. "So what would be the first step?" she asked, sounding as brisk and businesslike as an agent.

"Test shots. We could do them on the street, in the park. Or here in the studio. Wherever you're most comfortable." Andrea grabbed a card from a stack on a nearby table and handed it to Lizzie. "Here. Talk about it with your mom. See what she thinks. I'd be happy to speak to her."

Her mother. Suddenly Lizzie heard Natasha's spiteful voice. *Would you want your mother to think that you turned this into a career opportunity?*

"Can I have one of those, too?" Hudson said.

"Yeah, me too," Carina said, walking over.

She had to say no before this got out of hand. "Thanks, but I don't think I can," Lizzie said nicely. "It's not something I want to do. But I wanted to come by and just thank you for the interest."

Andrea gave her softest, gentlest smile, as if she were auditioning to replace the Dalai Lama. "Okay, I respect that," she said. "I know it's a lot to take in. But...just hang on to the card." She shrugged. "You never know, right?"

Lizzie didn't say anything, but Carina and Hudson gave her *are-you-crazy?* looks as Andrea led them to the door.

"I'm so glad you guys stopped by," Andrea said, opening the front door. "And if you happen to see a Dean & Deluca guy with my lunch out there, send him in." She put her hand on Lizzie's shoulder. She had a crooked, but utterly trustworthy smile. "Great to meet you, Lizzie. And good luck."

Andrea closed the door. For just the briefest second, Lizzie felt a sharp wave of regret.

"Are you totally insane?" Carina exploded as they walked down the hall. "You were just *discovered*!"

"And she was so cool!" Hudson exclaimed, almost jumping up and down. "And so talented! Did you see her stuff? How real it was?"

"You guys know I hate cameras," Lizzie said feebly as she pressed the elevator button.

"That's the whole *point*," Carina emphasized. "This would be like your own personal *Fear Factor*."

"Exactly," chirped Hudson. "This is happening for a reason — to make you grow, to help you get over your issues."

"I told you guys what Natasha said," she replied, giving up on the elevator and opening the door to the stairwell. "Stay away from cameras. Lie low. Stay out of trouble."

"Your mom would never need to know," Carina suggested.

"How?" Lizzie asked as they clomped down the stairs. "How would this *not* get back to her?"

"There are ways," Carina hedged. "We'd figure something out."

"And what if she did find out?" Lizzie said. "How would I ever do what she does?"

She knew that Hudson could relate to this, but she was quiet as they reached the lobby and walked back onto the street. Hudson never wanted to talk about her potential music career.

"It's not like you'd be following in her footsteps," Hudson finally said as they turned toward the corner. "This is completely unlike what she does. You'd be doing your own kind of modeling."

Carina put on her Oakleys. "Just do it. What do you have to lose? You could be the next Coco Rochas. Or whatever her name is. And I'll say I knew you when."

She said goodbye to her friends on the corner of Crosby and Prince and watched them walk west, feeling the raised type of Andrea's business card in her hand. She could still smell the piney scent of Andrea's studio on her clothes. Something inside of her felt lighter, almost proud. Andrea had said she was pretty. She turned and looked back down the street to Andrea's building and up to the fifth-floor windows and smiled. Maybe she'd be back there one day after all.

Suddenly she had a thought. She started walking down Spring Street. A cool breeze blew against her face as she picked up speed. She rounded the corner onto Broadway. Thankfully, the crowd of shoppers and tourists had thinned. It only took a few seconds to reach the doors to Big Drop.

Inside, she maneuvered her way past the teenage girls straight to the stack of lace-trimmed camisoles. The lavender one was right on top, back from the fitting room. Yes, it had been a little low-cut, and yes, it would show her white arms, but right now she didn't really care.

"Just this, please," she said to the woman behind the cash register, handing her a credit card.

As the woman ran her card, Lizzie's gaze wandered to the wall behind her. There, facing her, was a framed photo of her mother. She was on the street, coming out of this very store, dressed in aviator shades, dark toothpick-thin jeans, and a crisp white shirt. It was one of those "In Their Own Clothes!" features from one of the tabloids, and the store had framed it to show people that Katia Summers was a customer. WE SELL THESE JEANS! someone had written in gigantic capital letters with a huge arrow pointing to Katia's legs. Lizzie was definitely used to seeing her mother's picture in the most random places, but now for some reason it was jarring. Maybe because she still hadn't heard from her since their fight two days ago — and the release of the clip. Thankfully, Natasha had managed to pull it off the Internet.

The saleswoman handed Lizzie back her card and put the top in a plastic bag. "Enjoy," she chirped, bringing Lizzie back to the here and now.

On her way out, Lizzie checked her watch. Only six more hours until she and Todd were alone together inside his house. She walked out of the store into the crowds, swinging the bag, and she already knew that she'd remember this night for a very long time.

chapter 8

By the time the elevator doors closed on the lobby of Todd's building, the butterflies in Lizzie's stomach had morphed into tiny exploding grenades. It didn't help that she'd been nervous for hours during her Ava-worthy grooming routine. She'd showered, shaved her legs, scrubbed herself with loofah gloves, and slathered on perfumed body lotion. She'd straightened her hair, and then curled it with a curling iron for those soft, Pre-Raphaelite, Nicole Kidman–like waves. She'd dusted her lids with gold eye shadow and applied at least two coats of mascara. By the time she was done, she had to say that she looked pretty good, enough so that her old doorman had barely recognized her. But what if Todd thought she'd overdid it? Maybe he honestly just wanted her help as a friend. And she did look a little glamorous to be putting out pretzels and dip.

As the elevator raced upward, Lizzie checked inside her beaded pouch for her phone. Carina and Hudson had both promised to be on call for any emergencies until they came over to the party. But there wouldn't be any emergencies, she told herself. Everything was going to be just fine. Everything was going to be amazing.

When they reached the penthouse, the doors opened. Todd stood right in front of her — apparently, the elevator opened right into the middle of his house. In scruffy jeans and a light blue cowboy-style shirt, with a wet forelock of hair falling over his eyebrows, Todd's hotness was on fine display. "So you remembered the address," he said.

"Hi," she said, trying to breathe as she stepped out into a marble-floored foyer. Todd's new apartment looked like a castle. Large modern canvases hung on the walls, while a grand, marble staircase led to the second floor. A chandelier that looked like an explosion of crystal hung from a long skinny chain above their heads. And branching off from the foyer were at least five different rooms, all of which were dark and unoccupied. It was three times the size of Todd's old place, but it also felt oddly empty, as if people hadn't yet moved in.

"This definitely isn't your old apartment," she said, craning her head to take it all in.

"Yeah, it's nice," he said casually, looking around. Then his eyes returned to her. "You look nice, too," he said.

"Thanks." Her stomach did a little flip and she prayed that she didn't blush. "So, what can I do? I *am* here to help, right?"

"Actually, let's go upstairs."

"Upstairs?" she asked warily.

"Yeah, I want to show you something." He grinned the way he used to when he suggested anything that could have gotten them in trouble. "Come on. I think you'll like it." He bounded up the stairs in his bare feet. "I promise."

She followed him up the carpeted steps to the second floor and down a thickly carpeted hallway.

"I feel like I'm at the Met," she kidded, looking around. "Did your dad change jobs or something?"

"No, the company's just doing really well," he said vaguely.

At the top of another staircase he led her down a hallway and up to a closed door. "Okay, you ready?" he asked, almost giddy, as he slipped his feet into some flip-flops by the door. Whatever it was he had to show her had Todd really excited.

"Yes," she said.

"Well, close your eyes. And I mean, *really* close 'em."

She shut them. "Okay."

She felt his hand on her arm, and it sent a lightning flash of electricity all the way up to her shoulder. Then she heard the creak of a door opening. Gently he pulled her forward, just as she felt a breeze against her face.

"Okay, open," he said.

She opened her eyes. She was standing in the most beautiful roof garden she had ever seen. Bushes of pale pink roses and milky-blue hydrangeas swayed in the breeze. Purple and white and red impatiens bobbed their heads in wooden barrels. Ivy crept up the walls of a small water tower, and magenta bougainvillea dripped down from a trellis. But even more beautiful was the view: Central Park stretched out in front of them like a soft emerald carpet, and above it, the setting sun carved a deep pink gash in the sky.

"Oh my God," she breathed. "This is amazing."

"Yeah," Todd said, surveying the view. "That one's your building, isn't it?" He pointed to the other side of the park. "That one just to the left of us?" From here, the Central Park West skyline looked almost fake, like a painted backdrop of craggy, turreted prewar buildings crammed next to modern brick and glass condos.

"Yep," she said. "That's it."

"Just like Daisy's green light, huh?" he asked, glancing at her over his shoulder and grinning.

Daisy's green light, she thought. Gatsby had stared lovingly across the water to the green light on the dock of Daisy Buchanan's house in East Egg. Was he saying what she thought he was? *Get a grip on yourself,* she thought.

She turned around and saw a long table laid with drinks and snacks. "Hold on. I thought I was supposed to help you with that."

"You are helping me," he said. He pointed to a comfy-looking pair of padded deck chairs. "You had to approve everything."

"Well, I approve," she teased.

"Good, then have a seat. I'll get you something to drink."

She sank into the chair and leaned back so far that her gaze was at the hot pink sky. From below them on the street came the soothing white noise of traffic. Already, this Date/Planned Hang-Out was more than she'd expected.

"It's so peaceful up here," she said when he came back. "I feel like I'm in a movie."

Todd handed her a plastic cup of Coke. Then he sat down and laid his head back on the soft fabric of his chair. "It's a great place to think. And it's definitely cool for a party. I just hope people come."

"Oh, they will," she said. "Especially Ava."

Todd gave her a quick, careful glance. "What does that mean?" he asked.

"Just that she likes you," Lizzie said. "It's obvious. You don't see it?"

Todd turned away and rubbed his hands on his jeans. "Not really," he muttered.

Lizzie sipped her Coke. *Guess that was the wrong thing to bring up*, she thought.

"Hey," he suddenly said. "I read your story."

In her excitement about tonight, she had completely forgotten about her story. "You did?"

"I thought it was great. The fight between the mother and daughter was really well done. And the ending worked — it was sweet but not sappy." He cradled his head with his hands and tilted his head toward her. "It was about you and your mom, wasn't it?"

Her chest tightened with embarrassment. "Sort of," she admitted, turning her eyes to the sky and watching a plane slice through a cloud. "My stories tend to go that way — you know, toward the real. Though I've never had the urge to cut my hair." *For obvious reasons*, she wanted to add.

"Mine are like that, too, even when I try to write about other stuff," Todd said, rubbing his hands on his jeans again. He seemed jumpy. "I don't know, it's just the way I write. Oh, I've been meaning to tell you. I saw the YouTube clip."

"You did?" she asked, horrified.

"It really wasn't that bad, you know. It was kind of cute."

"*Cute?*" she asked, turning to look at him.

"I could tell it just slipped out," he said. "I don't blame you. It must be hard, being around that all the time. I couldn't do it. No way." He stretched out his legs and contemplated his feet.

"But it's funny," he went on. "I always thought you were prettier than your mom."

"What?" she asked, almost giving him a deathstare.

Todd frowned. "Sorry, does that offend you or something?"

"No, it doesn't offend me. I just…" She shook her head. "You *do?*"

"Hey, don't get me wrong — your mom's still hot," he said. "But so are you."

"You're a psycho, you know that?" she said.

"Why is that psycho?" he asked.

"Because it is. And you don't have to say that because of the YouTube clip —"

"I'm telling you this because that's what I think," Todd said. "I think you're prettier than her."

"Stop it!" she laughed, smacking him on the arm.

In a flash, he caught her hand and covered it with his own. Lizzie froze. Todd held her hand, and then, carefully, turned it this way and that, examining it, stretching out her fingers, like it was a piece of treasure he'd just found. She watched him, afraid to move, feeling the warmth of his skin over hers. When he finally braided his fingers with her own, she stopped breathing. His hand was so warm it sent chills through her body. Her skin tingled. Something was about to happen.

He looked up at her. With the smoothest movement, he began

to lean in, closer and closer, his lips headed straight toward hers, until…

She scrambled out of her chair and up onto her feet. "Where's the bathroom?" she asked, almost breathless.

A red flush began to spread over Todd's bewildered face. "Uh, what?"

"Where's the bathroom? Sorry," she added.

"Downstairs," he said quietly. Then he got to his feet and cleared his throat. "I'll take you."

She knew that she had just made one of the biggest mistakes of her life, but it was too late. He was on his feet. She had no choice but to follow him. They walked through the door and trudged down the steps in silence. *You are a moron*, she thought. *A complete and utter moron.*

At the bottom of the stairs he pointed to a door. "It's right here," he said.

"Great. Thanks." She threw herself inside as quickly as possible and shut the door. Then she stood over the chrome sink and turned on the water full blast.

Todd Piedmont liked her. He had just been about to *kiss* her. And she had bolted. For no reason. Well, she knew the reason. She was scared. Scared to death. But why? And most importantly, how was she going to walk out of here, pretend this never happened, and hopefully get him to kiss her again?

Carina would know what to do, she thought, reaching for her iPhone. Carina would supply her with a witty retort, a way to wriggle out of this mess.

When she pulled out her phone, she found that she already had a text from her.

HELP!
HUGE FIGHT WITH THE JURG!!
COME OVER NOW!!!!

Without a second thought, she threw the iPhone back in her bag and whipped open the door. Out in the hall, Todd jumped.

"I'm so sorry, but I have to go," she said. "It's an emergency."

If Todd had looked surprised when she walked into the bathroom, now he looked utterly confused. "Okay," he said carefully.

"It's Carina. She needs me."

"What's wrong?"

"I don't know yet," she said. "I'll try and come back later, though."

She wanted to say *I'm not blowing you off,* but then that would have only made it more obvious that this was exactly what she was doing. Why was she such a freak?

Instead she walked to the elevator and punched the button. "I'm sure the party'll be great," she said lamely.

"Yeah," he said, sounding as if he couldn't care less.

The elevator doors opened. She stepped inside. There had to be something she could say to explain.

"I'll see you later," she said, just before the door closed. *Brilliant,* she thought as the elevator dropped down to the lobby.

She leaned against the wall and sighed. That had been a grade A disaster. Just a few minutes ago he had been about to do something so incredible that she would probably never have to watch *The Notebook* again for the rest of her life. And now it was gone, as fleeting as the sunset they'd been watching upstairs. And it had been all her fault.

Lizzie sighed deeply as the elevator coasted to a stop.

She had to come back tonight to the party. She just had to. Otherwise she wasn't sure if she'd ever get back to that moment ever again.

chapter 9

When Lizzie walked into the lobby of Carina's futuristic glass high-rise on Fifty-Seventh Street, Hudson was already waiting on the bench by the cascading waterfall. An overnight bag was at her feet. They knew from experience that when Carina and the Jurg had a fight, it usually took a while to cheer Carina up.

Lizzie wanted to spill every detail about what had just happened at Todd's house, but it seemed more important to ask Hudson about Carina. "Do you know what happened?" she asked.

"I only know what you do," Hudson said as she rose from the bench. "They had a fight, and she's freaking out. But bad this time. Really bad." Hudson looked beautiful in a smoke-colored, sleeveless top with sequined straps, and an extra-skinny pair of purple Genetic jeans. Lizzie could never pull off the skinny jeans look. They made her look like a giraffe.

They got out at the sixty-fifth floor and walked down the hall to the only door. Out of habit, Lizzie glanced up at the security camera above the door. The Jurg's apartment was protected by a full-time security guard named Otto, who only buzzed in approved guests. They heard the buzz, and then the heavy door unlocked. Lizzie pushed it open.

Otto sat behind his desk in his suit and tie.

"She's in the den," he said, pointing down the hall.

"Carina?" Lizzie called out.

All they could hear was a Coldplay song coming from the den. Lizzie and Hudson looked at each other. Whenever Carina listened to Coldplay, she was in trouble.

They walked into the room. The Jurg's collection of rare Picasso sketches hung on the gold walls, and on the mantel just under the flatscreen was a display of Fabergé eggs. On one of the leather couches sat Carina, her blond head bent, her tiny frame shaking underneath a pale blue T-shirt. Her hair hung in damp, ragged chunks around her face. In her hand, she kneaded one of her dad's stress balls ferociously.

Lizzie went straight to the stereo and turned down the dial. "Why are you listening to this? No wonder you're crying."

"What's going on, C?" Hudson asked gently, letting her bag drop to the ground and taking a seat beside her on the couch. "Just tell us. It's okay."

Carina kept her head bowed so they couldn't see her face, but a tear splashed silently onto the leg of her cargo pants. Carina rarely cried, and when she did it was with a quiet, graceful dignity that Lizzie almost envied.

"He wants me to work for him," she finally said, raising her tear-stained face. Big red blotches spread underneath her eyes, which were shriveled from crying. "He says I'm going to inherit his company one day, so he wants me to start *now*."

"Where?" Hudson asked. "At one of his magazines?"

"Nope," Carina sniffed, wiping her freckled nose with the back of her hand. "The corporate office. Wednesday and Friday after school and all day on Saturday." She sniffled again. "No more soccer. No more surfing on the weekends. No more Model UN. No more hanging out with you guys. No more anything. Wednesdays and Fridays. Till *eight*. And Saturdays. All so I can watch him and his creepy manservant plot more world domination."

"Ugh. You mean Ed Bracken?" Hudson asked, visibly horrified.

Carina nodded and tied her damp hair into a sloppy bun. Ed Bracken was the Jurg's right-hand man and all-around suck-up. He was so good at sucking up Carina also called him the Anteater. He had slumped shoulders, a weird shuffling walk, and gray hair that was so thin and greasy that it looked painted on his head. Rumor had it that he lived with his mother, even though he had to be in his mid-fifties. Lizzie believed it.

"So what'd you say?" Lizzie asked.

"What could I say? You know how he is." Carina picked at her hemp bracelets. "He's always wanted me to learn the business, even though he knows I'm not interested and it's totally not me. He doesn't care. He pretty much ran his own newspaper when he was sixteen. So…it's my turn now."

"Did you say no?" Hudson inquired.

"I tried. There's no arguing with him."

"But you're the best arguer I know," Lizzie pointed out.

"Not this time. He's got me totally beat." Carina shook her head, and her hair drifted back around her ears. "And the worst part is, this is my life. He said I'm his sole heir," she said, using finger quotes. "Which means I'm gonna do this the rest of my life, like it or not."

"So just tell him that you don't want to inherit his business. Tell him there's other stuff you want to do," Hudson counseled, taking an elastic band off her wrist and putting Carina's hair in a ponytail.

"Like what? Lead Outward Bound trips?" Carina's chin quivered with a building sob. "Stuff like this just reminds me that he doesn't even know me. I'm just this kid who lives in his house. He doesn't have a clue who I am. He doesn't see me. He looks at these paintings more than he looks at me." She continued to knead the stress ball. "And now I just have to do what he says. Like everyone else."

Hudson threw her arms around Carina. "We'll figure this out," she whispered, hugging her. "Don't worry."

Lizzie crouched down next to Carina, too. "You're going to be okay, Carina. You really are."

Carina sniffled and got to her feet. "Well, if he's gonna make me do this, I'm gonna get back at him. That's for damn sure." She shoved her feet into a pair of Havaianas. "All right, you guys, let's go. Time to get out of here."

"Where are we going?" Lizzie asked, alarmed.

"Montauk," Carina said. "We'll have the place to ourselves. My dad went to LA. And it's my last chance to go there till I start indentured servitude."

"But —" Lizzie started.

"What?" Carina asked, wiping her puffy eyes. "You can't go?"

Lizzie felt Hudson watching her tensely. Of course she had to go. She couldn't desert her friend now. Not even to go back to Todd's house and try to rescue her evening. "No, that's fine, I mean..."

"Oh my God, Todd's party!" Carina realized, grabbing her arm. "I forgot! If you want to go back, Lizbutt, you totally can."

"No, let's go. It's not a big deal."

"You sure?" Carina held on to Lizzie's arm.

"Totally. Let's go."

When they reached the lobby, the Jurg's massive black Range Rover was waiting for them in front of the building. Carina could summon it whenever she wanted, along with Karl's driver, Max. As Lizzie followed her friends into the backseat, she reached into her bag for her phone. She'd have to just send Todd a text. She didn't have a choice. She couldn't desert her friend.

Can't make it back to the party, but have a great time! I'll explain later...

Clearly, she wasn't going to get into Carina's drama with him in a text.

For that night and most of Sunday, the three of them walked on the beach, watched an entire season of *Project Runway*, and swam in the Jurg's lagoon-shaped pool. Little by little Carina began to show progress. By Sunday she was almost back to her old, bossy self, criticizing Nina Garcia's comments and pointing out how much better her version of a dress made from car parts would be. But Lizzie couldn't get her mind off Todd. She played the scene on the roof over and over in her mind. She checked her iPhone every five minutes.

On Sunday afternoon, she couldn't take it any longer. During a break in the *Runway* marathon, she stole into the Jurg's office and wrote Todd a message on Facebook.

How was the party??

For the rest of the day, she checked her e-mail inbox frantically. He never wrote back.

chapter 10

Lizzie sat on the edge of her desk in homeroom, her eyes locked on the doorway like a Marine-trained sniper. It was Monday morning, and Todd still hadn't written her back. A thousand possibilities had begun to race through her head, but only three seemed likely. He a) was offended by her bizarre last-minute exit, b) thought she was crazy because of her bizarre last-minute exit, or c) had suddenly moved back to London.

Madame Dupuis stood at the front of the room in one of her heinously authentic pantsuits from the seventies. Her clothes were so bad that sometimes you could barely look at her. Why were teachers so clueless?

"Allez, allez," she called out in her French Canadian accent, furrowing her unibrow over the class list. "Lisa Angelides."

"Here."

"Bryan Buka."

"Here."

"Lizzie, relax, he'll be here," Carina whispered on her left. She had made a full recovery since Friday night, and was now doing her geometry homework at the last minute. Hudson was reading a copy of *Teen Vogue*.

"Ava Elting," Madame droned.

"Here!" Ava yelled from her corner, lifting her auburn head. Then she went back to whispering with the Icks. The bunch of them had been in a huddle since homeroom had started. Something big had gone down this weekend, that was for sure.

The sound of hurried footsteps in the hall made Lizzie look back toward the door, and suddenly Todd rushed into the room, his pale cheeks flushed and his hair wet and piecey. He looked completely embarrassed and a little groggy, as if he'd overslept. "So sorry," he stammered politely. "Really. So sorry."

"Bonjour, Monsieur Piedmont," Madame said with an edge in her voice, gesturing for him to sit down. *"Asseyez-vous."*

Over here, Lizzie thought, watching him as he moved into the room, looking for a seat. *Just look over here…*

But he stepped past her without a glance. All the way to the back of the room, right into the knot of desks that held the Alpha Male triad of Ken Clayman, Eli Blackman, and Chris Eaton.

Lizzie turned forward in her desk.

"Since when is he friends with that crew?" she whispered to Carina.

Carina looked back at Todd and shrugged. "He's a guy," she said.

For the rest of homeroom, Lizzie tried to construct a cool, clever, and hopefully funny apology. *I'm sorry I never made it back,* she thought. *Yes, I totally bolted from your house but I really* would *like to kiss you. When can we get back to that?*

When Madame had finally reached the end of the list and the bell had rung, Lizzie turned to Carina and Hudson. "I'll meet you guys in history," she said, packing up her stuff.

"Just be friendly," Hudson said.

"Yeah, don't be all tweaked out that he didn't write you back," Carina put in. "Make light of it."

Um, as if, she thought as she scrambled to catch up with Todd in the hall. "Hey," she said when she was just behind him. "How was the party?"

Todd turned around. He seemed surprised, as if they were the sort of friends who waved hi to each other but never really talked. "Hey," he said, slinging his bookbag over his shoulder. "What's up?"

"Sorry I never made it back," she said, plunging right in. "I really wanted to, but we ended up going to Montauk and it was kind of an emergency —"

"Hey, no worries," he said, holding up his hand to stop her, as if he were some cool surfer dude. "Things were a little crazy this weekend." His eyes darted around the hallway, looking for something, or someone. She waited for more of an explanation, but he didn't give one.

"Was it fun?" she asked.

"What?"

"The party."

"Oh, yeah," he said distractedly, still looking around. Suddenly he cocked his head as if he'd just had a brilliant thought. "Hey. I think we need to get to English, right?"

Before she could answer, he turned and started walking up the hall. Lizzie watched him, dumbfounded. This wasn't like Todd. He never acted uninterested in talking to her. Was he mad at her?

"Hey, you still owe me a story," she teased as she followed him down the hall. "Don't think I'm gonna forget about that."

"Hey, Piedmont!"

She looked over. Ken Clayman was waving him over to where he and Eli and Chris were standing near the lockers. "Get over here!" he yelled. "We're doing fantasy football!"

Todd glanced back at her. "We'll talk later. Okay?"

She just nodded and watched him walk over to his new friends. A moment later the whole pack of them moved down the hall, nudging and jostling and laughing. She couldn't believe it. Fantasy football? He'd been living in England for the past three years. What did he care about the NFL?

At a loss, she turned to see Sophie Duncan and Jill Rau emerge from the girls' bathroom, shoulder-to-shoulder, both of their kilts hanging unfashionably to the knee. Sophie and Jill weren't the coolest girls in the class — they wore bright pink lip gloss and had huge public crushes on Zac Efron — but they were nice enough, even if they were constantly gossiping about people.

"And are you totally *sure*?" Sophie asked, pushing her glasses up her nose.

"Yep, Kate and Ilona were talking about it at the deli," Jill confirmed, rubbing a lip gloss wand over her lips. "It happened after everyone else went home. So I won. I said they'd hook up the first week."

"They hooked up the first *weekend*, not the first week," Sophie countered.

"Same difference," said Jill.

They were all walking in the same direction, so Lizzie fell into step beside them. "What'd you guys bet on?" she asked.

"Oh, how soon Todd and Ava would hook up," Jill said casually, smacking her lips together. She gestured to Sophie. "And now this bee-yatch owes me a Mac Lipglass."

Lizzie had to force herself to keep moving. Her legs felt like they'd been filled with concrete. "They hooked up?" she asked as nonchalantly as she could.

"Yeah, at Todd's party," Sophie said. "Which is technically *not* the first week of school, by the way," she reminded Jill.

"Yes, it is," Jill said back to her.

"Todd's party?" Lizzie asked in disbelief.

"I knew it would happen," Jill put in. "I mean, she was all *over* him last week. And who else is Todd gonna go out with?"

The two of them turned into a classroom, leaving Lizzie in the hall. The bell rang. Doors shut. Everything went quiet. She couldn't move.

Todd and Ava.

Hooking up.

At his party.

Hours after she'd left him there.

She stood for minutes in the deserted hall, letting this sink in. At first it didn't seem possible. But then she remembered the distracted look in his eyes, the way he'd practically run away from her just now, and it made a sick kind of sense.

Finally she hitched her bookbag further up her shoulder and made her way up the hall. Todd had thought Ava was a cool girl. Cool enough to hook up with only a few hours after she'd left his house.

But he likes me, a small voice inside of her said. *He likes ME.*

And then another voice spoke up and drowned that first voice out.

Not as much as you thought he did.

Lizzie held it together until lunch, when she and Carina and Hudson slid into a booth at the diner around the corner on Madison.

"So he's about to kiss you, you leave, and then he hooks up with Ava the same night?" Hudson asked, her fork poised over her cottage cheese and melon. "It just doesn't add up."

Lizzie glumly plunged her straw up and down in her iced tea. "Maybe he *wasn't* about to kiss me," she said.

"It's my fault," Carina said quietly over a gigantic platter of fries. "I should never have sent you that text."

The diner was so packed with kids that it was hard even hearing herself think. In the next booth over Lizzie could see the Icks, sharing a plate of fries and giving them steely cold stares.

"It's not your fault, C," Lizzie said, trying to sound positive. "I'd already freaked out. He probably thought I was grossed out by him or something."

"You could tell him you weren't," Carina suggested, dragging a fry through her ketchup.

"Now?" Lizzie asked. "You know how it is when a guy starts

going out with Ava — they're lost forever. She's like the Bermuda Triangle." She poked at a floating lemon slice with her straw. "And maybe he wasn't that into me in the first place."

"Well then, that's his loss," Carina concluded, placing both elbows bossily on the table. "*He's* the idiot here, not you. *You* are hot and smart and completely *un*forgettable. Ava was probably throwing herself at him. Just because he was dumb and unoriginal enough to take her up on it doesn't say anything about *you*."

"I know, but it still feels awful," Lizzie said quietly, swallowing back the tears.

"Hey." Carina's trademark smile of mischief appeared as she leaned back against the vinyl booth. "Call that photographer. It's the perfect reason to do it."

"*Now?*" Lizzie gave Carina an are-you-totally-insane scowl.

"Yeah. It'll make you feel better."

"I think I still have that card...," Hudson said, diving into her bag.

"Wait! I can't just decide I'm going to be a model because some guy turned out to be a jerk."

"You're *not* gonna turn into a *model*," Carina moaned, dramatically rolling her eyes. "We're talking about getting some pictures taken. To boost your self-esteem. And to put up on your Facebook page and make him insanely jealous."

"Oh, and another thing," Hudson added, still digging in her bag. "Jupiter's in your tenth house right now, which is *huge* for your career."

"But I don't have a career."

"Here it is." Hudson produced the card from her bag. She handed it to Lizzie. "See? It's not even wrinkled."

Lizzie ran her fingers once again over the bumpy type that spelled out Andrea's name.

"I still don't get it," Carina said, shaking her head. "What were your reasons for saying no again?"

Lizzie put the card back down on the table. "Natasha said not to."

"Do you really think it'd hurt your mom to get a few shots taken?" Hudson asked sweetly. "You haven't even spoken to her since the fight."

Lizzie mulled this over. Carina was right. There was no reason for her to be worried about embarrassing her mom anymore. But then there was the reason Carina and Hudson didn't know, and the one that she didn't want to mention to them: what her mother really thought of her. That she was weird-looking. That she was someone to feel sorry for. And she trusted her mom's opinion more than she trusted Andrea's.

But maybe that was even more reason to do this, she thought. Maybe she needed to prove her mother wrong. To prove *herself* wrong. To prove that someone out there thought she was pretty, at least in kind of a twisted way. And doing this sure beat analyzing the Todd Piedmont Fiasco until the end of time.

Lizzie shrugged. "Fine."

Carina handed Lizzie her phone. Her friends didn't take their eyes off her face as she dialed. It rang three times, and then someone picked up.

"Hello?"

Lizzie recognized Andrea's friendly voice. She thought of the best way to put this.

"Hi, this is Lizzie Summers," she said.

"Lizzie!" Andrea said warmly. "What's up?"

Her friends were staring at her, waiting, daring her to chicken out. She knew, finally, that she didn't want to.

"I think I want to do it."

chapter 11

"I hope she doesn't think I'm a pro at this because of my mom, you guys. Or that I even know what I'm doing."

Flanked by Carina and Hudson, Lizzie turned off Fifth Avenue and entered Central Park. It was a beautiful Indian summer day, with clouds that looked like pieces of torn cotton candy and a light, mild breeze that made the tree branches sway in slow motion. It was a perfect day to get pictures taken, Lizzie knew, even though, five days after the call to Andrea, she suddenly wasn't sure if she wanted to do this.

"You're gonna rock this," Carina assured her as they walked by a harpist sitting on one of the benches near the Seventy-Second Street entrance. "You have the genes. You could catwalk Naomi Campbell under the table, for God's sakes."

"Um, I've never even *tried* to catwalk," Lizzie replied.

"You're doing this for you," Hudson reminded her, retying

a vintage Hermès scarf around her head. "Think of it as a self-affirmation exercise."

"Oh God," Carina sighed as they waited for some speeding bicyclists to pass. "You're going to have to stop reading your mom's New Age-y books, okay?"

"Thanks for coming with me, you guys," Lizzie said.

Hudson took her by the wrist. "And miss history in the making?" she asked, winking. "No way."

They walked the shaded, winding path that ran along the Boat Pond until it bottomed out into the redbrick-paved plaza in front of Bethesda Fountain. "There she is," Carina said as they walked into the open plaza.

Andrea sat perched on the edge of the fountain, an ice cream sandwich in one hand and her BlackBerry in the other. A square-shaped camera bag lay at her feet. When she saw them she stood up and waved her sandwich in the air.

"Okay, I didn't know what all of you wanted, so I got a Drumstick, a Fudgsicle, and a King Cone," Andrea said as they walked up, and she pointed to the ice creams she'd laid out on top of her bag. "Who wants what?"

Carina went right for the Drumstick — she loved anything with nuts — and Hudson took the Fudgsicle. Lizzie grabbed the King Cone. It was the first time Lizzie had ever seen a photographer actually encourage a model to eat.

"Isn't it gorgeous out?" Andrea gushed, looking up at the sky. "It's the perfect day to take some shots." She tossed her wrapper into the trash, unzipped her camera bag, and hefted a weighty

Mamiya camera the size of a volleyball into her hands. Looking at it, Lizzie could see why Andrea's arms were so toned.

"All right, where do you want to get started?" Andrea asked, pulling off the lens cap. She squinted in the sun. "Maybe we'll start in front of the fountain and then just move around?"

"Just so you know," Lizzie said, swallowing her ice cream, "I'm not like a pro at this or anything."

"Good!" Andrea exclaimed, smiling. "That's what I like to hear!"

Lizzie finished her cone, handed her bookbag to Hudson, and sat down on the rim of the fountain. She could feel the coolness of the water behind her. The floor of the fountain glittered with what looked like a thousand drowned pennies.

"Oh, Lizzie? Can I ask you to let your hair down?" Andrea gestured with her camera. "I want to be able to see it."

Lizzie reached up and pulled out her elastic, releasing her Brillo curls. Out here in the heat it was only a matter of time before they swelled into a helmet.

"Great," Andrea urged, holding the camera to her face. "Your hair is so beautiful!"

Are you nuts? Lizzie thought as she settled into the Pose: back straight, chin tucked in, shoulders down. It was the very first rule of modeling, and one that Katia had taught her years ago, even though she'd never really used it.

"Wait, wait," Andrea said, lowering her camera. She bounced over to Lizzie on her Chuck Taylors. "Don't worry about sitting straight up like that. Just sit the way you normally would. Like, the way you would if your friend was taking a picture of you."

"So, you mean, just kind of…" Lizzie let herself slump a little and relaxed her chin. "Like this?"

"*Perfect.*" She leaned closer. "I want you to forget anything you ever may have learned about doing this. You and I are gonna make our own rules — cool?" She turned to Hudson and Carina and yelled, "Okay, who wants to get things started for me?"

"Me!" Carina happily trudged over.

Lizzie watched in disbelief as Andrea handed her camera over to Carina. This woman was going to let one of her friends take her picture? With her fancy camera that probably cost thousands of dollars? Andrea wasn't crazy, Lizzie decided. She was totally cool.

"You just press that button there," she instructed, handing the camera over to Carina. "It'll do everything else."

Carina positioned herself in front of Lizzie as if she'd been taking pictures with a five thousand–dollar camera her entire life. "You ready, sexy thing?" she asked, hoisting it up to her face. "Make loooove to ze *cam-e-ra.*"

Lizzie laughed. Before she could stop, Carina pressed the button. *Click.*

"Great!" Andrea urged. "Keep going!"

"Work it, own it, *work it,*" Carina sang. Lizzie laughed again. *Click.* Carina pressed the button just at the right time.

"Perfect!" Andrea crowed.

"You are *fabulous, darling,*" Carina crooned, coming up close to her. "You're a *natural.*"

"Carina, stop!" Lizzie said, still laughing.

Then it was Hudson's turn. "To the left! To the right! You are so beautiful it *hurts*!" she yelled.

Click-click-click went the camera, as Lizzie smiled and laughed so hard her sides ached.

Finally Andrea stepped in and assumed control. "That was great, Lizzie," she said, suddenly the cool, calm professional. "Now look straight at me and smile."

Still giddy from laughing, Lizzie didn't have time to get nervous. She smiled broadly into the camera.

Andrea pressed the button. *Click.* "That's great!" Andrea called out.

Lizzie tilted her head just slightly to the right, smiled even bigger this time, and Andrea clicked.

"Yes!"

She tilted her head to the left.

"Perfect!"

Before she knew it, Lizzie had eased into a rhythm. She had a vague idea that her hair was starting to climb toward the sky but she didn't really care. A tiny voice told her to stiffen up, but she let it go. All that mattered was that she was getting her picture taken, and it didn't just feel okay — it felt natural. Fun. This wasn't anything like the onslaught of paparazzi at Fashion Week. This didn't feel invasive. It felt easy. Even exhilarating.

Meanwhile Andrea bobbed and weaved on her Chucks, coming closer, backing up, teetering to the side, capturing Lizzie from all angles. "That's great, Lizzie! Perfect!"

With every click, she actually felt something inside of her soar. *This woman is taking pictures of me. And this is actually fun.*

"Okay, let's try some serious ones," Andrea said, lifting her camera. "Let's have fierce Lizzie."

"Fierce Lizzie?" she said.

"Brave Lizzie," Andrea called out. "Says-her-mind Lizzie. The Lizzie from the clip."

The clip. The clip had started this all. Maybe, she thought, it hadn't been the worst thing in the world. For the first time, she remembered what it felt like just before she opened her mouth to speak to that reporter. That delicious feeling of letting go, of taking her hand off the wheel, of just being herself—with no filters, no voice in her head telling her no. She put her hands on her hips and leveled her gaze at the camera. She let her smile fade away.

"*Yes!*" Andrea moved closer as she pressed the shutter. "That's amazing! Keep going!"

It was almost like acting a part, and it was working. Behind Andrea, a crowd of tourists began to form. A little girl in the group caught her eye. She was a little chubby, ghostly pale, and her T-shirt said I HEART NY. She stared at Lizzie with wide, fascinated eyes, as if she were a unicorn or some other kind of mythical creature.

Finally, after Lizzie had taken a few more solo shots, Andrea lowered her camera. Her cheeks were flushed and there was a glistening layer of sweat at her hairline. "That was amazing! Did you have fun?"

"That was the most fun I've ever had in my life," Lizzie said. "Thank you."

"No, Lizzie, thank *you*," Andrea said, giving her a hug. "You're a natural. I knew you would be."

"Oh my God!!" Hudson yelled, running over. She grabbed

Lizzie and shook her arm. "You were amazing! You can do this, you know that? You're *good* at it!"

"You crushed it, Lizbutt," Carina announced.

"I felt so comfortable," Lizzie whispered.

"And you have it in you," Hudson assured her. "I could see it as you were posing. This other side of you just came out. You could really do this."

"For reals," Carina added.

"You do," Andrea seconded. "You really do. I'd be interested to hear what you think of the shots. I'll send you some, okay? I bet you'll love them."

They said their goodbyes to Andrea, and Carina and Hudson kept up their excited banter as the three walked toward Sheep Meadow and the west side.

"Well, you guys, let's not get carried away yet," Lizzie cautioned.

"No, I think I want to get carried away," Hudson said. She turned toward the Meadow on their left, filled with sunbathers and kite-flyers and people sitting on blankets in their work clothes, soaking in the last rays of the sun. "Hey, everyone!" she yelled. "This girl's gonna be a star!"

Needless to say, nobody turned around, but Lizzie beamed anyway. She looked past the Meadow, up at the crowded skyline of midtown just beyond the park and the hotels along Central Park South hovering above the trees. You couldn't hear the traffic this far into the park, and for a moment, the city didn't look real. New York was always changing like that. One moment you were overwhelmed by the in-your-face hustle of it — the traffic, the garbage, the noise, and the people scrambling down the streets — and then you entered the park, or looked out the window of Carina's penthouse, or stood on the roof of Todd's building, and the city could look as insubstantial as a dream. Inside Lizzie, something stirred. Maybe her friends were right. Maybe she could do this. Maybe Hudson's words might prove true.

"You have to do that again, okay?" Carina asked as they walked past the hansom cabs lined up in front of Tavern on the Green. "If you don't, I might not be able to be your friend anymore."

"Well, I will say this, I'm exhausted," Lizzie said. "I don't know how my mom does this."

"Get used to it," Carina said, her chocolate eyes twinkling.

She said goodbye to her friends on Central Park West and turned down her block, feeling the wind caress her face. At the corner of Columbus she looked across the street and saw paparazzi gathered in front of her building. They'd been gone for a while, ever since her parents left for Paris, but now they were back, and something had them excited, pressing their cameras to their faces. A black stretch limo with the trunk still popped open idled at the curb.

Her parents had just come home.

She rushed past the photographers calling their editors, and took the elevator upstairs. She opened the front door and almost tripped over her mother's gargantuan Louis Vuitton suitcase in the foyer. They were definitely home. Lizzie felt jittery. She wasn't sure if she was ready to see her mom yet. Or tell her about what she'd just been doing. But she knew that she would probably have to apologize for her dramatic outburst the night before they left.

"Mom?" she called out.

There was the terse *clip-clip* of spike heels approaching from down the hall, and then her mother appeared in the hallway. "Hi, honey," she said. Even after a nine-hour flight, she looked stunning in full-legged tweed trousers and a sleeveless silk chiffon blouse. Not one blond hair had escaped the updo she always wore on planes.

"How are you, honey?" Katia asked, coming toward her. She leaned down and tentatively wrapped her delicate arms around Lizzie's shoulders. Lizzie breathed in her mom's trademark scent — a tuberose and lily perfume blended exclusively for her by a perfumery in Paris — and realized how much she'd missed her.

"I'm good," Lizzie said. "How was the trip?"

"Productive." Katia straightened up and pushed some of Lizzie's hair off her forehead. Her mother was still at least three inches taller than her. "I got Katia Coquette into Bon Marché and Galeries Lafayette. And the L'Ete shoot went well. I missed you, though." Lizzie looked up at her, waiting. Even though she wanted nothing more than to apologize and put the fight away forever, she had no idea what to say.

"Look, honey," Katia said, laying a hand on her shoulder. "I spoke to Natasha. I know you went down to see her. And I've thought about the fight we had, and, well, maybe you're right." Her greenish-blue eyes were steady and sincere. "Maybe I haven't thought of how difficult it must be for you. The attention, the cameras. Sometimes I forget that I chose this life for myself and you didn't." Katia touched Lizzie's hair tenderly. "And I'm sorry about what I said. I hope I didn't hurt your feelings."

"I'm sorry, too," she said quietly. "Really."

"So from now on, you don't have to be a part of those events anymore if you don't want to be. That's my life. Not yours."

Lizzie blinked. For a moment, she wondered if her mom had taken too many melatonin on the plane. "Okay," she finally managed to say. "Thanks."

Katia hugged her again. "So, no more fighting. Oh, I brought you back some things from Paris. Just some makeup from L'Ete."

Lizzie never wore the buckets of makeup her mom brought back for her. She usually just gave it all to Hudson. "Great," she said.

"And I'm ordering in pizza for you and Dad," she said, backing up toward the kitchen. "He's in desperate need of junk food, he says. We can catch up more at dinner. I'm glad I'm home, honey," she murmured, and then she pressed through the door and her statuesque frame disappeared.

Lizzie hurried down the hall to her bedroom, still in shock. She hadn't expected her mom to apologize first. Now she felt a little embarrassed about the photo shoot with Andrea. If her mom knew that what she'd said had been hurtful, and apologized for it, then had Lizzie really needed to get those pictures taken by Andrea, just to prove a point about what her mom had said? And what if Natasha was right — what if the pictures got out and somehow made her mom look bad? After the YouTube clip, the last thing she wanted to do was embarrass her mom again. So for now, she wouldn't say anything, she decided. It was just a one-time thing, anyway.

Lizzie walked into her room, dropped her bag on the white shag carpet, and kicked off her shoes. On her computer was a message from Hudson.

U WERE AMAZING!

Lizzie smiled.

Couldn't have done it without u, she wrote back.

Then she lay down on her bed next to Sid Vicious and patted him on the head. He opened one cranky blue eye.

"Today was a good day," she told him softly, just before she drifted off for a nap.

chapter 12

The only problem with playing the game I Completely Forgot I Knew You is that eventually the person you're trying to ignore sits down next to you in English and forces you to talk to him.

A week after her shoot with Andrea in the park, Lizzie was busy proofreading the second draft of her short story and listening to the rain patter against the classroom windows when she heard someone sit next to her.

"Hey, Lizzie. What's up?"

She looked up. Todd eyed her cautiously as he took out his books. It was the closest she'd been to him since that night at his house two weeks ago, and her heart did a little flip. Ever since that horrible morning when she'd heard about him and Ava, she'd done a complete Todd-ectomy, cutting him out of her life. She breezed past him in the hall without eye contact; showed up late to every class so she could choose a seat as far away from him as possible; smiled at him only when she had to in the vaguest, I'm-just-being-polite way.

She'd even stopped looking at his Facebook page, just in case there was some way he knew how many times she looked at it and also because the gifts and hugs and cute wall posts from Ava were just too much to handle. Her cold-shoulder routine had worked. She could tell how nervous he was now.

"Not much," she answered.

"That your story?" he asked eagerly.

"Mr. Barlow read the first draft and had some notes, so I just did a second draft," she said coldly, but giving him a slight smile. "I'm turning it in today."

"Cool," he said, nodding. "I turned mine in already. But maybe I should have given it to him to look at first —"

"Oh my God!" a voice shrieked. Lizzie looked up to see Ava walking toward them.

"Kate's telling me that I have some weird bug in my hair! Do I? Look!" She dropped into the seat on the other side of him, and as Todd turned his attention to Ava's possibly contaminated curls, Lizzie went back to her story. Ava had turned into Todd's warden. Every class she sat next to him; every free period she followed him to the computer lab or the lounge. After school, they hung out for hours at Goodburger with Ken and his friends. Even if Lizzie had wanted to still be friends with Todd, she wouldn't have stood a chance.

The classroom door closed with a bang, and Mr. Barlow crossed the room on his stilt-like legs. His hair looked even whiter than usual.

"All right," he said, perching his bony posterior on the edge of the desk. "Who wants to tell me the difference between a myth and a story? Anyone?" His watery eyes searched the room as if looking for enemy fire.

Lizzie and Todd both shot up their hands.

"Mr. Piedmont," Barlow replied as he folded his arms and raised one white eyebrow. "Have at it."

"A myth tells a story about human nature," Todd ventured. "The ancient Greeks told them to each other to explain what it meant to be human. So it's more than just a story, because it's true."

As usual when Todd spoke, the rest of the class craned their heads back at him, giving him their full, wide-eyed attention. His mild English accent didn't hurt, either.

"Very good, Mr. Piedmont," Mr. Barlow said. "That's correct. Myths illustrate human nature, which is why they're still being told today, but with updated details, of course. Almost all the stories we read or see on television have some root in classical mythology. Which is why I've devised this fun little project. Each of you will update a myth into a modern-day story, and bring it to life using modern details. And you'll be working in *pairs*."

The room went abruptly quiet.

"And I've assigned them already, just to make it easier," he added with a slightly sarcastic wink. The room went even quieter.

He flipped his pad open. "Ilona Peterson."

Lizzie looked down the row. At her desk, Ilona had frozen in mid–hair flip, and was giving Mr. Barlow her most advanced deathstare.

"You'll be working with Harrison Chervil," he said cheerfully. "On the Icarus myth."

Heads whipped over to the other side of the room, where Harrison Chervil bent over what was probably one of his Lord of the Rings drawings, blushing through his acne.

"Sophie Duncan," Mr. Barlow announced. "You'll be with Ken Clayman. The myth of Sisyphus."

Sophie pushed her glasses up her nose, while next to her Jill patted her on the back as if she'd just won the lottery. Across the room Ken looked queasy.

"Lizzie Summers," Mr. Barlow barked. "You're with Todd Piedmont. You'll be doing Cupid and Psyche. The love myth."

Somebody somewhere giggled. Lizzie looked straight down, feeling her cheeks burn. The love myth. She was going to kill Mr. Barlow.

When he had finished going down the list, Mr. Barlow surveyed his panicked, bewildered class. "This project will count for a third of your grade this term," he said. "If you choose to write a play or a script, it should be at least ten pages. Same for a short story. And I suggest you get together with your other half to figure out the themes as soon as possible."

She refused to look at Todd. For the rest of class, Lizzie could feel him just a few inches away on her right, making that whole side of her body hot with embarrassment. As soon as the bell rang, she sprang to her feet and began to furiously pack her bookbag.

"If you want to come over tomorrow night and talk about this, that's cool with me," Todd offered. His maturity in the face of all this was impressive, she had to admit.

"Okay, great," she said, managing to look at him for a second or two. Then she sprinted out of the room, walked into Mr. Barlow's office, and shut the door.

"Is there a problem, Summers?" he asked wryly, reading a few phone messages on his desk.

"You can't put me with Todd Piedmont!" she exclaimed.

He stifled a smile. "But just the other day you were begging me to be his tour guide," he said.

"That was *three weeks ago*," she said. "Everything's different now. *Everything*."

"I see," he said, nodding.

"You don't understand," she said, edging closer to his desk. "He's going to think I put you up to this or something."

"Why would he think that?" Mr. Barlow asked, cocking his head.

She realized that she didn't want to explain. Her right leg started to shake.

"Summers, this is an English project, not a setup," he said. "I doubt very much that Mr. Piedmont thinks you were the mastermind behind this entire assignment."

"Can't you just put him with Ava Elting?" she asked. "That's who he really wants to be with. That's who *I* want him to be with."

"No, I can't," Mr. Barlow said, dropping into his chair. "I'm not switching anyone. It's just an English project. You'll survive. And how are we doing on that short story?"

We? she thought. Lizzie pulled the story out of her bag and handed him the pages. "*We're* done," she huffed, then opened the door and trudged out of the office.

"Good luck!" Barlow yelled after her.

She hated Mr. Barlow. That was the problem with becoming friends with a teacher. There was always a price to pay.

She was so annoyed that she barely felt her iPhone vibrate as she stalked down the hall. With just a couple seconds to get to French class, she unzipped the side pocket of her bookbag and pulled out her phone. It was an e-mail from Andrea Sidwell.

She clicked on it.

Hey! You're a natural!! Want to do another?

Lizzie clicked on the photo attached at the bottom. In it, Lizzie slouched against the gnarled trunk of a tree, the dark-blue Boat Pond behind her. She gazed straight ahead, bored and defiant, and her expression said *Try me.* This girl was nothing like the deer-caught-in-the-headlights Lizzie that she was used to seeing in the tabloids. This was Fierce Lizzie. Brave Lizzie. Cool Lizzie.

Without even thinking, she hit reply.

Sure! When?

By the time she walked into French, she had another shoot scheduled for the next day. Meanwhile, Fierce Lizzie was on her way to Carina and Hudson's inboxes. She had a feeling that they were going to love her.

chapter 13

"We're gonna try something a little bit different this time," Andrea said the next day, as she ran up the steps of the Canal Street subway station in her purple suede Pumas. "We're gonna do a little styling. Not that I don't love the school kilt, but we need to jazz it up a bit. Make your look a little more *you*."

They reached the street, and Lizzie sidestepped a delivery guy threading through the crowd on a squeaky bike. Chinatown had been Andrea's idea for the second shoot — "the energy down there is awesome," she'd said over the phone — but now at four o'clock, Lizzie thought that there might be *too* much energy. Honking cars choked the intersections, and waves of pedestrians squeezed past the vendors selling fake designer bags, jewelry, and bootleg DVDs. Lizzie felt a cool fall breeze wrap itself around her bare legs under her kilt. She wanted to ask Andrea what she meant by making her look more her, but instead she just asked, "Styling? Do you mean accessories?"

"Yep," Andrea said, and Lizzie scrambled to follow her down the street, past an open seafood stand with tanks of swimming eels. Even with her square camera bag bumping against her hip, Andrea projected an air of calm, or maybe it was that her black hoodie had a huge green lotus symbol on the back. "Now we just need to find the right store," she said over a woman yelling in Cantonese out the door of a storefront.

"Down here?" Lizzie asked skeptically. From what she could see, this slice of Canal Street was a jumble of discount electronic stores, fish stands, fast food places, and stores that sold everything from I LOVE NEW YORK keychains to ten-dollar sundresses. Hudson might have been able to cobble together a cool look down here, but Lizzie doubted that she could. She had a hard enough time picking out things at Urban Outfitters.

Andrea stopped in front of a store with a red awning that said HSU-FAT EMPORIUM. "Let's try here," she said, walking inside.

Lizzie looked around. Stacks of flashlights, personalized key-chains, tube socks, and value packs of batteries vied for space amid racks of hats, scarves, dresses, and metallic tops.

Andrea reached into her camera case and pulled out some bills. "Just find some cool accessories. Stuff that speaks to you."

"Accessories really aren't my thing," she admitted.

"They don't have to be," Andrea said, pressing a twenty and a five into Lizzie's hand. "Just grab whatever looks good to you. Trust your instinct. I'll wait here."

Lizzie wanted to say that she didn't have instincts for this, but she quietly wandered past the flashlights over to the hat rack. She'd never been a hat person. Hudson could wear those cute newsboy caps, and Carina could rock a baseball cap anytime with a ponytail, but hats on her always made her look a little deranged and dressed from another time, like one of those old ladies she sometimes saw in the park, dressed in a ballgown and pushing a shopping cart. And these hats weren't cute, girly hats. They looked like the kind of hats men wore in old detective movies.

Her eye gravitated to a gray fedora with a shiny black leather band. She pulled it off the rack and clapped it on her head. In the mirror it looked a little odd, but so odd it almost looked cool. The tag said it was eight bucks. *Huh,* she thought. *Why not?* She put it back on her head and kept going.

Underneath a shelf of white tube socks, she hit on a pile of beautiful Indian scarves with delicate metallic threads. She unfolded one, and wrapped it around her neck. This time she didn't even look in the mirror. She kept going.

Next, she spotted a pair of thick, fake-gold hoops the size of small tangerines. Lizzie grabbed them. Finally she spied a purple vest in a brocaded faux-velvet. That seemed like enough.

She paid for her stuff at the cash register, got her two-fifty in change, and put everything on: the brocaded vest, unbuttoned, over her white oxford; the skinny Indian scarf wrapped once, bohemian-style, around her neck, then the hat and the enormous gold hoops.

When she walked out, Andrea's eyes lit up. "Now *that* is what I call jazzed up," she said, holding up her hand for a high-five. "You look awesome."

"You don't think it's too much?" Lizzie said, touching the earrings.

"It's perfect. It's you." Then Andrea glanced at her tank watch. "Come on. We're gonna lose the light."

They crossed Canal Street and walked north up Broadway to a quieter corner. "Let's try here," Andrea said, gesturing for Lizzie to stand against a wall in between a dingy walk-up and a dry cleaners. Lizzie piled her hair underneath the hat, or as much of it as she could, then folded her arms and slouched against the wall, as if she were waiting for someone who was going to be in serious trouble when they showed up.

Andrea stepped backward. "Okay, Lizzie. Look right at me. And just give me exhilarated. Give me confident."

Suddenly that wasn't so difficult. She put one foot against the wall and cocked her head. In the hat and the scarf and the earrings, she felt like a different person. A confident person. An intriguing person.

Before she could think too hard, Andrea pressed the button. *Click.*

"Yes!" Andrea cried.

She pressed the button again. *Click, click.*

Before Lizzie knew it, she and Andrea had started their dance again — Andrea bobbing and weaving, Lizzie standing still but giving her as much as she could with her eyes. People stared as they walked by but Lizzie kept her eye on the lens. It was easier to concentrate than she thought.

"Great!" Andrea kept yelling. "Perfect!"

Each time Andrea pressed the shutter, Lizzie gave her something just a little bit different.

"Perfect, that's perfect!" Andrea yelled.

I'm doing my mom's job, Lizzie suddenly thought. *I'm doing my mom's job and I'm* good *at it.*

When the light began to fall behind the buildings on Broadway, Andrea let the camera drop against her chest. She had the same radiance in her eyes that she did after the last shoot, as if she'd just run a few miles. "Wow, Lizzie, the camera *loves* you. You must get it from your mom." A strand of Andrea's hair whipped in the wind and she pulled it behind one ear with her pinky. "And *speaking* of your mom," she asked, placing her camera back into her bag, "she *does* know about this, right?"

Lizzie took off her hat for a moment and let her hair fall back down to her shoulders. This was the moment of truth. If she lied, it would only buy her time. And the idea of lying to Andrea seemed gross and deeply unethical, like shoplifting, or cheating on a test. "Not yet," she confessed.

Andrea barely blinked. "Why not?"

Lizzie looked down at the sidewalk. "I know it sounds lame, but at first, she was out of town," she said, choosing her words carefully. "And we had this big fight right before she left."

"About the clip?" Andrea prompted.

"Right," Lizzie said. "And when it came out, her publicist told me that it wouldn't look good for me to be doing this. And that my mom wouldn't approve. That it would look like I was, you know, using the clip to…"

"To what?" Andrea asked, looking genuinely puzzled.

"To turn this into some kind of career opportunity," Lizzie mumbled. "And that my mom might be offended by that."

Andrea zipped up her camera bag and slung it over her shoulder. "That's not what you're doing here," she said, her blue eyes radiating warmth. "I came to *you*. You only did me the courtesy of responding to my crazy message. And your mom wouldn't think that about you, I promise. She'd be proud of you. I know she would be." She touched Lizzie's shoulder. "Hey. I'd love to send a few of your shots over to *New York Style*. Would you have a problem with that?"

"*New York Style*?" Lizzie wasn't sure she'd heard Andrea over the keening sound of a car alarm a few blocks away.

"I know the photo editor and I think you'd be perfect for them. They're always interested in real people and different looks. I can't guarantee anything, but it's just a way for them to get to know you."

"Sure," she gushed. *New York Style* was the city's weekly fashion bible. "New designers, new looks, new faces" was its motto. Lizzie had been reading it for years.

"Except I'm going to need this signed," Andrea added, pulling out a folded piece of paper from the outside pocket of her camera bag. "By your mom. Before I can give them any photographs."

Andrea unfolded the paper. At the top was written NOTICE OF PARENTAL CONSENT FOR MINORS. It was a permission slip.

"Which means you're going to have to tell her," Andrea warned as they started to walk up Broadway. "And if you want me to talk to them, I'd be happy to —"

"No, that's okay," Lizzie cut in, taking the permission slip out of her hands. "I'll tell her tonight."

"You sure?"

"Yeah, it's time," she said, folding the piece of paper and dropping it into her bookbag.

"I'll be away next week — I have a shoot down in Austin — but just fax me the release and we'll talk when I get back." At the corner of Prince Street, Andrea leaned down and gave Lizzie a quick, piney-smelling hug. "Good work today. And tell Carina and Hudson they really missed out."

"I will."

"And don't worry about your mom." Then she gestured to the Dean & Deluca on the corner. "All right, gonna go flirt with the cute barista. He always gives me a discount, thank God. That place is a fortune." She cracked a warm smile just before she turned away.

Lizzie rushed down the steps into the N and R subway, her head spinning. *New York Style*? Was Andrea serious? She needed to talk to her mom immediately. If Andrea was really going to send in her photos, then hopefully her mom would be supportive.

"Mom?" she yelled when she walked in the door. "You home?" She pushed through the swinging door and walked into the kitchen.

In her excitement about her own photo shoot, she'd forgotten about the one that *Celebrity Living* was doing on their apartment that day. Through the archway to the living room, Lizzie saw her mom posed on the beige suede sofa, her arms splayed out on either side of her and her chin tilted in the air, smiling expertly. Her white Grecian-style dress fluttered in the air from a fan. A photo assistant held a silk in his hands to bounce off the light from a stand. And a makeup artist hovered nearby with a tray of lip glosses and powder. A bearded photographer wearing a skullcap stood behind his tripod and snapped another picture.

"Lizzie? Where've you been?" Katia asked. Years of experience had given Katia an almost supernatural ability to speak through a smile.

"Um, just hanging out with C," she said. This clearly wasn't the time to spill the beans.

The photographer snapped another picture and Katia released her statue-like pose. "It's six o'clock," she said. "And what is that?" she asked, noticing the hat.

Lizzie snatched the fedora off her head. "Just something I bought after school."

"Is that your daughter?" asked a voice, and Lizzie turned to see a redheaded woman with quick, eager eyes walk into the living room. Lizzie could tell she was the reporter.

"Fiona, this is Lizzie," Katia said, standing up. "Lizzie, this is Fiona Carter. The writer doing the piece for *Celebrity Living*."

The woman pumped Lizzie's hand eagerly. Perhaps a little too eagerly. Lizzie wondered if she'd seen the clip.

"What about a picture with your daughter?" Fiona asked. "The both of you on the couch. It'd be adorable and her uniform is just darling —"

"No, I don't think so," Katia answered quickly.

"It's okay, Mom," Lizzie said. "I can do the photo."

"No, really, it's just not something we're interested in," Katia said firmly, giving Lizzie a confused look. "Honey," she said, "don't you have homework?"

"Yeah," Lizzie said as she turned and walked out. Sometimes it felt like she and her mom would never, ever get on the same page about anything. Just as she was starting to accept the camera, her mom thought she wanted to avoid it. Now it would be even more confusing for Katia if she heard what Lizzie had been doing.

"Your father and I are going out tonight," Katia called after her. "Want me to order something for you?"

"No, thanks," she yelled back.

On the way to her room, she stopped in front of the enormous gold-framed mirror that leaned against the hallway floor. She looked exactly the same as she did most afternoons when she came home — kilt crooked, hair in a thick mass around her face, her nose shiny — but something was different.

It was her mind. It was quiet. The chorus of voices that usually rose up in her head whenever she looked in the mirror — the voices that said *I'm so weird-looking, I have to get rid of that, I wish that was different* — all of them were gone. Now it was just her and her reflection staring back at her. No chatter.

But things with her mother were clearly more tentative than she thought. Lizzie turned into her room and dropped down on the bed, burying her head in Sid Vicious's fur. Maybe telling her about the modeling gig — and asking for her permission to take it even further — was asking for trouble. Suddenly she remembered that she had to go over to Todd's tonight to work on that project. Two weeks ago she would have prayed for this. Now she wished there was any way she could get out of it.

"Sid . . . can we just trade places for a day?" she asked her cat.

Sid stood up, arched his back, yawned, and jumped off the bed. "I take that to be a no," she said.

chapter 14

When she stepped off the elevator into Todd's apartment a few hours later, Lizzie was surprised to see that the foyer was dark.

"Hello?" she called out.

"Up here," a voice called out.

She looked up to see Todd standing on the second floor, leaning over the banister and looking extremely cute in a red Vampire Weekend T-shirt and faded Levis. "There's pizza," he said. "Pepperoni and plain. You hungry?"

"No, thanks." She walked up the stairs, feeling her knees tremble a little with nerves. "We should just get started on this. I've got a lot of other homework tonight."

At the top of the stairs he looked her up and down and smiled. Unlike the last time she'd been to his house, she was wearing her decidedly unsexy ripped jeans and an extra-large Mr. Bubbles T-shirt. "Hey, lemme take that," he said, reaching out for her book-bag. "That looks heavy."

"That's okay, I got it," she said, stepping back. She wasn't going to let him be all charming. "So . . . where shall we go?"

"Uh, in here," he said, as he led her into his room.

Lizzie looked around in awe. Todd's old bedroom had been just big enough to fit a set of bunk beds and a built-in desk and bookshelf. But this room looked like the presidential suite at the Mercer Hotel — and was just as cool. Half of it was set up like an office, with a chocolate leather sofa along one wall, a sleek glass coffee table, and an imposing steel desk topped by a gleaming Mac Pro. The other half had a king-size bed, a flatscreen, and a large, bleak painting of an orange spot against a gray background.

"Wow," Lizzie remarked, dropping her bookbag on the couch. "This is your *room*?"

"And look at this," he said, gesturing toward a door. He led her into an adjoining room and flipped on the light. "What do you think?" he asked, grinning.

It was a room lined with books, *crammed* with books, hardbacks and softcovers, new and old, on shelves that rose all the way to the ceiling. Lizzie had never seen so many books in her life, not even at the Strand bookstore downtown.

"You'll never have to go to Barnes & Noble again," she said, turning around in circles. "This is unbelievable. It's like Gatsby's library."

"It's my little hobby," he said.

"Hey, what are these?" she asked, walking over to a pair of glass bookcases that stood separate from the rest of the shelves.

"*This* is what I really wanted to show you." Todd bent down next to her, so close that one of his arm hairs sent her skin bristling. He opened one of the cases and she saw a series of boxes with one familiar title after another stamped in gold on the spine. *The Old Man and the Sea. Nine Stories. The Catcher in the Rye.* "They're all first editions," he said. "I collect them. Some of them are even signed."

"You have a first edition of *Catcher in the Rye*?" she asked, agape.

"Yep." Todd slid one of the boxes out. "Here."

He opened the box and nestled inside was a goldish-brown book. She took it out. The dust jacket felt soft and velvety, as if years of being held had ground it down into something more precious. "How'd you get this?" she stammered.

"My dad used to take me to this dealer in Camden Town. He had everything."

Lizzie flipped the pages, breathing in the smell of old ink. She wondered if Ava was as impressed by this as she was. She doubted it.

"This is the coolest thing I've ever seen," she said, handing the book back to him. "But why don't you have *Gatsby*? That'd be my first pick."

"I tried," he said, taking back the book. "It was always the one book the guy didn't have. And I wanted a signed copy. Those are pretty hard to find." He put the book back on the shelf with special care, as if it might disintegrate.

"This collection is amazing," she said.

Todd smiled sheepishly as he turned back toward his room. "I guess there are some perks to my dad's midlife crisis."

"What do you mean?"

"You know we didn't always live like this," Todd confided. She followed him back into his room. He fiddled with his iPod on his desk. A soft, slow rock song began to play on the speakers on either side of his bed. "He thinks spending money'll keep him young," he went on. "Or dating a twenty-two-year-old model."

Lizzie sat on the edge of his bed. His bed. Almost without thinking, her pulse began to rise. *Calm yourself*, she thought.

He flopped down on his back next to her. "Her name's Chloe," he said, grimacing. "Fake boobs, fake teeth, and she's really into India." Todd made a *yecch* sound. "My dad used to laugh about guys like that. Now he's one of them."

"Maybe it's just a phase." Without thinking about it, she leaned back on the bed so that they faced each other.

"Except I get to watch him in it day and night." He stared past her at the painting on his wall. "It's just depressing. Seeing him so different. Sometimes I think I shouldn't have come back here."

"*I* think you should have come back here," she said.

Todd's enormous blue eyes looked at her so closely she almost stopped breathing. "You do?" he asked.

"Hey, this song's pretty," she said abruptly. "What is this?"

"Band of Horses. I saw them in London at the Hammersmith. Wait." He touched her arm. "Listen to this part. Right here."

Just then the song opened up into a shimmering chorus:

When eyes . . . can't look . . .
At you any other way . . .
Any other way
Any other way

"Such a good part, right?" he asked. His face was so close that she could see his white front teeth just past his parted lips.

"It's pretty," she murmured.

The chorus repeated:

When eyes can't look . . .
At you any other way

She lay on her side, her head resting in her hand, facing him while they listened together. The music crowded around them both, enveloping them, carrying her softly away . . .

Until the squawk of a cell phone made her jump. It was a sped-up version of the James Bond theme. Todd's phone on the desk was ringing.

"Hold on," Todd said, sitting up. He reached past her for the phone. For a quick second, she saw the name on the screen. AVA.

She sat straight up. The room spun as she felt a massive head rush.

"Hey," he said quietly into the phone. "Can I call you back in twenty minutes?"

She got up, went to the couch, and sat down next to her backpack. Of course it was Ava. He had a girlfriend. How could she have almost forgotten that?

"Okay, I'll call you right back," she heard him say, and he hung up.

"So do we want to do a short story, a play, a screenplay?" she asked, all business, unzipping her bookbag. "Or a television series? That might be more fun."

Todd seemed taken aback. "Um, a screenplay might be cool," he said, sounding a little disappointed.

"Great," she said, taking out her notebook. "Just what I was thinking. Okay, what's the premise?"

The music had changed into something loud and jangly. Todd got up and turned it down with his remote. The moment was definitely over. She wasn't a girl who stole guys away from their girlfriends. She and Todd were going to be just friends if it killed her.

But as they plotted out a story for their project, she scribbled an urgent note to herself at the top of the page.

BUY THAT BAND OF HORSES SONG!!!

chapter 15

"So there's *one* good thing about working for my dad," Carina declared the following Saturday as the three of them stood in line at a Korean deli. "Remember I said I'd get back at him? Well, I think I figured out how." She placed her toasted sesame bagel and Snapple bottle on the counter and handed the elderly woman behind the cash register a hundred-dollar bill. "Can I get change?" she asked.

Hudson and Lizzie traded a look behind her in line. "You're gonna 'get back' at him?" Lizzie said, holding her turkey and Swiss wrap. "Are you serious?"

"What are you going to do? Draw on his Basquiats with Magic Marker?" Hudson asked, taking a green apple from the basket on the counter.

"This isn't a joke, you guys," Carina said, unwrapping her buttered bagel. "Coach Reynolds was so upset I couldn't play this season he actually called my dad up — at home — and *begged* him to let me stay on the team. But he didn't even listen. And then today

I had to practically give blood so Creepy Manservant would let me leave the office and come meet you guys. And it's Saturday!" Carina brushed her hair off her shoulders and took another buttery bite. "It's insane. I have no *leverage* in this family at all!"

Hudson and Lizzie looked at each other again. Lately Carina had started to use corporate lingo, like the word *leverage*.

"But it's more than that," Carina argued. "He's forcing me to turn my back on the stuff I love. And forcing me to live *his* life. And there's nothing I can do about it. Nothing. It just makes me so angry."

They walked out of the deli and onto Sixth Avenue. It was the first brisk day of the fall, and the city air had that autumn smell of woodsmoke and peppermint.

Lizzie pulled the black fedora closer to her head and zipped up her corduroy cropped jacket. "So what's your big plan?" she asked.

"Okay," Carina said, dropping her voice as if she were planning a bank heist. "I came across this file on Jurgensenland. You know, that charity thing my dad does in Montauk? Well, they supposedly raised two million bucks from it for Oxfam. But it looks like they really raked in *three* million."

"So what does that mean?" Hudson asked. "What happened to the rest of the money?"

"I think he took it," Carina said. "I mean, I'm not entirely sure yet, but it looks that way."

"But your dad doesn't need another million dollars," Lizzie said. "That's like pocket change to him."

"*Duh*," Carina said. "I know. That's the point. But where else could it go?"

"Do you really think he would do that?" Lizzie asked. "I mean, I know the Jurg is obsessed with making money, but would he do something that unethical?"

"My dad loves money more than he loves people," Carina assured them, tossing her bagel bag into the garbage. "He totally would."

"So what are you gonna do?" Hudson pressed.

"Just let it slip out," Carina said slyly. "Send in the file to the Smoking Gun. Just put it out there. No one'll know it's from me. And people'll finally see who he really is."

"But if he finds out it's you, he'll kill you," Lizzie said, pulling open her bag of chips. "Not to mention it would really suck for him."

"I know," Carina said, trotting along on her new suede Adidas. "But it'd be so worth it. Just for the look on his face."

"Oh, C," Hudson groaned, unwrapping her string cheese. "Can we talk about this when I'm done with this album? My mom's been stressing me out about it."

"I thought she was going to be 'hands off,'" Carina said, making air quotes.

"Uh, right." Hudson gave a rueful chuckle in between bites of apple. "She's never been hands-off anything in her whole life. Especially me. And *especially* music."

"But this is *your* album," Lizzie pointed out, wrapping her new Indian scarf closer around her neck. "You're not even on her label."

"I don't have to be on her label. I'm her *kid*. But don't worry,"

Hudson said. "I've talked to her. And I have the coolest producer ever. He's a genius. *And* a Pisces."

"How old is he?" Carina asked, getting right down to it.

Ever since her crush on their sixth-grade art teacher, Mr. Thurber, Hudson had always liked older guys, and even adult men. Lizzie and Carina thought it had something to do with the fact that she'd never met her father.

"Twenty-eight, and no, I *don't* like him," Hudson said, nudging Carina. "And speaking of *guys*," she said, taking Lizzie's arm, "you haven't said a *thing* about your Todd Piedmont study date."

Lizzie hadn't stopped thinking about that moment in his room for days. But she wasn't quite sure how to talk about it. "It was good," she said casually. "He was really nice. I think we're friends now."

"Friends?" Carina looked at her skeptically. "Really?"

"Yeah. We talked. And listened to music in his room."

"What'd you listen to?" Carina asked, tossing her empty bagel wrapper into the trash.

"That song 'Detlef Schrempf' by Band of Horses."

"*What?*" Carina shrieked, stopping in her tracks. "Hel-*lo*! That's totally a hook-up song!"

"What?"

"He was trying to be romantic!" Carina cried. "Don't you see that?"

"I think he does still like you," Hudson said more diplomatically.

"He doesn't. And Ava called right in the middle of it, anyway," Lizzie said.

"So *what*?" Carina blurted. "You should have *jumped* him!"

"You guys, *no*. I'm just gonna be friends with Todd Piedmont. He has a girlfriend. End of story." She ate her last bite of turkey sandwich and threw it out. "What's a lot more important right now is this release I have to give my mom. So Andrea can send in my pictures to *New York Style*."

"You still haven't told her, right?" Hudson said, applying a wand of Chanel lipstain to her lips.

"I can't. *Hey, Mom, I know you're a supermodel, but guess what? Someone wants me to be an ugly model!* I can't do it."

"Where's the release?" Carina asked as they turned west on Twenty-Fifth Street.

Lizzie pulled it out from her purse. "Why? Do you understand lawyer-talk?" she asked.

"I don't have to," she replied, unfolding it. "You got a pen?"

"C, what are you doing?" Hudson asked, concerned.

Lizzie gave Carina a pen. Carina walked over to a mailbox, spread the piece of paper on it, and signed it with a flourish. "There you go," she said simply, handing it back to Lizzie.

"Carina!" Lizzie said. The signature said KATIA SUMMERS with a bunch of overdone curlicues and flourishes.

"What?" Carina asked defensively. "The photos are just for the editor to look at, right? She's not gonna do anything with them."

"That's forgery, C," Hudson said, astonished. "People go to jail for that."

"It's making something *easier*," Carina groaned. "I mean, Lizzie's gonna tell her mom eventually, right?"

"Right," Lizzie said, folding the slip. "I guess," she added, less convinced.

"It's still wrong," Hudson argued. "Lizzie, why don't you just tell your mom? I'm sure she'd be fine with it."

Lizzie shrugged, looking at the slate-gray Hudson River in the distance. "If you guys remember, I had a hissy fit about getting my picture taken at Fashion Week. Now it's like I'm totally changing my mind."

Hudson came to a stop in front of a sleek glass-fronted gallery building. "Okay, guys, we're here." Both Carina and Lizzie had hung out with Hudson in recording studios before, but this was the first time they'd be seeing Hudson, and not her mom, lay down tracks. Supersonic Recording Studios was on the fifth floor, behind a pair of smoked-glass doors that clicked open when Hudson typed in a security code. Inside, the studio's large reception area-slash-lounge was filled with things to pass the time when recording an album: a flatscreen TV with Xbox, neon-lit pinball machines, piles of magazines on the coffee table, and bowls of Chupa Chups and Hershey Kisses. Carina swiped a handful of Kisses before they turned down the hall to the studio. "This place is awesome," she muttered.

Hudson took off her jacket. She looked adorable in skinny jeans, ballet flats, and a black-and-red-striped trapeze top. "Okay, you guys promise not to make funny faces at me through the glass?" Hudson asked. "C?"

"Swear to God," Carina said, eating a Hershey's Kiss.

"I'm so proud of you," Lizzie said, squeezing Hudson's tiny shoulder. "Your first album. This is so cool."

"Tell me that after you hear the first track," Hudson said nervously, but her green eyes shone with pride.

As they walked into the recording studio, a guy with strawberry blond hair and amiable blue eyes looked up from the mixing board. "Hey superstar," he said to Hudson with a smile.

"You guys, this is my producer, Chris Brompton," Hudson said. "Chris, these are my best friends in the whole world, Carina and Lizzie."

Hudson hadn't been exaggerating, Lizzie thought. Chris was hot.

"Hey, welcome," Chris said, getting up and shaking their hands. "Hudson's told me so much about you guys."

As Chris grinned at Hudson, Carina and Lizzie traded looks. *"Oh my God,"* Carina mouthed.

"I know," Lizzie mouthed back.

"You guys wanna make yourselves comfortable?" He pointed to a sofa at the back of the room, but Chris's eyes and smile were so mesmerizing Lizzie almost forgot to sit down. Carina had to gently nudge her.

"So we're just gonna have you lay down the vocal," Chris said to Hudson. "How's the throat?"

"Kind of scratchy." Hudson fluttered a hand over her neck. Lizzie could already tell that Hudson had a crush on Chris, and she didn't blame her.

Chris handed Hudson a bottle of water. "Or do you want me to get you some hot water with lemon?"

"That's okay, I'll be fine." She took the water, blushing.

Lizzie and Carina exchanged a look. *Uh-oh.*

"Okay, guys, I'll see you in a bit," Hudson said, turning to them.

Carina and Lizzie gestured excitedly toward Chris's turned back. Hudson rolled her eyes as if to say *calm yourselves,* and left the room.

Chris turned around to face Carina and Lizzie. "Have you guys heard her yet?"

They nodded.

"She's gonna be a big star," he added before swiveling back around to the board.

Carina grinned with pride. "Damn straight," she whispered.

Through the window above the mixing board, they watched Hudson and her band enter the recording booth. The guys picked up their guitars, took their places behind a double bass and a drum set, and Hudson slid behind a shiny Yamaha piano. She slipped on a pair of earphones, as if she'd been doing this for years, and gave Chris a thumbs-up sign behind the glass.

A moment later they began to play. The soft rat-tat-tat of a snare drum poured through the studio speakers. Then the thump of a jazz bass, and the soft trills of Hudson's piano. Lizzie recognized it right away. It was a song Hudson had written last year and played for Carina and Lizzie on the Steinway in her apartment, fumbling a little over the keys. Even then Lizzie had known it was beautiful. Now with the addition of drums, bass, and electric guitar, it was gorgeous.

Hudson closed her eyes, swayed a little on the bench, and as her fingers pressed the keys, she began to sing.

There is just one place in my heart
Just one place in my heart
For you, my love, for you...

Goose bumps rose up along Lizzie's arm. Hudson's voice was perfect for jazz and soul: deep, throaty, and evocative. It was the complete opposite of her mother's, which was like a sonic Pop-Tart: yummy and sweet and made for Top Forty hits. Holla's voice made you want to get up and dance, but Hudson's made you want to slow dance with some guy who was bad for you.

When the song faded out, Lizzie and Carina shot to their feet, clapping wildly.

"Yeah, Hudson!"

"Woo-hoo!"

Hudson couldn't hear her friends going crazy, but she gave them an embarrassed half-wave through the glass.

Chris leaned into a microphone on the board and pressed the intercom. "That was amazing, you guys. Let's play it back."

And just then the studio door burst open.

"That was so good!"

Before anyone could fully prepare themselves, Holla Jones — *the* Holla Jones — marched into the room. "Great job, baby," she yelled to the glass, waving her hands with their long manicured nails. "Great *job*!"

At the piano, Hudson's face dropped. Clearly her mom's visit had been a surprise.

Holla turned to Carina and Lizzie and held out her arms. "Gir-*irls*," she said in a singsong, like she always did, and both of them went up to hug her.

Holla couldn't have been more than five foot one and ninety-five pounds, but her presence was as large and overbearing as Godzilla's. She was darker-skinned than her daughter, with large, almond-shaped brown eyes, lush lips, and a high, commanding forehead that was remarkably smooth. Today her long caramel hair was twisted in a bun and swept off her face with a pair of enormous D&G sunglasses perched on top of her head. Holla was known almost as much for her supremely fit body as she was for her voice, and today she wore a sleeveless pink tank top and hip-slung yoga pants that showed off her fearsome biceps and six-pack. A sparkling pendant of three diamond monkeys, one covering its eyes, another covering its ears, and another covering its mouth, hung from her neck. It was easy to see where Hudson had gotten her love of jewelry.

As Lizzie and Carina took turns giving her a hug, two twiglike women with sunken cheeks and fake eyelashes and one beefy man dressed in black quietly walked into the room. Lizzie didn't recognize them, but she knew exactly who they were: Holla's assistant, stylist, and bodyguard. Holla never went anywhere without her entourage, but the trio was always different — none of the three ever lasted long in their jobs. They leaned against the wall, took out their BlackBerrys, and expertly melted into the background.

"All right, Chris, I've got some thoughts," Holla said abruptly after greeting Lizzie and Carina. She pulled up an empty chair and sat herself next to him. "I know what you're going for with the whole low-fi thing. I get it. But I've told Hudson a million times — that whole rootsy, brown-sound, Norah Jones thing is totally over."

Chris rubbed his chin. "O-kay," he said carefully.

"We should track all these guys separately," Holla said, gesturing to the band behind the glass. "Maybe sample in some beats. Put her voice through a sequencer, use some compression, take out the scratches. Go sharper and glossier."

146

Chris glanced hesitantly through the glass. Hudson sat on the edge of the piano bench, her brows knitted with concern.

"I think your daughter really wants *this* kind of sound," he said, sounding a little terrified.

Holla sat back in her chair. "I know what she wants," she snapped. "But I'm telling you the way it *should be*."

Just then the door opened and Hudson walked into the room. "Hey, Mom, what's going on?" she asked casually, coming to stand by her chair. Lizzie could hear the panic underneath the sweetness.

"Oh, nothing, baby, I'm just having a talk with your producer," Holla said gently, taking Hudson's wrist in her hand. "I think we need to start over with this. Go with what we talked about. Something sharper. Fuller. More radio. Less . . . easy listening."

Hudson darted a here-we-go look at her friends. "Mom, we talked about this," she said. "I'm not Britney."

"Thank God," Holla laughed, swinging Hudson's arm. "I'm not saying that. I just want you to have the career you deserve. And if you're stuck behind a piano on tour, nobody's gonna see you dance. And you're such a *good* dancer —"

"Mom," Hudson cut in, her voice darker. She darted a look at Chris. "I told you I didn't want to do this unless I could make the album *I* want to make," she said in a low voice.

"Honey, what do you want to be?" Holla said, sitting back in her chair and letting go of her daughter. "A girl who sells a hundred thousand records? Or a star who sells millions and wins Grammys? Who's going to have little girls dressing like her and singing her songs? You have that in you, honey. I know you do."

Hudson chewed her bottom lip and looked anxiously at her

friends. *I don't care,* Lizzie wanted Hudson to say. *I don't want to be like you.* But she knew Hudson couldn't bring herself to say that in front of her mom.

"How soon do you think we could move to a new studio?" Holla asked Chris, as if the issue had been settled. "One with the digital capability we might need?"

"I'm not sure. We'll have to talk to the label about that."

Holla's hands were already moving over the board. "Can we play it back? I just want Hudson to hear what I'm talking about."

Hudson stared at Chris imploringly. But he was no match for Holla Jones. With a sigh, Chris pressed a button and the music started.

Lizzie knew that this was only going to get worse. She looked at Carina. *What can we do?* she asked with her eyes. Carina gave a sad shrug.

"You guys are probably bored," Hudson said, sensing her friends' discomfort. "You can take off if you want."

Carina and Lizzie traded a look. They didn't want to abandon their friend, but it was obvious Hudson wanted them to leave. They knew that nothing was more mortifying to Hudson than a public power struggle with her mom, because she'd always lose.

"Thanks for having us," Lizzie said to her as she leaned down and gave her friend a hug. "You were so great."

Carina hugged her, too. "You kicked ass," she whispered.

"Thanks, guys," Hudson said with downcast eyes.

"Stand up to her," Lizzie said under her breath.

Hudson only shook her head, her green eyes faraway. "Right," she wisecracked.

They mumbled a goodbye to Holla, but she was too busy manipulating the faders on the mixing board to notice their exit.

Out in the hall, Carina and Lizzie walked to the elevator in silence.

"I hate watching her do that to her," Carina finally said, punching out a piece of gum and putting it in her mouth. "It's so unfair."

"Maybe she should have waited to do this," Lizzie said.

"Waited for what? Her mom's always gonna be like that," Carina said.

"But maybe she could handle it better in a few years."

"Well, the sooner she learns to do it, the better," Carina said, pressing the button. "But what do I know? I'm my dad's slave."

The elevator door opened and they walked inside.

"You know what? This is the year we stand up to our parents," Lizzie announced. "You need to let your dad know that he's being unfair, Hudson needs to do the album she wants to do —"

"And you need to not be so afraid, Lizzie," Carina said pointedly. She punched the lobby button. "It's *your* life. Do you want to spend the rest of it in your mom's shadow or not?"

The doors rumbled shut. Lizzie didn't answer, but she thought about Carina's words all the way down to the lobby and out onto the street. That's what this was all about. As long as she could remember, this had been the implicit bargain of her life: to live on the sidelines, in the shadows, out of the spotlight, and off the red carpet. To be known to everyone — and even to herself — as Katia Summers's daughter. Her weird-looking daughter. To be quiet, to be unseen, and to hope nobody noticed her.

But that couldn't last forever. Didn't she deserve her own life?

A few minutes later, out on the street, she stopped in front of a Kinko's on Twenty-Third Street. "Hold on," she said to Carina, and ran inside.

At the counter, she pulled the permission slip out of her bag. Andrea's fax number was at the top. She handed it to a clerk behind the counter.

"Just fax that, please," she said.

As she watched him feed the slip into the fax machine, she felt a niggling sensation of doubt. But she knew that Carina was right. It was time for her to start being Lizzie. Even if doing that scared her to death.

chapter 16

Four days later, on a rainy Wednesday a few minutes before French, Lizzie looked up from reading *Tender Is the Night* and saw Todd standing over her, looking like he either had something important to say, or had completely forgotten her name.

"Hey," he finally said, and cleared his throat. "What's up?"

Now Todd was giving *her* the cold shoulder. He didn't look at her in class. He passed by her in the halls — with Ava and her rolled-up kilt glued to his hip. Lizzie knew that she had no reason to be hurt — they were just friends, after all — but his decision to ignore her ever since their study session didn't make any sense.

But, it seemed, he'd changed his mind. Again.

"Uh, just reading," she said, putting down the book.

Todd nodded and looked down, as people streamed into class behind him. *God, he could be awkward*, Lizzie thought.

"So we should meet again for the English project," he said haltingly.

She closed the book. "Sure."

"And is it okay if I ask you a favor?" he asked.

"All right," she said.

"Actually, it's not for me," he said, letting his weird English book-bag slide off his shoulder. "It's for Ava."

Lizzie felt something drop inside her, as if her heart had just been torpedoed.

"She wants to ask you something but she's kind of embarrassed," he said, staring at the ground, as he swept the floor with his shoe.

Ava embarassed? she thought, just as Ava blew into the room.

"Hey, Lizzie!" Ava cried, walking over. Her cheeks were rosy from being outside, and she'd left on her knit hat with devil horns, which immediately got on Lizzie's nerves. "I *sooooo* didn't want to bother you, but you know I'm the chairperson for the Silver Snowflake Ball, and we're doing a raffle for prizes, and, well, I was wondering if we could get your mom to donate something."

Her torpedoed heart made a crash landing in her gut. "Um, like what?" she asked.

"It could be anything," Ava shrugged crazily. "Dinner with her, a dress, going with her to a photo shoot, hanging out with her and Martin Meloy, what*ever*. Oh, and you're totally gonna get an invitation, just so you know." She smiled radiantly and glanced at Todd, who still seemed fascinated by the floor.

"Uh, well, I'll ask her," she said, deliberately sidestepping Ava's invitation.

"Great!" Ava exclaimed. She tossed her curls off her shoulder and squeezed Todd's hand. "Todd said you wouldn't mind. And you know, he said your mom is really cool and everything."

"Glad he helped you out with that," she said thickly.

Just then Madame Dupuis stalked through the doors in a hideous chartreuse pantsuit.

"Okay, well, see you later!" Ava chirped.

She and Todd scrambled to the back of the room just as Madame Dupuis called class to order with her usual *"Shhht!"*

Lizzie opened her book, feeling let down and confused. She was used to people asking her for things, but this just depressed her. Didn't Todd know how annoying it was to be used as a "connection" to her mom? Then again, he hadn't made eye contact with her once during that entire interaction. Hopefully he felt like an idiot.

After class she found Carina and Hudson waiting for her on the bench in the lobby.

"So I got hit up by Ava Elting for her dumb charity ball," she said, pushing open the main door and walking out to the sidewalk. The rain had turned to a soft drizzle. "Todd even did the intro for her. Yecch."

"Ugh," Hudson sniffed, opening her see-through plastic umbrella. "She hit me up, too. For concert tickets. Or dinner with my mom. As if my mom would ever sit down with a stranger and have dinner. She barely has dinner with *me.*"

"What a weenie," Carina confirmed, pushing a wide blue headband through her blond hair. "She's got him totally by the you-know-whats."

"He *has* to know she's a tool," Lizzie argued. "So how can he stand it?"

"I'm pretty sure I know the answer to that," Carina said dryly.

They turned the corner onto Madison Avenue and walked into the deli. Carina and Lizzie got in line to order toasted bialys with butter, while Hudson went to the magazine stand. White flour had been banned in the Jones's home a long time ago, and she'd lost her taste for it.

"Oh my God," they heard Hudson mutter. "Lizzie. Come over here."

"What?" Lizzie stepped out of the line and walked over to the magazine rack. "What is it?"

Hudson stood in the middle of the aisle, with the latest issue of *New York Style* open in her hands. "You're in here," she said to Lizzie, as if she didn't quite believe it herself.

"What?" Lizzie stepped closer.

Her mouth open in shock, Hudson turned the magazine to show her. The first thing Lizzie saw was the headline: THE NEW FACE OF BEAUTY.

Underneath it was her picture. Her. Lizzie. Wearing the black fedora and the gold hoop earrings and the crazy pink scarf, leaning against the brick wall in Chinatown. The picture took up almost the entire page.

Her eye fell to the caption:

Seems like arresting looks run in the family. Lizzie Summers, the 14-year-old daughter of supermodel Katia Summers, is the latest discovery of photographer Andrea Sidwell. She calls her "the new face of beauty." We couldn't agree more.

"Oh my God," Lizzie said.

"You look amazing!" Hudson screamed. "Carina? Come over here!"

Carina walked over. "I'm just about to order."

"Did you see this?" Hudson shrieked, holding up the magazine.

When Carina saw the picture, her mouth dropped open. "Holy *shnit*! That's *you*! You look incredible! Look at you!"

"You're the New Face of Beauty!" Hudson yelled, jumping up and down. "Did you know they were gonna do this?" she asked.

Lizzie could only shake her head. "Uh. No."

"You're the new face of beauty! Oh my god!" Hudson's excited green eyes searched Lizzie's face. "Wait. What's wrong?"

"You're screaming, that's what's wrong," said Carina.

"I sent in the forged release," Lizzie replied, still in shock. "I never told my mom. Anything. She's gonna flip out."

Just then she felt the ominous buzz of her iPhone in her bag. Someone had just texted her. She pulled it out. It was from home.

COME HOME NOW.

"Lizzie?" Hudson asked warily. "You look scared."

"I think I should be." Lizzie showed them both the message.

"Yikes," Carina said.

"Do you want us to come?" Hudson asked, her brow knitted with concern.

Lizzie shook her head. She felt like she was standing at the edge of a high-dive board, and trying to get the courage to jump. "No, that's okay. I should do this alone." She started to go to the door.

"But it's lunch period," Carina said.

155

"I'll come back," she said.

"Don't worry, you're gonna be fine," Hudson said as she followed Lizzie onto the street. "They're gonna love it. You'll see."

"I don't think so," she said as she raised her hand to hail a cab.

"Just remember," Hudson said, twisting Lizzie around by the waist. "This is a huge, huge deal." She stood on her tippytoes and threw her arms around Lizzie's neck. "And you deserve it."

Lizzie squeezed her back, and for the first time felt like jumping up and down, too. She was the new face of beauty? This was unreal.

After hailing a cab, she got inside and gave the driver her address. Then she leaned against the backseat and watched the brown and gold leaves whiz past the windows as they crossed the park. Quickly, she tried to formulate an excuse. But she couldn't come up with one. She'd lied to Andrea, forged her mom's signature, and gotten her pictures in a national magazine without her parents' permission. She'd probably be grounded for the rest of eternity.

But she was also the new face of beauty. *Her—the new face of beauty!* she thought, gripping the metal bar on the cab door as she smiled to herself. How had *that* happened?

When she got out of the cab she quickly bypassed the paparazzi and ran through the beginning rain into the lobby. In the entry hall to her family's apartment she dropped her bag.

"Hello?" she called out, and pushed through the swinging door into the kitchen.

Bernard, Katia, and Natasha sat in grim silence around the kitchen table, as if someone had just died. Katia was pursing her lips so tightly that her cheeks looked hollow, and her hair had been hastily pulled back into a severe, schoolteacherish bun. Natasha flicked the fringe of her bangs out of her eyes and gave Lizzie a scowl. Her dad glared at her from under his bushy eyebrows as he touched the magazine that lay in the center of the table.

"Explain *this*," he said, pushing the copy of *New York Style* toward her. "I'm assuming you can?"

"It wasn't supposed to come out," she started. "They were just test shots —"

"You're a minor!" Bernard exploded, his eyes becoming dangerously buggy. "Didn't Natasha explain to you why this wasn't a good idea? Didn't she?"

"Clearly she didn't want to take my advice," Natasha said haughtily, drumming her eggplant-colored fingernails on the table. "Your daughter's quite a strong-willed girl."

"It was just to have the editor look at my photos," Lizzie said. "They weren't supposed to print them. I swear."

The house phone trilled on the kitchen wall. Bernard leaped up out of his chair and grabbed it.

"Yes, send her up, please," he directed, then slammed the phone back down. "Your photographer's here. And you can bet I have a few words to say to *her*," he said.

Of course they'd tracked down Andrea. Now she'd have to explain that she'd lied — not just to her family but to the coolest woman in the universe.

Katia finally unpursed her lips. Her eyes had turned a deep shade of purple, which meant that the situation was dire. "I didn't think you liked cameras," she said.

"Mom." Lizzie searched for the right way to put it. "It started while you were in Paris — I just wanted to try it — and then when you came home I thought you'd be upset and think it was weird, and think I was trying to take advantage of the YouTube clip thing so I didn't say anything —"

Katia looked down at the cup of espresso in her hand, unmoved.

"I don't know what I was thinking," Lizzie went on. "I never thought that it would end up somewhere, I never thought there was any chance, and I *was* going to tell you —"

She heard someone come in through the open front door, and then Andrea walked into the kitchen, stepping carefully on the tile in her wet sneakers. Her blond ponytail was dark and bedraggled-looking from the rain. Her zip-up yoga jacket was soaked. She barely glanced at Lizzie, but in the millisecond their eyes met Lizzie could feel all of her betrayal and disappointment.

"I'm so sorry about all this," she launched right in, speaking to Bernard and Katia. "I was out of town, my BlackBerry wasn't working, the editor and I weren't in touch —"

"Do you know that she's fourteen years old?" Bernard demanded.

"Shhh, Bernard." Katia placed her hand on Bernard's arm.

Andrea put her messenger bag on the counter. "I wanted the photo editor just to *see* Lizzie's pictures. I never thought she'd print them. She did e-mail me to ask my permission but, as I said, my BlackBerry wasn't working —"

"What you did is illegal," Bernard cut in.

Natasha snickered.

"I gave Lizzie a release before I sent in her photos," Andrea said calmly. "When I got it faxed back to me I thought she'd spoken with you." She shot Lizzie a reproachful look, her friendly blue eyes flat now. "I was wrong."

"So you forged your mother's signature," Bernard said, turning to Lizzie. "Wonderful."

"No, this is my fault," Andrea said quietly. "Lizzie said that she was going to tell you. I never thought that she wouldn't. I never thought she'd lie to me."

It killed Lizzie to see Andrea take the responsibility for this. "Mom, Dad," she broke in, "I shouldn't have sent the release back in. I just wanted to see if I could do it without you." She bowed her head so she wouldn't have to look her mother in the eye. "I wanted it to be my own thing. If that makes any sense."

When she looked back up, Katia's face was still pale, but her eyes were just blue enough to indicate that this might end okay. "You have to see why I feel a little surprised here," Katia said to Andrea. "Especially because this is my world. I would hope that I'd be included in any decision Lizzie has to model. I had no idea she even wanted to try it."

"She didn't want to," Andrea confessed with a sigh. "In fact, she turned me down at first. But she's good at it. And I think she has something. I think her face is a work of art."

Katia and Bernard glanced at each other, as if they weren't sure they bought this.

"I'd understand if you never want her to be in front of a camera again," Andrea went on. "But I'm shooting a layout for *Rayon* in a couple of days. It's that music and entertainment magazine for college kids and twentysomethings." Andrea turned to Lizzie and finally eked out a proud smile. "They *flipped* over her picture in *New York Style*. And they'd love for her to be the model in the shoot."

"Absolutely not," Bernard announced.

"Bernard," Katia said, touching his arm again. She stood up from the table, and pulled her cashmere wrap closer around her shoulders. "Lizzie, you should probably get back to school now. And starting tonight you're grounded. For the next two weeks."

"Wait," Lizzie said. "*Rayon*? Mom . . . Can I do it?"

Katia glanced back at Bernard. Her dad threw up his hands, as if saying he was going to sit this one out.

"Look, I know that I lied to you, and I'm so sorry, Mom, I really am. But can we at least think about this?"

Katia pulled her wrap closer, but the stony look on her face was gone. "We'll *think* about it," she said. "Now, go back to school."

That was good enough for now, Lizzie thought. They would all need some time to recover from this. On her way to the front door, Lizzie brushed past Andrea. "I'm sorry," she whispered.

Andrea patted her on the shoulder as if to say "Okay."

At the front door she heard her mother behind her. "Lizzie?"

Her mother stepped out into the hall so that they were finally alone. Even in bare feet, she still towered over Lizzie.

"Promise me that you'll never do that again," she said in a quavering voice. She seemed so hurt.

"I promise," Lizzie said. "I'm sorry, Mom. Really, I am."

Katia reached out her slender arms and Lizzie stepped into her hug. She smelled the tuberose and lilies and felt an overwhelming sense of relief.

"But I'm proud of you," Katia said into her ear. "Do you really want to do this shoot?"

Lizzie nodded into her mom's shoulder. "Yes. I really do."

Katia let her go. "It would be just this once, Lizzie. *If* we do it."

Lizzie nodded again.

Katia smoothed Lizzie's hair. "Okay, get back to school."

Lizzie walked out to the elevators, feeling dazed and stunned, like she'd just survived a plane crash. The worst thing had happened, and somehow, everything was okay. Everything was more than okay, actually.

She checked her iPhone and there was a text from Hudson.

How does it feel to be the new face of BEAUTY???

Lizzie smiled.

AMAZING, she wrote back.

chapter 17

Psssst! The Evian mist felt cool against her skin. When she opened her eyes, the makeup artist with the tangerine-colored hair and pierced nose was crouched down in front of her face, swatting at Lizzie's damp cheeks with a makeup sponge. Her green T-shirt said EVERYBODY LOVES AN IRISH GIRL, and she smelled like patchouli. "This'll give you dewiness," she said, still swatting. "God, you barely need foundation. Who does your facials?"

Lizzie sipped her green tea. She thought about the time she and Hudson had tried to use Holla's weird microdermabrasion kit and gave up. "Nobody," she said.

"Really?" The makeup artist leaned back on her heels and studied her. "What's your secret then?"

Lizzie shrugged.

"She's only fourteen, Marisa," quipped the bald, stubbly-faced hairdresser standing behind her. "*That's* her secret." He twisted a piece of her hair around the barrel of a curling iron. "Is this your real color?" he asked.

"Yep." Lizzie nodded.

He whistled to himself. "Gor-geous," he muttered.

Only two days had passed since the *New York Style* meltdown with her parents and Andrea, but now everything was different. People were telling her that parts of her were gorgeous. She'd been allowed to skip school — just this once — to actually be paid to model. And while her friends were suffering through geometry, she was sitting in a makeup chair in a sun-drenched studio at Chelsea Piers, bopping her leg to Kanye West and getting her eyelashes curled. It was almost too much to wrap her head around, Lizzie thought, but she knew that she couldn't exactly get used to this. Bernard had allowed her to do this shoot for *Rayon* on two conditions: that this be a one-time thing, and that Katia be there to supervise it. Even though her mother still hadn't shown up.

"How're we doing, Lizzie? We good?" Andrea strode over, more keyed-up than usual, her blue eyes dancing and her wavy blond hair down around her face. She wore faded boot-cut jeans, a hoodie, and boots instead of sneakers. "Don't do too much to her, okay?" she said to Marisa. "Just a little powder and eyeliner. That's it. And Serge, not *too* corkscrewy, all right?" she said to the hairdresser, looking at Lizzie in the mirror. "She looks best when she looks like herself."

And that's something I've never heard before, Lizzie thought, getting out of the chair.

The *Rayon* fashion editor helped her get dressed in her first "look": a sheer floral-printed sundress layered over a C&C

long-sleeved cotton tee, with red paisley tights and oxfords. A little busy, Lizzie thought, but then again, *Rayon* was an edgy kind of fashion mag.

"Perfect. Just perfect," pronounced the editor, shaking her head as she stroked her long silver chain necklaces. "Let's get you some accessories." She pulled out a box of different pieces of jewelry, each of them wrapped in plastic, and picked out a necklace made up of big chunky pieces of glass that looked like candy. When she fastened it around Lizzie's neck she grinned. "There. *Now* you're perfect."

Lizzie looked at the portable full-length mirror on wheels. She would never have worn this outfit in real life, but, like her mish-mash of accessories from Chinatown, it all kind of worked.

Lizzie walked over to Andrea, who was standing near a gigantic computer monitor, flanked by two of her assistants. "What do you think?" she asked her.

Andrea looked her up and down. "I love it. And I think we're ready to go here. But should we wait for your mom?"

"I don't know. She had a meeting with her designers in the garment district. It might be a while."

"I'm here!" trilled a familiar voice.

The heavy door of the studio slammed shut, and Katia glided into the studio brandishing a BlackBerry in one hand and her daily Venti green tea chai from Starbucks in the other. "I'm so sorry I'm late, the traffic was *terrible*," she said. Her hair dangled over her shoulder in a long, thick braid, and she was dressed in an attention-getting black metallic tunic, corset-style jeweled belt, and a pair of tight, sleek black leather leggings that made her legs look twice as long. With a sinking feeling, Lizzie realized that Katia was going to do anything but fade into the background here.

"That's what you're wearing?" she asked Lizzie, stopping short when she saw her and scanning her with turquoise eyes.

"The story's called 'Crazy for Layers,' " Lizzie explained, slightly irritated. "They like to do edgier stuff."

"Uh-huh." She peered at Lizzie's face. "Are you wearing *any* makeup?"

Before Lizzie could say anything, Andrea rushed over to her. "I thought I'd keep it minimal," she said, walking over. "I want her to look like her, after all."

Katia's eyes narrowed just the slightest bit. Lizzie could tell she didn't approve.

"Okay honey, when you're up there, remember the Pose," Katia instructed. "Shoulders back, chin down, neck long —"

"It's okay, Mom," Lizzie interrupted. "Andrea and I kind of have our own style. But thanks."

Katia stared at her as if she didn't quite understand what she'd said.

"Oh, and can you kind of stand in the back? If that's okay?" she asked.

Her mom nodded. "Fine. Have fun. Because we're only doing this once, remember. It's just a trial run —"

"I know, Mom." Lizzie swallowed. She didn't want to be reminded of that just this moment. "I know."

"Okay, Lizzie! Let's do this!" Andrea called out, and Lizzie went to take her place in front of the camera. Behind her the whitewashed wall curved right into the floor, so that it looked like a blank white backdrop. Two light stands stood on either side of her, and at her feet was a small, powerful fan that blew her hair off her shoulders. Someone had turned up the music so that the hip-hop beats thudded behind her eyes and made her want to move. The fashion editor, the makeup artist, the hairdresser, and Andrea's assistants gradually made their way to the area behind Andrea to watch. *They're all watching me*, she thought. *What if I can't do this?*

"Okay, Lizzie, for this, I want movement!" Andrea yelled, holding her Mamiya. "Running! Jumping! Kicking! Dancing! The works! Don't be afraid to be crazy." Andrea hoisted the camera up to her face. "Let's go!"

As soon as Lizzie saw the black eye of the camera lens, something clicked inside of her. *I can do this*, she thought. The camera was her friend now. It wasn't going to judge her anymore.

She gave it all of her attention, gazing straight at it, leveling her eyes.

"Yes! Perfect!" Andrea clicked.

Slowly, she started to move. The music surrounded her, blocking out the chatter in her head. The breeze from the fan tickled her neck, and she had the vague sensation that her hair was blowing out behind her, but she didn't even notice. It was like she had tunnel vision — all she could see was the camera, and it was all she cared about. The people standing behind Andrea disappeared. Even Andrea disappeared. It was just her and the camera.

"Yes!" Andrea yelled as she snapped away. "That's great! Just like that!"

She jumped. She kicked. She twirled. She actually broke a

sweat. Every so often, Andrea would take a break, and the makeup artist and the hairdresser would jump up and press powder on her nose or smooth her hair with some styling lotion. When she had to change into her second look, and then her third, she scurried off the set, panting, and the fashion editors wordlessly handed her the clothes. Then in a flash, she'd be in front of the camera again. She was in a groove. She was untouchable. Powerful. In charge.

She could have gone on for hours when Andrea finally handed her camera to one of her assistants and started clapping. "That was great, Lizzie!" she hollered, breaking into a little dance of her own. "Your best yet!"

Lizzie grinned and limped off the set, cheerfully exhausted. Her legs ached like she'd just run five miles. Who knew that modeling was so much exercise?

As she walked out of the glare of the lights, and her eyes adjusted to the sunlight, Lizzie did a quick visual sweep of the room. She'd almost forgotten that her mom was here. Realizing that she'd just danced in front of her for an hour and a half to hip-hop, she was a little embarrassed.

But Katia sat perfectly still in a canvas folding chair, her long, leather-covered legs crossed, and her BlackBerry lying untouched on her lap. She was so still that for a moment, Lizzie wondered if she was okay. And then her mom smiled, slid to her feet, and started clapping as she walked over. "Well done!" she yelled. When she reached Lizzie, she threw her arms around her. "Well done!" she said again, squeezing her.

"Thanks, Mom," Lizzie said, a little unsure what to make of this.

"I had no *idea*," Katia said, letting her go. "I had no *idea* you were so good at this!" Katia looked at Andrea. "She can really do this, can't she?"

Andrea reached out and touched Lizzie's hair as if she were her own kid. "She's very talented," she agreed.

"Did you have fun up there?" Katia asked.

"The most fun ever," Lizzie said.

"Well, I have some news I was saving," Andrea informed them. "*New York Style* loved Lizzie's look so much they want to use her again. But this time they want her on the cover."

The cover. Lizzie's heart did a somersault. "Oh, Mom, can I do it?" she pleaded. "Please? Can I? "

Katia took a deep breath. "I don't know, honey —"

"But I can do this," she argued. "I feel like I'm actually *good* at this. Please?"

Katia bit her lip. She was still beautiful, but there were tiny frown lines around her mouth, and the crow's feet under her eyes looked deeper than Lizzie had ever noticed before. For the first time, she realized that her mother was getting older.

"I *am* very impressed," Katia conceded, narrowing her eyes as she thought. "Let's talk to your father."

Without Katia saying it, Lizzie had her answer. For the first time in years — maybe *ever* — she and her mom were finally on the same side of something. All this time, she had been her mother's daughter, too, and neither of them had known it.

chapter 18

The first school dance of the year always reminded Lizzie of Christmas: lots of exciting lead-up, and then a somewhat anticlimactic main event. Before the big night, she and her friends always had the crazy hope that given mood lighting, a DJ, and the ability to wear their own clothes, romance might suddenly strike with one of the guys in her class. And then, at the dance, they'd remember that romance really wasn't a possibility when there were only sixty people in your grade, and you'd known most of them since pre-K.

But for Lizzie there was still one exciting prospect. Even if that prospect had a girlfriend he was surgically attached to, and he wasn't actually here yet.

"Lizzie, he's going to show up, I promise," Carina said as she leaned over the snack table and grabbed a handful of Fritos. "And you're *stalking* those doors."

Lizzie guiltily tore her eyes from the double doors to the assembly hall and sipped her 7UP. "I wasn't *stalking* them."

"Ugh. C...," Hudson said, wrinkling her nose. "You put your hands in that bowl? And Fritos? Really?" Hudson had taken one of her famous fashion risks tonight with a purple and yellow silk Matthew Williamson shredded-hem tunic and a deconstructed feathered headdress. It actually worked.

"I'm under a lot of stress at the office," Carina said defensively, crunching her Fritos. "My dad actually made me take a quiz on his different companies. A *pop* quiz. Like he doesn't think I pay attention while I'm there. It's so condescending." She pulled at the strap of the black dress she'd bought at Big Drop. "So I checked, you guys. Almost a million bucks definitely *didn't* get to those charities. And I found some weird file showing that one of his companies got a sudden influx of cash." She snapped her fingers. *"Busted."*

"So you're gonna blow the whistle on him?" Lizzie asked. "Just like that?"

"He's a cheater," Carina said. "People need to know that."

"No, they don't," Hudson said, shaking her head. "Please promise me that you'll call me before you do this. So I can try to stop the madness before it's too late?"

Carina only winked. "I promise."

Even though she was the most extroverted of the three of them, Carina would sooner sell her soul than give up a secret — hers or someone else's. It was one of her best qualities — except when she chose to withhold info from her best friends. And Lizzie knew that there was more going on behind Carina's decision to do this than she was going to admit.

"So, what'd your dad say about the cover shoot for *New York Style*?" Hudson asked Lizzie. "Did he come around?"

"Amazingly, yes," Lizzie said. "I'm doing it next week. It was all my mom. Now she's totally on board with the modeling thing."

"Except they still grounded you for two weeks, right?" Carina said.

Lizzie shrugged. "I got them to lift it a few days early for the dance," she said. She looked out onto the empty dance floor and saw a little person crossing the room through the weird pink and blue lighting. It was Hillary Crumple. From the steely, woman-on-a-mission look in her eyes, Lizzie knew she was coming straight toward them.

"Oh no," Carina said, spotting her. "Incoming."

"Yeesh," Hudson sighed.

Before the three of them could turn around toward the snack table, Hillary was right in front of them, staring at Hudson expectantly. "Hey, Hudson. Awesome headdress."

"Thanks," Hudson said delicately. "I like your sweater."

"Really?" Hillary looked down at her pink knit sweater embellished with sparkly flowers. "I just got it."

"It's cute," Hudson said, trying as always to be nice.

"So, I saw you in *Life & Style* the other day," Hillary said, launching into verbal attack mode. "It was a photo of you coming out of a Starbucks with your mom. You had on this purple jumper thingie with the black fishnet tights. Where'd you get them? And where are you at with your album?"

Hudson darted a nervous glance at Lizzie. "It's in the beginning stages right now."

"Is your mom helping you?" Hillary pressed. If Lizzie didn't know better, she'd think Hillary was interviewing her.

"My mom and I have different styles," Hudson said cautiously. "So she is, but she's kind of in the background, if you know what I mean."

Hillary nodded. "This dance is totally lame," she announced, craning her little head to take in the empty dance floor. "Why aren't you guys at Ava's? I heard she's having a party."

"Ava's having a party?" Lizzie asked. No wonder Todd wasn't here.

"Are you going?" Carina asked Hillary.

Hillary shook her head. "My mom won't let me," she said, rolling her eyes. "What-*ev*."

"Well, I think we need to go to the bathroom now," Carina cut in, taking Hudson by the arm. "Sorry, Hillary."

"Just one more thing," Hillary said to Hudson, pulling out her cell phone. "Want to give me your number? Maybe we can go shopping sometime?"

"Um," Hudson paused, biting her lower lip.

Don't do it, Lizzie tried to say with ESP, but Hudson took Hillary's phone and punched in her number.

"Cool!" Hillary gushed, taking the phone back. "Thanks!"

Carina finally managed to yank Hudson toward the doors. "You gave her your number?" she asked in disbelief.

"You're way too nice to her, H," Lizzie said. "Especially since she's obsessed with you."

"She's not obsessed with me," Hudson countered. "She's obsessed with my mom. What else is new?"

"Yeah, but I'd still be careful," Carina whispered. "She's crazy as a freakin' loon."

"You guys, let's go to Ava's," Lizzie declared, before she'd even really thought about it.

Hudson and Carina traded looks. "We weren't invited," Hudson said.

"And I thought Ava was driving you crazy," Carina pointed out. "She'll probably hit you up for something for her stupid party."

"Yeah, but the dance is kind of lame," she said. "And Todd'll be there."

Just then they saw Hillary Crumple walk out of the assembly hall and make her way toward them. The three of them looked at each other. It wasn't even a question.

"Let's take a cab," Carina said as they headed toward the doors.

Lizzie hadn't set foot in Ava's brownstone in years, but she remembered every inch of it: the chandeliers, the steep, creaky staircases, the thick Persian carpets, the tufted couches and chairs done in that curved Louis XIV style. Ava's mom was a famous interior designer, and every year, Ava would get a new bedroom. In first grade, the theme had been Sleeping Beauty, which meant that she had a graceful canopy over a painted iron bed and luxurious pink and purple velvet pillows. In fifth grade it had changed to Moroccan Casbah, with rich tapestries and a curtain of mosquito netting surrounding her bed on the floor. Now Lizzie wasn't sure what it was — she hadn't been invited over to Ava's since the seventh grade.

"You think this is a good idea?" Hudson whispered, as Lizzie rang the doorbell.

"I'm sure she won't care," Lizzie said.

"You're so ballsy all of a sudden," Hudson said admiringly.

Lizzie let the compliment sink in. Maybe she was different now, she thought.

Finally a defeated-looking housekeeper answered the door, and with a shrug she gestured for them to step into the foyer. The party was in full swing. People from Chadwick and other schools milled around with red plastic cups. Music came from the dining room in the back. Lizzie heard feet trampling the stairs above them. As usual, Ava's party had drawn most of the entire fourteen-year-old population of Manhattan.

"So what's the plan?" Hudson asked.

"Let's look for food," Carina announced. "Where's the kitchen?"

Lizzie scanned the crowd for Todd. He had to be here.

"Oops." Hudson dug her BlackBerry out of her purse. "Chris just texted me."

"Your lov-ah?" Carina asked.

"My *producer*. We're moving studios. He just booked us another one."

"Does he know you're in love with him?" Carina teased.

Hudson put her BlackBerry away. "Please. We have a completely professional relationship. And he's twenty-eight."

"Just don't let Ava know that you like him," Lizzie quipped, just as Todd walked into the hall holding a red cup and wearing a blue button-down shirt.

"Lizzie," he said, stopping in his tracks.

Before she could say anything Ken Clayman tumbled out of the kitchen behind him and plowed right into Todd's shoulders. He stumbled toward her. A moment later Lizzie felt something cold spill all over the front of her dress.

It was from Todd's plastic cup. She looked down. A large purple stain was quickly spreading across the front of her brand-new dress. It had a familiar smell.

"Is this *grape juice*?" she asked, sniffing.

Todd blushed. "I'm so sorry," he said stiffly. "Here, let me help you."

"You still drink that?" This suddenly struck her as unbelievably adorable.

"Once in a while," he mumbled. "Hold on. There's a bathroom upstairs."

Taking by the hand, he led her up the steps and into a small powder room at the top of the stairs. He closed the door behind her, then turned on the faucet and ripped some Kleenexes out of the tissue box. "Really sorry about that," he said once more.

"Okay, stop. You've just said sorry about forty-five times." She grabbed a washcloth and wet it under the water. "You're so *English*."

She wanted to tell him that he could have spilled six glasses of grape juice on her. All she cared about was that they were alone together in a small space.

A very small space, it turned out. The powder room was just big enough for a toilet and a sink. He sat down on the counter, trying to fold his long legs in toward himself, with his feet on the toilet lid.

"I'm glad you guys came by," he said. "I was gonna tell you about it but I thought you wouldn't want to come."

"Why not?" she asked, dabbing at her dress.

Todd didn't say anything for a moment. "I got the sense you weren't so keen on Ava after she asked you to help with her party." He picked up an expensive-looking vanilla candle and studied it.

"No, I didn't mind," she said. She couldn't bring herself to criticize him.

"Hey, I saw that picture of you in the magazine," he said, putting the candle down. "I told you you're hot. You didn't believe me."

She rolled her eyes at him and tried not to blush. "It was just one picture."

"It was a good one. I bet you become just as famous as your mom."

Lizzie looked down at her dress. Suddenly this seemed like a little too much. Why was Todd always flirting with her? "I doubt it," she said. "And what'd Ava think of it?"

Todd stared at her. "What?"

"Did she like it?"

Todd looked completely thrown. "I don't know...I guess so. We didn't exactly talk about it."

"Are you guys, you know...in love?" She couldn't resist. And why couldn't she ask him this anyway, if they were just friends?

"In love?" He started to fidget on the counter. "We just started hanging out."

"Well, you guys do spend a lot of time together, so I just thought I'd ask," she said casually. "And if you are, I'm really happy for you."

Todd furrowed his brows and hunched his shoulders. "You are?" he asked.

She'd dug herself into a hole, one that was about to collapse over her. "Uh...well," she started. "Yeah..."

And then the door suddenly opened.

"Todd?"

Ava stood in the doorway, wobbling on her snakeskin heels.

Her saucer-shaped eyes looked glassy, her cheeks were flushed, and her normally bouncing curls looked deflated and flat. Lizzie could smell the beer on her.

"What are you guys doing?" she asked suspiciously, her eyes darting from one to the other of them as she fingered her necklace.

"Oh, I just spilled something on Lizzie's dress," Todd explained, springing to his feet.

"Yeah," Lizzie chimed in. "I was just getting a stain out —"

Ava's injured glare stopped them both cold. "I've been looking for you everywhere," she snapped at Todd. "Can I talk to you?"

Ava lurched past Lizzie into the room. Lizzie had no choice but to step outside into the hall, and before she knew it, the bathroom door slammed in her face. Through the door, she could hear Ava's and Todd's muffled voices. It sounded like they were having a fight. A bad fight.

Oh my God, she thought. Ava Elting was *jealous*.

She marched down the steps. Luckily, Hudson and Carina were waiting for her right at the bottom.

"We're out of here," Lizzie said, heading straight for the door.

"What happened up there?" Hudson asked.

"Nothing good," Lizzie replied.

All she'd wanted to do was finally talk about Ava with him, instead of pretending that he didn't have a girlfriend. So why did she get the feeling that bringing her up had hurt his feelings? And why had she felt bad about it?

"Did you see Ava?" Carina asked as they walked out onto the street. "She can barely walk. She's hammered."

"Classy girl," Hudson chimed in.

"I give that relationship two more weeks," Carina observed. "Anyone want to bet?"

"Or maybe they'll stay together forever," Lizzie said cryptically as they walked to the corner. "I kind of hope they do at this point."

Out of the corner of her eye, she saw Hudson and Carina look at each other as they walked to Park Avenue. "Guess that's the last time we crash an Ava Elting party," Carina said.

chapter 19

"Lizzie, honey? I was thinking, should we do that shoot with Andrea in London over Thanksgiving? Or do you have too much work to do over the break?" Katia leaned past Bernard's shoulder in the backseat, her diamond and ruby drop earrings glittering in the dark. "I don't want to overload you."

The town car made a right onto Park Avenue, and Lizzie swayed against the door in a crunch of organza. "No, let's do it," she said.

"You said that you were going to take this slow," Bernard said, attaching a pair of mother-of-pearl cufflinks to his shirt. "She should be at home right now doing homework."

Katia patted Bernard's knee. "We are taking it slow, don't worry. I'm still not sure that signing with my agent is the best thing for you, Lizzie. We need to find someone who specializes in what you're doing."

What she was doing was still a little unclear, Lizzie thought, looking out the window at the passing office buildings. She had done the *Rayon* shoot and posed for the cover of *New York Style*, and now the offers were starting to pour in from advertisers and editors alike. Could she do a spread in *i-D.* magazine? Could she do a print ad for a new, eco-friendly face skincare line that was looking for a "different" face? Could she do a spread for *Teen Vogue* about "real beauty"? Before this started, she'd never known how hot "real beauty" was. Now it seemed everyone wanted to do a story on the New Pretty. And they wanted Lizzie to be the poster girl for it.

She still didn't have an agent or a manager. She still hadn't worked with anyone but Andrea Sidwell. And she still wasn't clear if she was getting this work because of her weird looks, or because of her celebrity pedigree. But Katia seemed genuinely proud of her, and this made Lizzie happy. Over the past three weeks, ever since the *Rayon* shoot, she and her mom had gotten along better than they had since Lizzie was in the fourth grade. Katia had even invited her to go tonight to the American Fashion Awards, the most prestigious fashion event of the year. It hadn't even occurred to Lizzie to say no.

"Do you want to walk with us, honey?" Katia asked as the car pulled up to the curb in front of the Waldorf-Astoria Hotel. "Or do you want to meet us at the entrance?"

The red carpet at the AFAs was extra-long and extra-notorious, and walking it was almost the entire point of going. Every fashionista, stylist, entertainment reporter, and fashion blogger breathlessly covered the carpet, making and breaking careers based solely on people's wardrobes. Lizzie knew that it would probably take Katia a good half an hour to get down it.

"I'll meet you by the doors," she said.

"You can hang with me, Fuzz." Bernard patted her hand. "Thank God I finally have a date to one of these things."

"You sure you're okay?" Katia asked.

Lizzie gazed out at the gauntlet of paparazzi and cameras and wildly revolving floodlights. "I think I can handle this now," she said.

Her mom winked at her. Something had happened that day at the *Rayon* shoot, and now, it seemed, the two of them were a team.

Bernard turned to Lizzie. "See you on the battlefield, soldier," he muttered.

Katia opened the back door of the town car. The usual flurry of flashes started, as did the chorus of voices. It was just like Fashion Week.

"Katia!"

"Over here!"

"Katia!"

Her parents got out of the car and Lizzie waited inside, watching the flashes light up the open car door.

Here goes, she thought, hauling herself and her long, purple, full-skirted Zac Posen dress out of the car with all the gracefulness she could muster. She'd just need to get to the doors as quickly as possible. Out on the carpet, she squinted in the bright lights, looking around at the sea of cameras when —

POP.

A flash went off in front of her face. She blinked.

POP.

Another flash went off.

POP. POP. POP.

Clickety-clickety-click.

Someone was taking pictures of her. She held her hand up to her face, shading her eyes so she could see.

Clickety-clickety-click.

A *lot* of people were taking pictures of her. Alone. Just her.

And then she heard her name.

"Lizzie!"

"Straight ahead!"

"Over to the right!"

"Lizzie! Look to the left!"

She didn't know where to look first. There were too many flashes.

"Lizzie! Who are you wearing!"

"Lizzie! Over here!"

In what seemed like half a second, she was swarmed.

"Lizzie! What's it like to be the next big thing?"

"Lizzie! Did you always want to be a model?"

"Let's get Katia! *Katia!*" someone called. "Can we get one with your daughter please?"

She couldn't move. None of this could really be happening, she thought. Through the flashes, she saw Katia glide toward her in her strapless red gown. Then she felt her grab her hand.

"That's great!"

"Beautiful!"

"Mother, daughter, look over here!"

A female reporter with a frozen, swirly hairdo leaned out of the crowd and pointed a mic at Katia's face. "What do you think of your daughter's success?" she demanded. "Did you ever think that she'd be a model?"

Lizzie watched all of this in slow motion. Over and over, she had to remind herself that this was really going on.

"Lizzie, I'm from FTV," said another girl with a camera and a microphone. "Please tell us. Who are you wearing tonight?"

"Uh, Zac Posen," she stammered, almost forgetting.

Then the midst of the frenzy her mother let go of her hand, and she was on her own. For a moment the clicking sounds of the cameras called up the same panic of Fashion Week, that feeling of vulnerability, of exposure. And then she remembered Andrea. How many times she'd put her at ease behind the camera. And then she relaxed. *It's just like modeling*, she thought. *I can do this.*

When she reached the end of the carpet, her cheeks ached from smiling, and shooting rays of light bobbed in her vision. Katia and Bernard were waiting for her at the door.

"You okay?" Katia asked, putting her arm around her daughter.

Lizzie nodded. "I wasn't really expecting that."

"We weren't, either," Bernard said.

"You did great, honey," Katia assured her, patting her shoulder. "Like a pro. Come on, let's get inside."

They walked up a set of steps into the high-ceilinged lobby and

183

joined a stream of tuxedoes and swirling Technicolor gowns headed for the ballroom. Lizzie caught up to her dad and took his arm. "That was seriously the craziest thing that's ever happened to me," she whispered.

Bernard gave her a kiss on the top of her head. "I have a feeling that's just the beginning, Fuzz," he said.

They were almost at the ballroom doors when a familiar-looking man with close-cropped platinum hair and liquid brown eyes approached them with his arms outstretched.

"Katia!" Martin Meloy cried, throwing his arms around her mother with desperate force. He shut his eyes as they hugged. He was so small that he barely cleared her neckline. "Oh, darling, congratulations again on the line. I never had any doubts."

"Oh thank you," Katia said, unpeeling herself from his embrace. "You remember my husband, Bernard?"

"Of course, of course," Martin said, vigorously shaking Bernard's hand. "I love your column."

Bernard shook back, but there was a cold detachment in his eyes. "Good to see you," he said gruffly.

"And my daughter, Lizzie," Katia said, putting a hand on Lizzie's back. "I believe you've met?"

Lizzie stepped forward, bracing herself for a fake hello, or at least a severe lack of interest. But this time Martin Meloy clasped his hands under his pointy chin and shook his head faintly, as if he'd just encountered a vision. "Well, hello, Lizzie," he said softly. "I've become quite a fan of yours."

"You have?" she asked, thinking she'd misunderstood him.

"I saw the *New York Style* cover. Fantastic." He reached down and took her hand. "*You* are a revelation."

"Uh, thank you," Lizzie said, almost numb. Going from invisible to revelation was quite a shock.

"I would love for you to come down to my studio," he went on, his liquid eyes fixed on her. "Maybe tomorrow?"

Lizzie glanced up at her mom. She wanted to make sure that she wasn't dreaming this.

"That's very sweet of you, Martin," Katia said, smiling tightly.

"It's just that Lizzie has never seen my studio," he said.

"We're so flattered," Katia said, placing a hand firmly on Lizzie's shoulder. "But we're just trying to take things one step at a time. I'm sure you understand."

"Oh, of *course,* but just think about it," he said, pressing Lizzie's hand. "It would mean so much to me for you to see the new collection I'm working on."

There was something odd about his persistence, but she couldn't help but be flattered. Martin Meloy wanted her to see his collection?

"It sounds kind of fun," Lizzie said. "Can we?"

"Okay, then," Katia said nicely. "We'll come by after school tomorrow." But her tone was unsettled, as if she was saying something that she knew she might have to take back.

"Oh, wonderful!" he cried, clapping his hands with delight. "I look forward to it. *A demain.*" He did a little bow as he stepped back into the crowd, and then he was gone.

A headset-wearing assistant walked up to them and announced that she could lead them to their table. They followed the assistant into the immense gold and crimson–colored ballroom, and past tables decorated with flaming votives set around an exploding centerpiece of pink and purple roses.

Lizzie took her seat in between her parents and pulled the silk napkin out of its ring. Before she could say anything to her mom about what had just happened, the skeletal editor of one of the fashion magazines swanned over to their table and started air-kissing her mother.

"This is all kind of bizarre," she said in her father's ear.

"Tell me about it," Bernard agreed, straightening the forks next to the gleaming china plates.

"I mean, about what just happened with Martin Meloy," she said. "He's never looked at me twice before."

Bernard knitted his bushy eyebrows together and studied his water goblet. "Look, Fuzz. You've always been beautiful to me. But sometimes it doesn't take much to change people's opinions. A shoot here, a cover there, a mention on Page Six in the *Post*…"

"And suddenly, someone's cool," she prompted.

"Exactly," her dad said, smiling at her. "Just like in school. Things don't really change, I'm afraid," he sighed. "And from what I can tell, that goes double for Martin Meloy."

A man on her father's left tapped his shoulder and started speaking to him about the stock market, leaving Lizzie to think about his words. She stared at her name written in fancy black calligraphy above her plate. Of course her father was right. There was something a little high school in all of this.

Under the table, Lizzie pulled her iPhone out from her clutch. Normally she would have rather done this with a gun to her head — she never really enjoyed tabloid coverage, thanks to her daughter-of status — but now she googled her name, along with the name of the cruelest, snarkiest celebrity gossip blog she could think of. She needed to see what came up.

"CHIA PET TURNS CHIC!" cried the headline, just over her cover photo from *New York Style*.

Underneath, the caption read:

Is it just us, or has our favorite supermodel-spawn gone from horrible to HOTTIE?

She dropped the phone back in her bag and a thrill ran through her. *She* was a *hottie*?

Her father was definitely right. People *were* too easily swayed. But was it bad for it to feel wonderful?

The orchestra started to play at the front of the room, and the first awards presenter walked stiffly out onto the stage. She leaned back in her chair and smiled. At last, she wasn't on the sidelines anymore.

chapter 20

"Martin Meloy?" Hudson repeated. *"Martin MeLOY?"*

Lizzie smiled as she popped the lid off of her hot chocolate and licked the dollop of whipped cream on top. She should have been spending her free period going over her algebra homework from last night — she had barely finished it after getting home from the Waldorf — but filling her friends in on last night was so much more fun.

"Yep," she said, blowing on her hot drink. "We're going over there after school."

"I can't believe it," Hudson said, pulling her collar closer against the chilly October wind blowing down Madison. "Martin Meloy's studio! *Nobody's* allowed in there. Not even the Olsens."

"Wait, I thought you said he was a creep," Carina broke in, tearing open a Balance Bar with her gloved hands. "Or a tool."

"Well, he is a little fake," Lizzie conceded. "But they all are."

"And you still want to work with him?" Carina asked skeptically as the wind blew the ends of her blond hair.

"C, this is a *huge* deal," Hudson piped up on Lizzie's other side. "You could be the face of his line! His *muse!*" Her ivory coat matched the color of her teeth as she smiled. "Do you know which campaign you're doing?" she asked breathlessly. "Fragrance? Accessories? Clothing?"

"Hudson, I don't even know if I'm doing a campaign."

"And you're gonna get *such* a great discount," Hudson gushed. "And free stuff. You better give me whatever you don't want. What does your mom think? Is she psyched?"

Lizzie took a big sip of hot chocolate, unsure how to answer. Katia had seemed a little cool toward Martin's invitation. "I think so. But she wasn't jumping for joy or anything."

They walked into the school building and took the steps two at a time past a slow-moving group of middle schoolers.

"Maybe she's jealous," Carina said. "She's only human."

"Oh, come on," Lizzie said. "She's the World's Most Perfect Woman Ever."

"Yeah, but maybe she doesn't see it that way," Carina said.

Lizzie didn't say anything. The thought of her mom being jealous of her was almost too ridiculous to think about.

Hudson's phone rang. "Private number," Hudson said, looking at the screen. "Whoever this is, they've been calling me all morning." She put the phone to her ear. "Hel-*lo*?" she answered. Then she hung up. "Nobody there again. Weird."

"Maybe it's your lov-ah," Carina joked.

They walked up the stairs, and Carina and Hudson headed off to Spanish. Lizzie was on her way to the lockers when she heard Mr. Barlow call out from his office.

"Miss Summers? May I see you, please?"

Lizzie grabbed her French books. "Yes?" she asked, coming to stand in the doorway.

Mr. Barlow sat at his desk. The glow from his banker's lamp cast a green shadow over his white-blond hair. "Your story's about five hundred words too long for the contest," he said. "Two thousand words is the cutoff point. Just trim it a little and turn it back in. But it's very good. I think you have a shot at winning this."

"Really?" she asked. In all that had been going on in her personal life, she'd almost forgotten about the contest. "I was afraid it might be a little too...realistic."

Mr. Barlow shook his head. "Don't be afraid of that. The best writing always comes from your own experience. Even if you've never cut your hair to look like your mother's," he added with a smile as he handed the story back to her. "And how's the project going with Mr. Piedmont?" he asked, cocking an eyebrow.

"Fine," she said. She and Todd hadn't spoken since Ava's party a week and a half ago, but luckily they'd split their screenplay up into two parts — the same scene, told both from the boy's and the girl's point of view. Lizzie hoped that she could just quietly write her half and skip any more awkward study sessions.

"Well, look who's here," Mr. Barlow said, looking past her into the hall. "Mr. Piedmont! Would you come in here, please?"

Todd loped into the office. From the quick sideways glance she

190

stole of him, Todd looked a little more rumpled than usual, as if he'd slept in his navy-blue jacket and tie.

"I was just speaking with Miss Summers about your project," Mr. Barlow said. "Are you two making progress?"

"Sort of," Todd mumbled, looking briefly at her.

"Sort of?" Mr. Barlow barked.

Uh-oh, Lizzie thought.

"You know I think we have it under control, Mr. Barlow," she offered. "If we need to get together again —"

"You are required to meet *twice* for this assignment," Mr. Barlow pointed out. "Which, I may remind you, is due on Monday."

"Then I could get together tonight to work on it," Todd offered, sounding slightly defeated. He turned to her. "What do you think, Lizzie? You free tonight?" She couldn't help but notice that his hair was adorably messed up and the knot of his tie was askew.

"Yeah, that's fine. Tonight can work," she said coolly.

"Today's Wednesday so you two better get moving on it," Mr. Barlow said, unfolding himself creakily from behind his desk. "I was just giving Lizzie back her story. She did a very good job on it. As did you, Mr. Piedmont."

Todd suddenly swallowed and looked down at the acid green carpet. "Thanks," he said, looking mortified for some reason.

"Would it be okay if I kind of tweaked this a little bit?" she asked Mr. Barlow. "Maybe just smooth out some of the story? End up in a different place?"

"Sure, sure," Mr. Barlow said, getting distracted by the front page of the *Times* on his desk. "Good luck, you two."

They walked out into the hall, and when they got to French class, Todd sat in the empty chair next to her. It was the closest they had been to each other since Ava's bathroom.

"So tonight around seven?" she asked him. "We can do it at my place."

"Great. And hey, I want to show you something," he said, unzipping his bookbag. "Close your eyes."

"Where's Ava?" she asked him. Seeing him alone for this long was a rare event.

"She has the flu. Just close your eyes."

She sighed and shut them. She didn't seem to have any choice. "Todd, I really need to check my homework for a second —"

"Okay, open."

There was a blue box on her desk, like the ones she'd seen in Todd's bookcase. "Open it," he said.

She opened the box. Inside was a hardback book with a slightly tattered, familiarly blue dust jacket. It was *The Great Gatsby*. And it looked like a first edition.

"Oh my God," she said, almost afraid to touch it. The book's jacket was creased and wrinkled, and peeling apart at the edges. It looked ancient. "You found it?"

"Yep. You can take it out," he said.

She ran her fingers over the smooth, delicate dust jacket, and carefully opened the book. On the title page was a dark squiggle of ink. She stared, dumbfounded, at the signature. "You got a signed first edition?"

Todd smiled at her. "My hookup in London really came through."

She ran her fingers over the ink. Fitzgerald had touched this book, held this book, and signed this book himself. It was the most precious thing she had ever come across. "I can't believe you have this."

"I don't have it," he said. "*You* do. It's yours."

She gaped at him. "What? I can't take this! How much did this cost?"

A deep red blush pulsed in his cheeks. "Don't worry about it," he said, shrugging. "It's for you to start your own collection."

"I can't take this, Todd."

"Well, if you want, we can share it," he said, cocking his head and peering into her eyes in a peculiar way.

Her heart thudded in her chest. Her palms got sweaty. HE LIKES YOU, said a voice inside her, as loud as a siren.

"Okay," she said. "Thanks."

"Oh, and we're on for tonight then?" he asked cheerfully, taking out his French book.

"Uh, yeah," she managed to say. "Sure."

As she put the book carefully back into the box, and then into her bookbag, she knew that it was time to stop playing the We're Just Friends game. She was going to tell him how she felt — tonight. Ava or no Ava. After all the games and the missed signals and the weird broken pauses, she had her answer. And for the first time, she finally had the courage to give him hers.

chapter 21

Later that afternoon, Lizzie sprinted through the cobblestone triangle of the meatpacking district, her kilt flying around her knees and
the wind blowing through her unruly curls. She was fifteen minutes
late for her life-changing meeting with Martin Meloy.

Panting, she turned the corner onto Washington Street and saw
the low, block-long, aluminum-green warehouse, and on the bottom floor, the windows of the flagship Martin Meloy store.

She bypassed the store entrance, emblazoned with twin silver
M's, and ran around the corner to a nondescript glass door. Anyone
could walk into Martin Meloy's boutique and buy wallets and perfume and his coveted clothes, but only the chosen fashion elite knew
about this door, which led to Martin's private, multi-million-dollar
five-story studio. She felt a little shiver as she pulled the door open.
As Katia Summers's daughter she wouldn't have been able to swing
this invitation. But now that she was Katia Summers's model-daughter,
everything was different.

"Hello, Lizzie, Martin's expecting you," said a receptionist behind a steel sliver of a desk. She gestured toward the lobby with her fountain pen.

"Thanks," she said, unbuttoning her peacoat and hoping she wasn't too sweaty.

She walked into the spacious, white lobby. Tufted couches and chairs in purple and magenta dotted the room. A fake tree rose out of the floor, extending its branches in all directions. And in the center was a twisting gold and diamond-studded staircase. As Lizzie climbed the steps, she couldn't help but think of Mount Olympus, from the myths they'd been reading about in English class.

"Hello, Lizzie," said a girl who was waiting for her at the top of the steps. She was tall and thin, with expertly flatironed brown hair and a fresh-scrubbed, freckled face. Lizzie wondered for a moment if she was one of Martin's models. She definitely could be. "I'm Annalise, Martin's assistant," she said in a velvety smooth voice. "They're waiting for you in the salon."

"There's a salon here?" Lizzie asked, looking around the large open room, where designers hovered over drafting tables.

"No." Annalise smiled gently. "The *Salon*. As in, the French term for a gathering of creative people. Martin is a big fan of the French. Their history, their philosophy, their food...Can I take your bag?"

Lizzie eyed her dirty bookbag. "Uh, that's okay." The less that Annalise noticed her bag, the better.

"Well, then, follow me," she said, walking — or rather, floating — down the hall. "Martin is so excited to have you here," she whispered over her shoulder. "He's been talking about it all day. I've

195

been with him for years and I've never seen him so excited about one of his girls."

"His girls?"

Annalise gave her another sweet, patient smile. "I'll let him explain it." Annalise came to a stop at the open door. "Here we are."

Lizzie walked inside. Katia sat on the couch, dressed in a knee-length pencil skirt and high black boots, her blond hair drawn into a severe bun. She was frowning, but before Lizzie could reach her, Martin suddenly appeared in the doorway. In his distressed velvet jacket he looked like a punk Willy Wonka.

"Lizzie," he said, tugging her inside with both hands and giving her a European-style double-cheek kiss. "So good to see you. I hope you found it okay. I'm *delighted* to have you." Martin smiled, exposing his blindingly white teeth. "Your mother and I were just talking about you," he said kindly. "Please. Sit down. Can I get you a cappuccino?"

"No, thank you," she said.

The salon was actually just an office, with furniture that looked like it had been stolen from Versailles and then updated for the twenty-second century: suede chairs with gold-leafed legs, a gigantic armoire with filigreed pulls. A gold velvet sofa stretched against one wall in one long, undulating wave, and the window facing them looked out over the placid gray surface of the Hudson. But like the lobby, the room felt cold and untouched. Lizzie sat tentatively on the sofa next to her mom and kissed her hello.

"Martin has something he wants to say to you," Katia told her. "Go ahead, Martin," she said.

Martin took off his velvet jacket. Underneath was a simple black T-shirt that showed off his gym-sculpted arms. "When I saw your photo in *New York Style*, Lizzie," he said, pacing the floor, "I knew exactly what was going to inspire my next collection. *You.* Your face. The way it makes you think. The way it seizes your attention. The way it veers between awkward and stunning. The way it breaks all the rules."

Awkward and stunning? she thought. What the heck did that mean? Lizzie snuck a glance at her mom. She was watching Martin with an inscrutable expression.

"*You* are what my clothes are all about," he went on. "Straddling the line of what's acceptable, what's beautiful. Making people think. *Provoking* people."

He leaned closer to her, close enough that she could see the wrinkles and bags under his radiant eyes. She wondered for a moment if Martin Meloy actually slept. "Here, look at this."

He picked up a piece of poster board that was leaning against the wall. With a start, Lizzie saw that it was a collage of pictures of her. Her *New York Style* cover. Her *Rayon* shoot. The first photo that had run in *New York Style*. Plus every paparazzi shot that had been taken of her in the past five years: photos of her with her mother at screenings, at Fashion Week, at the supermarket. Pictures that had made her cringe. Pictures that had made other people cringe.

"You were my inspiration board this season," he said proudly. "The awkward trailblazer. The girl who doesn't know she's beautiful." He put down the collage and took a deep, meaningful breath. "I want *you* to be the face of Martin Meloy next year. I want you in my clothing ads, my fragrance ads. My accessories ads. Everything. All over the world. *You* are the face of the moment. And I want it."

It took a moment for this to sink in. *Her. Lizzie. Chia Pet. Muse?*

"What do you think?" he asked, crouching forward, as if his entire career depended on her answer.

"I...I would love to," she said.

"Lizzie," Katia snapped, breaking Martin's spell. "What about school?"

"I'm happy to work around her schedule," Martin replied.

"She's in *ninth grade*," Katia reminded him.

"I'm sure she has some free time," Martin said.

"I have free time!" Lizzie agreed.

"Annalise!" Martin called toward the door. "Can you bring in my book, please?" He turned back to them. "Just so we can take a look at Dietrich's schedule. Dietrich Hoeber," he said to Lizzie. "He's my photographer. A genius. First we'll do a fitting of some of the clothes — I just have a few pieces done — and then we have you do a shoot. Which is why we need to check Dietrich's availability."

"Martin, just hold on a minute —" Katia interjected.

But Martin didn't seem to hear her. Annalise hurried in carrying an appointment book the size of a small billboard. She opened it and Martin looked over her shoulder. "Let's put you down for a fitting tomorrow. Four o'clock. Does that work?"

"That's not good for me," Katia said, sounding exasperated. "I have a meeting with my designers."

"Well, I'd like to get Lizzie fitted as soon as possible so Dietrich can shoot her. He's leaving for Iceland next week." Martin glanced over the schedule again. "Yes, I'm afraid that's the best time. Of course, if that doesn't work for you, Lizzie, then perhaps we can move it."

"No, it works for me," Lizzie said.

Katia shot Lizzie a warning look, and Lizzie couldn't help but notice that her mom's eyes had gotten frighteningly purplish.

"You know, you don't *have* to be here for this part, KK," Martin said, the faintest trace of a smile on his pink lips. "It's just a fitting. Believe me, there'll be *plenty* of people here to supervise."

Katia glanced from Martin to Lizzie as her face reddened. "Fine," Katia agreed, but she didn't sound happy about it.

"Tomorrow at four," Annalise said, as she scribbled in the book with her red pen.

Katia snatched her purse from the couch. "In that case, I think we should go now. Lizzie has homework."

"Oh, Lizzie, before you go, I'd like to give you something."

If he knew that Katia was angry, Martin was pretending not to see it. Instead he strode over to a cabinet, opened the light-colored wood doors, and pulled out the most gorgeous white handbag Lizzie had ever seen. It was made of a soft, buttery white leather, quilted on the sides, and strung with shiny silver chains and buckles. There was even a pocket for an iPhone. "I'm calling it the 'Lizzie,'" he said, handing it to her. "Do you like it?"

She eased the bag onto her shoulder in disbelief. She'd never cared much about bags, but this was probably the most beautiful thing she had ever seen in her life. "Oh my God. Thank you."

"Katia, would you like one, too?" Martin asked.

Katia glared at him. "Come on, Lizzie, let's go," she said, tugging her by the arm toward the hallway.

Out on the street, Katia's stilettos struck the cobblestones like thunder. Lizzie lagged behind her for a few minutes, her new bag slamming against her hip. "Why are you so mad?" she asked.

Her mother wheeled around. "Why am I mad? I felt *completely* ignored up there. It was like I wasn't even there."

"Mom, he was talking to me. He asked me a question and I said yes."

"You said yes?" Katia repeated, rolling her eyes. "You're *fourteen*!"

"I don't get it," Lizzie said. "You're always kissing and hugging him and pretending to be his best friend. Now you hate his guts. For what? For wanting me to work with him? Why does that make you so angry?"

"Because he's a *parasite*, honey!" Katia yelled. "He's only concerned with making money. Trying to get people to buy his clothes and his perfume and his bags. He's part of a giant corporation now. He doesn't care about your career. He certainly didn't care about you before all of this started. And he doesn't care about how this is going to be for you. He just wants to use you."

"Isn't that the point? Isn't that what modeling is all about?" Lizzie's voice was getting louder. Tourists coming out of his store turned to stare.

"I know you feel very special right now, honey," Katia said carefully, struggling to stay calm. "And that's wonderful. But trust me, if you do this, you're going to be at the mercy of Martin Meloy and his corporation. And as soon this is over, he'll find someone else. He'll use you and move on."

"But...but..." She felt tears well up in her eyes. "But what's wrong with that?" she asked. "It's just a job."

Katia sighed and twisted one of the diamond studs in her ears. "It won't just be a job for you, honey," she said in a softer voice. "You're not a traditional model. You can't just do his campaign and then go pose for Dior or Yves Saint Laurent. You're not going to have those options. I don't want you to burn out before you even begin." Katia reached out and touched Lizzie's cheek. "Don't you see what's going on here? He's capitalizing on your story, too. Think about it — this isn't happening because you're anonymous, Lizzie. It's because of me. Do you think you'd be in this position if you weren't my daughter?"

Lizzie felt as if someone had punched her in the chest. She stared at her mother in silence.

On the street, a noisy truck barreled past them. "Katia!" yelled the driver, sticking his head out of the window. "I love you!"

"Let's go," Katia said, heading to the curb where she hailed a cab.

Inside, Katia gave the driver their destination and Lizzie turned toward the window and swallowed her tears. She wouldn't give her mother the satisfaction of seeing her cry. She looked down at her new white bag, resting in her lap. Now it seemed like more of a bribe than a gift.

"Look, it's just a *fitting*," Lizzie said thickly. "If it's a bad scene, I can always say no. Please? *Please?*"

Katia stared out the window. She took so long to answer that Lizzie wasn't sure she'd heard her. "Fine," Katia said, digging in her bag as her BlackBerry began to ring. "But just the fitting. Until I make up my mind about the rest of this."

As Katia answered her call, Lizzie clutched the white bag with relief. This wasn't over yet, and she was going to do everything she could to make sure this wouldn't be over. She pulled out her own phone and saw that she had a missed call from Andrea. She hadn't told her about Martin Meloy yet. Maybe it was better not to say anything until she knew exactly what was going on. And then she saw that she had a text from Todd.

NEED TO CANCEL TONIGHT. SORRY. TALK TOMORROW.

No explanation. No warning. No real apology. And it had been his idea to work together tonight in the first place. What a complete jerk.

As their cab rattled up the West Side Highway, she decided that Todd Piedmont could wallow in his bad relationship for the next four years for all she cared. She tossed her phone back into her bag and listened to her mother, chatting with her agent about her upcoming L'Ete contract. She wished they hadn't fought, but things were okay. They were more than okay. If Katia couldn't be there tomorrow for the fitting, she knew exactly who she'd bring.

chapter 22

"I've got one word for Todd Piedmont: *Loo-oo-SER*," Carina declared the next morning, making an L with her fingers and plastering it onto her forehead. "Who does he think he is?"

"A Scorpio," Hudson spat, tying a pink Hermès scarf around her black ponytail and knotting it with outrage. "And he probably has Pluto in his relationship house."

"And this after he gave me that book," Lizzie said, twirling her lacrosse stick in her hand. "Do you guys know how much it's worth? A hundred thousand bucks! I looked it up!"

"Well, my dad gives diamonds on the second date," Carina said, leaning against the gym wall. "Don't read too much into that."

Hudson sighed with disgust. "He's just way too screwed-up, Lizzie. I say move on."

"Oh, completely. I'm totally over him." She twirled her stick, watching the woven basket become a blur. "At least he's not in school today. Even though I wish I could ignore him."

"But hey!" Hudson said, nudging Lizzie, her green eyes suddenly alive again. "You're the new face of Martin Meloy! That's like the biggest deal in the world. Is your mom gonna be there today?"

"No, she can't go," Lizzie said, unsure how to explain the fight with Katia. Though they'd somewhat made up in the cab, they'd avoided each other the rest of the night, until her mom and dad went out to dinner. "She's not that into it. We sorta had a big fight about it."

Carina stopped scratching a mosquito bite. Hudson leaned against the wall and bit her lip. She had their full attention now. "What's her problem with it?" Carina asked.

"That he's *using* me," Lizzie said, using air quotes.

"What does that mean?" Hudson asked.

Lizzie shrugged. "I don't really know."

"You did say the guy could be fake," Carina reminded her.

"But that's not a reason to keep me from working for him," Lizzie countered.

"Then, like I said before, maybe she's jealous," Carina said, practicing cradling with her stick.

"No. She said I wasn't a 'traditional' model. That I wouldn't be able to keep working after this because my unusual look would be overexposed. It's like she thinks he'll turn me into some kind of freak and then I'll never work again." Lizzie looked down at her untied shoe. "Nice, huh?"

"Then maybe you shouldn't do it," Hudson warned, flipping her lacrosse stick from hand to hand. "She *does* have experience with this. And is it really worth screwing things up with your mom? You guys are getting along so well."

"But it's not fair. I'm her kid. She should be happy for me."

"I'm sure she *is*," Hudson assured her. "But she just doesn't want you to get in over your head. Hey, you're lucky," she said, stretching her quad muscle. "If this were my mom, she'd be on the phone with Anna Wintour right now, screaming at her to put me on the cover of *Vogue*."

"Summers!" yelled Ms. Donovan, Chadwick's permanently irritated gym teacher. "You're up!"

Lizzie reluctantly stepped to the head of the line. Ms. Donovan threw her a ball with her own stick and Lizzie was so distracted from Hudson's advice that she almost missed it. If Hudson, the most fashion-crazed person she knew, thought that being Martin Meloy's "muse" was a sticky idea, then maybe it was.

When she returned to the back of the line she found herself behind Sophie Duncan and Jill Rau, who leaned against the wall in deep gossipy conversation as usual.

"She must have been *so* mad," Sophie whispered, pushing her glasses up her nose. "It's kind of awesome."

"And I heard she *really* bitched him out," Jill added. "That's why he isn't in school today."

Lizzie perked up her ears. Trying to be discreet, she stepped a little closer.

"I just can't believe he *cheated* on her," Sophie marveled. "I mean, nobody has ever done that."

"I kind of think it makes him hotter," Jill added. "If that's possible."

"Who are you guys talking about?" Lizzie asked, casually leaning against the wall beside them.

Jill exchanged a proprietary look with Sophie, as if she wasn't sure Lizzie had earned the right to hear the news. "Todd and Ava broke up," she said flatly. "She dumped him."

The lacrosse stick almost fell out of Lizzie's hands. "What? How do you know?"

"Ilona and Cici were talking about it in homeroom," Jill added confidently, producing a tube of lip gloss from the pocket of her gym shorts. "He cheated on her."

"He *did*?"

Jill patted the gloss on her lips and looked at Lizzie closely. "Yep. He hooked up with some other girl at a party. And Ava's really upset," she said, sounding a little too gleeful about this. Then she narrowed her eyes at Lizzie. "Do you like him or something?"

"No," Lizzie said quickly. "Of course not."

The line moved up again, and Sophie and Jill went back to talking about Zac Efron. Lizzie leaned against the cold wall of the gym. Todd was a *cheater*? It didn't sound right. Ken Clayman? Of course. Eli Blackman? Definitely. But Todd? Insecure, mixed-up Todd?

But when she thought about the way he'd acted with her, it all made sense: his flirting, his mixed messages, the way he'd hooked up with Ava so quickly after that night on the roof. Lizzie suddenly felt sick. Hudson had been right all along. He was a player.

"Sounds like they deserve each other," Carina remarked later, buttoning her kilt in the locker room.

"See?" Hudson said, brushing out her hair. "This all worked out for the best. He's just as bad as we thought."

"You dodged a bullet," Carina put in.

"Yeah, seriously," Lizzie agreed, smoothing her frantic hair with some styling lotion she'd snagged from a shoot. But she felt that the bullet had lodged itself right in her chest.

On their way up the stairs, Hudson's cell rang again. "Oh God, private number," she grumbled. "Again." She put the BlackBerry to her ear. "Hel-LO?" she asked. This time Hudson's face morphed from placid to horrified, until she hung up.

"What happened?" asked Lizzie as they reached the third floor.

"Yeah, who was that? Your face is white," said Carina.

"That was *Celebrity Secrets*," she said, stunned. "That gross tabloid. They have my number. How do they have my cell number?" Hudson tossed the phone into her bag like it was suddenly covered in germs. "Ugh! Who would give it to them?"

"All they have to do is offer someone a hundred bucks," Carina said. "They could have gotten it from anyone."

Hudson's green eyes searched the ceiling as she shook her head. "Great. Now I'm going to have to change my number."

"Well, what'd they want?" Lizzie asked.

Hudson looked down at the floor. "Nothing," she muttered. "Come on, C, we have to go to Spanish."

As her friends headed off down the hall, Lizzie walked to the lockers. She knew from the look on Hudson's face that there was more to that call from the tabloid, but for some reason, Hudson wasn't telling.

Lizzie popped into Mr. Barlow's empty office to drop off her newly revised story — she'd changed a few things around the night before — and then, instead of going to the library to study, she went to the coat closet and threw on her peacoat. After the Todd bombshell, she needed some fresh air.

It was a chilly, damp late October morning, the kind that promised rain but refused to deliver. She crossed Fifth and walked into the park, squeezing her wool scarf tighter around her neck against the wind. Above her, the half-naked branches reached into the sky like dark gnarled fingers, as their last few leaves fluttered to the ground. She gazed at the craggy skyline of the Upper West Side across the park, and remembered the day when she ran into Todd on the street. It had only been six weeks ago, but now it felt like two years. She'd been so excited about him then, and so devastated when things hadn't worked out. Little had she known then that it would all be for the best.

As she neared the reservoir, Lizzie spied a figure sitting alone on one of the benches. She wore a camel-colored car coat over the Chadwick kilt, and a knit hat with devil horns. But she was bent over, and her tiny shoulders were shaking, and Lizzie instantly knew that speaking to her was the right thing to do.

"Ava?" she said, when she was standing in front of her.

Ava looked up. Her normally huge eyes had shrunken into tiny slits from crying. "Hey," she said, sniffling.

Lizzie had never seen Ava this upset — not even close. Maybe when you were used to getting what you wanted from guys, she thought, it felt even worse when they betrayed you. "Are you okay?" she asked gently, sitting down next to her on the bench.

Ava wiped her face with the back of her hand. "I'm fine," she said in a raspy voice.

"I heard about Todd," Lizzie said. "I'm so sorry."

Ava drew herself up, and pulled one wet curl away from her face. "It was Thayer Quinlan. She goes to Pomfret. *Total* slut."

Lizzie nodded as if this were fact.

"I was supposed to go to this party Saturday night but I didn't feel well," Ava went on. "So Todd was gonna come by my place after. And he didn't. And at, like, midnight, I get this text from Jackie Woodhouse that he was all over Thayer at this party, and that they went into the maid's room for, like, two hours. Can you believe it? The *maid's room*." Disgusted, she kicked at the bench underneath her.

"So what did you say to him?" Lizzie asked.

"Just that it was over," Ava said evenly, her eyes on the reservoir. She pulled her coat closed with one pink hand. "The crazy thing is, I wanted to end it a couple weeks ago. Things were starting to get kind of boring and I told him I needed some space, but we had a big fight and he freaked out. And then he does this." Ava fought another sob. "He's such a head case."

He certainly was, Lizzie thought as she watched a jogger in a maroon sweatsuit huff past them on the reservoir track. "I think Todd's a pretty messed-up guy," she announced.

Ava gave her a measured look, as if she wasn't quite sure she believed this. "I thought you guys were so buddy-buddy."

"We're not," Lizzie said. "I mean, we were, a long time ago. But now we just have to do that stupid English project together."

"Well, please don't say anything to him," Ava said, wiping her eyes again. "Really. Please don't."

"Of course not. You're gonna be okay, Ava," Lizzie said, patting her arm. "You're so much better off without him. I'm sure he feels like a colossal dumbass."

Ava stood up. "Now I just have to look at him for the next three and a half years," she said ruefully.

You and me both, Lizzie thought.

A soft drizzle started to fall as they walked back to school. The sky had turned a dark, gloomy gray, as if it, too, were utterly depressed about the state of events.

"You know, I think it's really cool what's happened to you," Ava suddenly said as they crossed Fifth Avenue. "You know, with the modeling and everything. I think you totally deserve it."

"Thanks."

"And hey, Ilona's having a Halloween party tomorrow night," Ava said, when they reached the school lobby. "You and Carina and Hudson should come."

"You sure?"

"Yeah. Definitely."

They trudged up the stairs. Maybe there was something good about all this Todd drama, after all, Lizzie thought. Maybe she and Ava might finally, actually, be friends.

"Okay, we'd love to," she said.

Ava left Lizzie at the door to the library. "Well, thanks for listening," she said. "And yeah, don't say anything."

"I won't."

Ava smiled weakly and then walked away. This time her kilt didn't swing back and forth with flirty confidence — it barely moved. Her trademark swagger had become a slouch, all because of some stupid guy. *Poor Ava*, Lizzie thought.

In the library, Lizzie saw that she had another missed call from Andrea. And a text.

Have you gotten my msgs?? Need to talk to you!

Between the fight with her mom and Todd's blow-off yesterday, Andrea's call had completely slipped her mind. She stepped outside the library and listened to the message.

"Hey, Lizzie, I have a job I want to talk to you about," Andrea's chipper voice said. "Can you call me back, please?"

She needed to tell Andrea about Martin Meloy. But she couldn't help but feel like she was cheating on her. After all, Andrea had been the first one to notice her. Would she be upset if she started working with someone else? Lizzie texted her back.

Sorry I've been MIA. Walking into class now. I'll call you later!

She just needed a little more time to figure out how to explain everything. Which she would. Eventually.

Work life. School life. Friend life. Suddenly all of these parts felt separate and too large to carry all at once. And figuring out which Lizzie she had to be for each one was starting to get confusing.

chapter 23

There was only one thing more amazing than your first fitting with a famous fashion designer, Lizzie thought later that day, nestled in between Carina and Hudson on the gold couch in Martin's salon. And that was having your best friends there to share it with you.

"Oh my God, I *worship* that dress," Hudson said, pointing at a page in the lookbook of his last collection. "I actually tried to get it but it was sold out everywhere but, like, Singapore."

The photo showed a model on the runway wearing a leather dress that could only be called Goth Swiss Miss. At the bottom of the skirt, just above the hem, the leather had been cut out in the shape of flowers and filled in with pink velvet.

"It looks like a cross between a waitress at a German restaurant and an extra in a Marilyn Manson video," Carina sniffed.

Hudson let out a dramatic sigh. "As usual, you just do *not* understand fashion," she murmured.

"So, what exactly does a muse do?" Lizzie asked Hudson. "No one's given me the job description."

"Well... you inspire him," Hudson said.

"But just make sure you don't inspire him to make something like *that*," Carina said, pointing to the models' headpieces in the photos, which looked like cut-up Slinkys topped with blue flowers. "And where is he? I thought he said to be here at four."

"He's a *designer*," Hudson said, excitedly flipping the page. "He's probably in the middle of a creative moment."

Carina wrinkled her nose. "Or in the middle of something illegal."

"Oh Lizzie, I am *so* sorry!"

Martin Meloy rushed into the salon, wearing a pinstriped blazer, purple jeans, and a shrunken top hat that made him look like the Mad Hatter. "I just couldn't get off the phone with Victoria Beckham. Sometimes she can be *so* tiresome. Oh! I see you brought some friends."

"This is Carina Jurgensen and Hudson Jones."

"Hello, ladies," Martin said graciously, pretending to tip his hat. "It's a distinct pleasure."

"I just want to say," Hudson gushed, "that I am a huuuge fan."

"Well, thank you. And I see you also have very good taste," he said, nodding toward the photo of the leather dress in Hudson's lap. "Would you like to try it on?"

Hudson's mouth fell open. "Uh, sure," she said.

"Christi-ahn?" Martin yelled toward the door. "Can you bring out the Leather Milkmaid?"

A tiny, petite girl with a blond pageboy and ruby red lips ran into the room with the Leather Milkmaid on a hanger and laid it in Hudson's lap.

"There we are," Martin said. "I think it'll look smashing on you. And if it fits, it's yours."

"R-r-reeally?" Hudson stuttered.

Then Martin turned his eager gaze on Carina. "And you, my dear. Anything I can offer you?"

Carina regarded him coolly as she played with her necklace. "No, I'm okay. Fashion's not really my thing."

Martin squinted at her neck. "What about accessories? Maybe *that's* your thing?" He turned toward the hallway and bellowed, "Annalise? Jewelry, please!"

A moment later Annalise ran into the room carrying a tray laden with gold and silver necklaces, bracelets, and earrings.

"On the coffee table," Martin commanded.

Annalise placed it directly in front of Carina on the purple glass table as Carina scooted closer. "I didn't know you did jewelry," she murmured, already devouring the tray with her eyes.

"Go ahead. Pick out your favorite piece," Martin said. "My little gift to you."

"Uh . . . thank you," Carina murmured, picking up a chunky gold charm bracelet. She gave Lizzie a disbelieving look as she slipped it onto her wrist.

"All right, Lizzie, up, up, up," Martin said, briskly clapping his hands. "We have some work to do."

Lizzie got to her feet. "See you guys in a couple minutes." She left her friends completely engrossed with their new gifts and trailed Martin down the hall. "That was so nice of you."

Martin waved the compliment aside. "My pleasure. That's Holla Jones's daughter, right? And Karl Jurgensen's?"

"Ye-es," Lizzie said carefully. She wondered if Martin had just been that generous for a reason. "You know, we're not really red-carpet types."

Martin chuckled and patted her shoulder. "Darling, please. I just *saw* you on the red carpet. And you'll be on it again — for *me*. Did I mention that I have a few store openings coming up? Oh, here we are. This is the *atelier*."

He steered her into a large design studio painted a bright magenta. Long worktables and dress forms were clustered here and there, and along the walls were more curved, velvet couches and footstools, interspersed with several floor-to-ceiling mirrors. And in the center of the room was a rack of clothing on satin hangers.

"These are the very first pieces of the spring collection," he announced in a reverent whisper, presenting them with a sweep of his hand. "Let's see how they look on you, and then we can make changes. If we need to." He touched the row of delicate silk dresses, tops, and skirts in shades of lilac and dusty pink. "Aren't they beautiful?"

"Absolutely," Lizzie said, but somehow she got the feeling that Martin expected her to say more. What exactly were you supposed to say to a designer about his clothes?

"All right, then." He gazed lovingly at the clothes one more time. "I'll be back to check on you in a few minutes. Have fun." He made a half-bow and closed the door.

Lizzie kicked off her shoes and approached the rack with little, worshipful half-steps, as if it were an altar. *How ironic*, she thought.

I would never ever even try these on in a store but now I'm going to be wearing them in ads. It was all too surreal.

There was a knock at the door, and then Hudson peeked her head into the room. "Oh my God," she whispered, looking around. "Can I come in?"

"Yes!" Lizzie whispered, waving them in.

She and Carina entered the room and shut the door. "This is just like *Project Runway* but a million times nicer," Carina observed, looking around.

"Are *these* the clothes?" Hudson made a straight shot for the clothing rack. "Holy manoli, Summers. These are *gorge*."

"What should I try first?" Lizzie asked.

Hudson pulled out a sleeveless lilac sheath, with tiny narrow spaghetti straps, a drop waist, and a hem of flouncy tulle. "This one," she said. "Definitely."

Sleeveless still wasn't Lizzie's favorite style, but she didn't care anymore about her arms. Andrea had helped her get over that.

Lizzie stepped out of her kilt and tights, leaving them in a tangle on the ground, while Hudson climbed up on a chair. "Ready?" she asked, holding the unzipped dress over Lizzie's head.

"Ready."

Hudson let the silk dress fall over Lizzie's arms — until Lizzie felt it come to a screeching halt at her shoulders.

"Huh," Hudson said. "It's not going down. Carina? Can you pull it down from the bottom?"

Lizzie felt Carina tug on the hem. "It's not moving," she said.

The dress closed in around her arms, and Lizzie stood there

with the dress over her face, feeling cold and drafty and a little embarrassed.

"Just scissor your arms," Hudson advised. "Move them back and forth."

"You sure?" Lizzie asked, her voice muffled.

"It'll help shimmy it down."

Lizzie waved her arms as if she were swimming. The dress moved just a few inches and then —

Rip!

"Oops," Hudson said.

"Oh *shnit*," Carina said, and then burst into giggles.

"What happened! Did I break it?" Lizzie asked.

"Hold on, I'm gonna just pull it off," Hudson said, as she tugged upward. There was another sound of ripping. "Oops. There go the straps."

Carina's giggles turned into out-and-out guffaws.

"Oh my God, we're destroying his clothes!" Lizzie shrieked.

"This is seriously the funniest thing I've ever seen," Carina said, still laughing.

"This is NOT funny, you guys!" Lizzie yelled.

There was an urgent knock on the door. "Lizzie!" Martin's voice came through the door. "How are you getting on in there?"

"Fine!" she yelled miserably.

"Do you have something on?" he yelled.

"Uh . . . almost!" she yelled back. "You guys, help!"

Finally, with Carina and Hudson both standing on chairs, they got the ruined dress off of her.

Lizzie ran over to the rack, covering herself and shivering. "I just need to get into something. Anything."

"Don't worry," Hudson said, rifling through the hangers. "What about this?" She pulled out a tiny pair of shorts.

"Are you *kidding* me?"

At last they settled on a lilac silk jumpsuit that looked a little bigger — and sturdier — than the rest of the things. Somehow she managed to get it up over her hips and pull the zipper up her back.

"Lizzie? You alright in there?" Martin yelled through the door.

"Coming!"

On her way to the door, she caught a glimpse of her reflection in one of the mirrors. "Oh my God. I look like a purple sausage."

"Open the door!" Carina whispered.

There was no turning back now. She opened the door.

Martin stood on the doorstep with Annalise, Christiane, and a short, plump older woman with a beady-eyed scowl and a tape measure around her neck. They seemed to be alarmed at the sight of her, and then Martin stepped into the room, appraising Lizzie with a fist under his chin.

"Hmmm. How did the other ones fit?" he asked.

"A little on the small side," she admitted. "Especially that one." She pointed to the silk heap in Hudson's arms that had once been a dress.

"We're so sorry," Hudson said, grimacing.

Martin let out an anguished cry and ran to the dress. He snatched it out of Hudson's arms and let it fall to its full length, staring at the broken straps and the gash in the fabric below the zipper. It looked like it had been through a war.

"Really, we're so sorry," Lizzie repeated.

"No problem," he said through a gritted smile. "I guess we're just going to have to recut them."

Annalise scribbled in a notebook. Christiane nodded her pert, blond head, and Lizzie tried not to think about what might be running through it.

"Magda," Martin said, nodding toward Lizzie, "would you please...?"

The short plump woman lurched toward Lizzie's chest with the measuring tape. Before Lizzie could stop her, the woman had flung the tape around her chest, her waist and her hips. "Humph!" she hissed, pulling the tape away. "She *not* a size four!"

"Hmmm," Martin said once more. "Well, I guess we'll just try and get everything ready for Monday morning."

"Monday morning? What's Monday morning?" Lizzie asked, feeling flustered and panicked.

"That's when we'll do the first test shots with Dietrich," Martin said.

"Wait. I can't do Monday morning. I have something due that day. In school. An English project." Lizzie was vaguely aware of Annalise and Christiane staring at her. She had a feeling that other muses didn't have English projects.

"Well, Dietrich has to fly to Iceland Monday afternoon, so it's the only time we can do it." Martin smiled more firmly, in a way that showed all of his teeth. "This will really be the only time we can't work around you, Lizzie. I promise."

Christiane and Annalise traded glances.

"Okay, fine," she said. "Monday." She had no idea how she was going to get Katia's permission, but she'd worry about that later.

Outside on the street, the three of them walked in the drizzle toward the subway.

"I'm gonna have to cut school," she said.

"You don't have to," Carina said. "They can't do anything without you. Just tell them you can't do it."

"I agree," Hudson said.

"He totally shot me down. And I can't make a big deal out of it after destroying his dress. Which he took pretty well, by the way." Lizzie looked over at Hudson, carrying her new dress in a thick black garment bag. "I thought when you were someone's muse, the clothes *had* to fit you. Instead, I end up looking like a purple bratwurst."

Carina started giggling. Hudson started giggling, too. Soon Lizzie was laughing so hard she had to stop in front of Pastis and bend over because she was laughing so hard.

"We *destroyed* his clothes," Lizzie said, gasping for breath. "I mean, I'm probably the first muse who's *ever* done that."

Maybe that was the other key to being a model, she thought: not losing your sense of humor. And keeping your friends with you at all times.

chapter 24

Forty-five minutes later Lizzie ran up the subway steps onto Broadway and hurried past the Starbucks on the way to her building.

"Hey, Lizzie!" called a voice. In the gathering dusk she saw the shape of a woman peek her head through the doors. "I don't mean to be stalking you," she yelled, "but get your butt in here!"

It wasn't clear how long Andrea had been waiting for her inside the Starbucks, but she'd been saving Lizzie a seat with her messenger bag. "Here, siddown," she said, moving the bag onto the floor underneath their table. Her blond hair was down around her face again and seemed extra-wavy from the rain. "Boy, *you're* a hard girl to reach," she teased, sitting down and putting both her elbows on the table.

Lizzie sat down. It was obvious she'd been avoiding Andrea,

and now she felt guilty. "You should have just called up to my apartment. You didn't have to wait for me down here. My mom would have let you upstairs."

"That's okay, I like overpriced and bitter-tasting coffee," she said, winking, as she sipped from a large takeout cup. "And the people-watching's insane in here. So far I think I may have found a couple new subjects."

"Well, things have been a little crazy," Lizzie admitted. "I was gonna call you tonight."

Andrea shook her head. "Don't worry about it. I wanted to tell you this in person, anyway. So guess what?" She leaned over closer on her elbows. "I've been offered my own show. At the Gagosian Gallery. And I'd like it to be entirely of you. It'd be a ton of shoots, and I can't offer you a lot of money, but it'll be fun. And we could just do weekends and maybe one day a week after school. What do you think? Do you mind being my muse?" she asked, grinning.

Now she had to tell her, she thought.

"Actually, Martin Meloy has asked me to be the same thing for him," Lizzie said.

"Lizzie!" Andrea gasped, grabbing Lizzie's wrist. "That's amazing! Why didn't you tell me! Oh my God, I'm so happy for you!" she squealed.

"You are?"

"Of course. Why wouldn't I be? Now you just have to always give me credit for discovering you, okay?" she said, pretending to wag a finger. "Your mom must be very proud."

Lizzie looked away, out the window at people walking by. "Yeah, sort of," she said.

"I knew this was all going to happen," Andrea said, leaning back in her chair. "You're gonna give thousands of girls out there a whole different attitude about themselves. Girls who think they're too tall or have too big a nose or hair that's too curly are going to realize they're *freaking cool* because of you. *And* Martin Meloy, I suppose," she added, tipping her drink to her lips.

"I'm not sure," Lizzie said. "Today, at the fitting, I actually *destroyed* a dress. I mean, destroyed it. Because I was too big for it. I don't know if I'm cut out for this."

Andrea chuckled. "Well, that's fashion for ya. They'll figure out how to fit you. But if you don't *want* to do this, Lizzie, then that's something else. Do you want this?"

Lizzie felt her right leg start to do its little nervous jig. These questions were always so hard to answer. "Of course I do," she finally said. "I mean, why wouldn't I?"

Andrea looked at her closely for a few moments. "Then if this is what you want, then you have to go for it and not be afraid. You can't be afraid of being different. Remember that." Andrea pulled up the hood of her jacket and pushed back from the table. "I gotta get home. I have a date tonight. Some guy who lives in Williamsburg and does installations. Wish me luck."

"Okay," Lizzie said, reluctantly getting to her feet. She didn't want Andrea to leave, but there was nothing she could do to stop her. "Thanks for coming by."

"Good luck, Lizzie. And keep in touch with me, okay?"

"I will."

Andrea gave her one last smile, and walked to the door. "Be fierce, Lizzie!" she yelled. "Always!" She walked out onto Broadway and blended into the dark stream of passersby, and Lizzie felt her throat get lumpy. She didn't feel fierce, although she knew she had every reason to.

Outside a cold rain had begun to fall. She bent her head and sprinted toward her building, ducking as two paparazzi pointed a camera at her and snapped.

When she was finally in her room, changing into jeans and a T-shirt, there was a knock on the door. "So how was the fitting?" Katia asked cautiously, standing in the doorway dressed in her gym clothes, and holding a copy of the *New York Times*.

"It went great," she said brightly. *No need to mention the ripped dress,* she thought.

Katia gently closed the door. "Look, honey, I've been giving this a lot of thought. And I don't think you should do this."

Lizzie sat on the edge of her bed, just hard enough that Sid Vicious stretched out a paw. "Why not?"

"Because of all the reasons I've already explained," Katia said, shaking her head. "If Martin's really that interested in you, he can wait a couple of years."

"What if he can't?"

Katia sat down beside her. "Maybe we should stop thinking so much about what's good for Martin, and focus on what's good for you. And right now, that's school. And having a normal life."

"A normal life?" Lizzie chuckled. "As if I've ever had that."

"You can still model a little, but I don't think a commitment to something as huge as Martin is a good idea," Katia said. "At least, not right now."

"Mom —"

"I've already called Martin," Katia said. "And I told him that we changed our mind."

"*What?*" Lizzie slid to her feet.

Katia held up her hand. "Lizzie, don't."

"How could you do that without talking to me first?"

"It's just temporary. It's not forever. When you're older you can still do this, honey —"

"What is your problem?" Lizzie asked, cutting her off.

"I've already told you my worries about this. I don't want him exploiting you, and you need to stay in school."

"No, there's something else going on here," she said.

Katia narrowed her darkening eyes. "Such as?"

"Maybe you're mad that I'm in your world now. Or maybe you don't like the fact that I'm not just your kid anymore. Maybe you still want me to be in your shadow."

Katia sat up and drew her shoulders back. "I'm on your side here, Lizzie."

"Mom, I'm finally myself," she said evenly. "I'm finally just Lizzie. Not Katia's daughter. Don't you know what that's like? To finally have that?"

Katia stood up. "You *are* your own person, Lizzie," she said sternly. "But part of who you are is being my daughter and no matter what you do, that's never going to change. *Especially* if you work with Martin Meloy." She walked to the door and paused with her hand on the knob, gathering herself. "Your father and I have to go back to Paris. L'Ete wants to meet with me —"

"Just go," Lizzie said, cutting her off. "Just leave."

Katia paused at the door. "Irlene'll be staying with you until Monday. We'll be back then."

Lizzie collapsed on her bed with her back to her mother. *Just go,* she thought. Finally she heard the door close behind her.

That night, Lizzie was too angry to sleep. She punched her pillow and tossed from side to side, as the pattering rain outside swelled into a thunderstorm. It wasn't fair, she thought over and over, feeling a burning in her chest. She was Lizzie now. Not the daughter of the supermodel. For the first time she knew what it was like to walk into a room and know that more of her was about Lizzie than it was about Katia. And now her mom wanted to snatch that away from her. It made her feel small and helpless and angry and trapped. But maybe there was a way for her to fight back.

The next morning, she found it.

"Annalise? It's Lizzie," she said into her iPhone on her way to the bus stop.

"Oh hi, Lizzie, how are you?" Annalise sounded cheery but tentative.

"I just wanted to say that there was some confusion last night," she said, hopping onto the bus. "I *can* make the shoot on Monday."

There was a pause on the other line. "Well, that's wonderful, Lizzie," Annalise replied crisply. "I'm sure Martin'll be thrilled."

A few moments later, Lizzie slipped the phone into her bag and snagged a seat by the window, feeling empowered and, yes, a little sneaky. But if you wanted something in life, you had to go out and grab it. No matter what stood in your way.

chapter 25

"And *who* are you?"

Ilona stood on the doorstep of her own Halloween party that night and looked Lizzie's costume up and down. "I sort of don't get it," she sneered.

From the flouncy black dress that barely covered her butt, the little white doily pinned to her head, and the pink feather duster in her hand, it was blatantly obvious what Ilona was supposed to be. A French maid. *How original*, Lizzie thought.

"Daisy Buchanan," Lizzie answered, adjusting her black feather headband. "She's a character in *The Great Gatsby*. Which you probably haven't read yet," she added with a smile.

If anyone at this party did know who Daisy Buchanan was, Lizzie thought, they'd be impressed. She'd worn one of Katia's blue silk Lanvin sheaths, with a lavender sash tied around the hips to give it a drop-waist look, and topped it off with a long strand of fake pearls, a painted-on beauty mark, and a wig with chin-length black hair that Hudson had swiped from Holla's extensive collection. Yes, she looked just like Daisy, but there was really only one person who would get it. And he certainly wouldn't be here tonight.

Ilona turned her attention to Carina. "Are you a zombie?" she asked, crinkling her nose.

Carina's pale gray face makeup and reddened circles around her eyes were at odds with her preppy pearls-and-cardigan outfit. "A zombie *Martha Stewart,*" Carina corrected.

"And I'm a Goth Swiss Miss," Hudson offered, gesturing to her braided pigtails and new dress from Martin. "Or a Leather Milkmaid. Either one."

"Is Ava here?" Lizzie asked, sensing that she should find the person who'd invited her to this as soon as possible.

"She's in the kitchen," Ilona said, waving vaguely with the duster toward an open door.

Lizzie, Carina, and Hudson headed into the kitchen. Inside they found Ava, dressed as Batgirl, squeezing a lime into something that looked like a gin and tonic.

"He-*ey!*" Ava cried out in her usual singsong. She seemed to have fully recovered from her crying fest in the park. "*Soooo* glad you guys could make it. Love your costume!" she said to Lizzie. "What are you?"

"Oh, it's something from *The Great Gatsby.*"

"Ohh," Ava said carefully but judgmentally, taking a sip of her drink. "That's cool."

Even though she knew he wouldn't be coming to this, Lizzie did a quick sweep of the kitchen for Todd. Ever since the day he'd given her the book, he hadn't come to school, and nobody knew where he was, or what had happened to him. The rumor going around was that Ava had shamed him into staying home ever since her dumping. He'd texted Lizzie earlier that afternoon, asking to get together that weekend to work on their project, so whatever was wrong couldn't be that dire. She hadn't written him back. If he'd been so concerned about the project, she figured, he wouldn't have cancelled on her the other night. And on Monday morning, she'd be at the photo shoot, so she wouldn't be doing the presentation anyway.

As Carina and Hudson poured themselves some cranberry juice, Ava pulled Lizzie aside.

"Have you heard from Todd?" she asked with an edge of desperation in her voice, her brown eyes glittering. "Ilona invited him but he didn't write back or anything."

Lizzie wanted to ask why Todd had been invited at all, and why Ava even cared, but she just shrugged. "He texted me this afternoon about our project, but I haven't written him back. Are you feeling better?"

"Oh yeah, totally," she said, knocking her drink back. "I mean, I wanted him out of my life anyway. So I should be happy, right?"

"Uh, yeah," Lizzie said, playing with the strand of pearls. She wasn't quite sure where this conversation was going.

"So . . . you're not gonna date him, right?" Ava asked suddenly. "I mean, you can if you want to, but you know he's bad news, right?" Ava stepped closer, and Lizzie could smell her cloying perfume.

"Wait — why would I date Todd Piedmont?" Lizzie asked.

Ava grabbed her arm and laughed like she'd said the funniest thing in the world. "Oh my God, Lizzie, don't take it so seriously! I was just kidding! Oh, and do you know if your mom is gonna come up with something for the charity ball? 'Cuz we kind of need those prizes pretty soon."

For a moment, Lizzie wasn't sure if she'd heard Ava right. "I really don't know yet," she said, seething. So much for hoping that she and Ava could actually turn out to be friends, she thought. Now that she was over her Todd trauma, Ava was back to her old self.

Ava turned away to say something to Cici, and Carina took Lizzie's arm. "Don't look now, but Carter McLean is staring at you," Carina whispered into her ear.

Lizzie glanced across the kitchen at the guys. Even in someone's apartment, the boys still clung to the opposite side of the room from the girls, and hardly any of them were dressed in real costumes. Sure enough, Carter McLean — the hottest guy in the tenth grade — was across the room with his friends, but he wasn't looking at Lizzie. Instead his sexy green eyes were trained on Carina.

"Um, he's looking at *you*, C," Lizzie said.

"Really?" Carina asked.

As they looked back at him, Carter smiled broadly, flicked his dark curls out of his eyes, and then turned back to his friends.

"Wow," Lizzie said. Even she had felt the heat of his look.

"Let's go out to the living room," Carina whispered. When they were back in the hallway, Carina leaned in close to her friends, her cheeks flushed. "Was it just me, or was he checking me out?"

"He really was," Hudson said.

"Yep," Lizzie agreed.

Carina waggled her eyebrows and grinned. "Well, *that's* interesting."

"I think Ava still likes Todd," Lizzie told them. "She kept asking me if I thought he was coming to this."

"Looks like she got her wish," Hudson said under her breath, nodding toward the living room.

Lizzie looked over. Todd, unbelievably, was here.

He stood by himself in the living room, holding a red plastic cup and looking deeply uncomfortable. Lizzie realized it was because he was the only guy in an actual costume. At least, she hoped it was a costume. He wore a crisp white tuxedo with a natty red pocket square, shiny black shoes, and his hair was slicked back with pomade, like a man from the nineteen twenties. Then she realized who he was. His blue eyes landed on her, and from the way they stayed locked on hers, she knew she had to go over and say hi.

"I'll be right back, guys," she said, and made her way toward Todd. Her right leg felt shaky, but she ignored it. She said a quick, fervent prayer that she wouldn't throw up. And then she was right in front of him.

"Hi, Todd," she managed to say.

"Hi," he said quietly, looking over her costume. "Lemme guess. Pearls, headdress. Beauty mark. Daisy Buchanan?"

"And you're Jay Gatsby."

"Or just very overdressed for this party," he said with a shy smile that made her heart seesaw. "So . . . ," he said, rocking back and forth on his heels, "did you get my text? About the English thing? It's due Monday, right?"

"I did, but . . . I won't be in school that day. I'm kind of working. I have a modeling job."

He frowned. "Wait. You're not gonna be in school?" He scratched his head, making a dent in his pomade. "What about me? Am I supposed to just fail it because you're not gonna be there?"

"*You're* the one who hasn't shown up. You blew me off the other night." She glanced around the party. Ava was liable to walk in and see them at any moment. "Let's go in here," she said, brushing past him through a pair of French doors into the dining room.

He followed her into the dark, quiet room. "I've had some stuff going on," he said in a low voice.

"Uh, yeah, I know," she said, letting her voice curdle with sarcasm. "I know all about it."

He cocked his head. In the dim light she could see the confusion in his eyes. "What do you mean?"

"I mean how Ava dumped you. After you *cheated* on her."

Todd gave a short, surprised laugh. "Is *that* what she said?"

"She said you hooked up with some girl at a party. Some girl from Pomfret. And that she dumped you. I'm amazed you even showed up here tonight."

"And you *believe* that?" he sputtered.

"It's bad enough that you play with *my* head, but to do it with your own girlfriend? What's your problem?"

"Wait — playing with *your* head?" he repeated.

"Oh come *on*," she said, rolling her eyes. "Flirting with me, telling me secrets, giving me a book that cost tons of money and that I don't even ask for? While you're going out with someone else?"

He didn't say anything. She stepped closer to him, and this time she was too angry to notice his dreamy scent.

"Who does stuff like that? Except a total player?"

Todd flinched.

"All this time, I thought you were a decent guy. The guy I used to know. Obviously, I was wrong."

She tried to walk past him to leave, but Todd stepped in front of her, blocking the way.

"No, *I* was wrong," he said. "I should never have gone out with her, but I did. And when I realized I'd made a mistake, I ended it. I probably should have done it sooner, but I didn't want to hurt her. I did it the night you and I were supposed to work together. I told her that I wanted to be friends. And she started to cry and wouldn't let me leave. *That's* why I couldn't come over to your house." He shook his head. "But no, you believe this crazy story of hers that I *cheated* on her." He took a step backward. "Do you really think I would do that, Lizzie?"

Her eyes had gotten used to the darkness now, and she could see the anger and hurt in his face.

"I thought you knew me better than that. I thought you were my friend." He shook his head. "Whatever. Have fun on Monday. And thanks for the fail." He turned on his heels and walked out through the French doors, letting them swing open behind him.

Lizzie didn't move. She stayed in the quiet darkness of the dining room, her hand on Ilona's dining table to keep her steady. Todd's disgusted voice rang through her mind like a howling car alarm. She had gotten it all completely wrong. Todd was a decent guy after all. And now he hated her.

Lizzie waited until she was sure Todd wasn't hovering right outside the French doors, and then made her way back into the party. She found her friends in the corner.

"What happened?" Hudson gasped. "Did you guys just get in a fight? Todd stormed out of the room."

"I have to go, you guys," she said quietly. "Now." Hot tears were dangerously close to filling her eyes.

"No problem," Carina said. "We're so out of here."

They followed Lizzie into the hall, where Ilona and Ava were standing over what looked like a shattered vase. Pieces of white porcelain were strewn across the carpet.

"Someone just slammed the front door so hard this fell down," Ilona said. "My mom's gonna *kill* me."

Lizzie instantly knew who it was.

"All I saw was some guy in white," Ilona said. "In some weird tux."

"It was Todd," Lizzie said.

"Todd?" Ava practically shrieked. "Are you sure?" She eyed the front door. "Why'd he leave?"

"And why was he in a white tux?" Ilona asked.

Lizzie averted her eyes. She didn't have the strength right now to explain. "I have to go, you guys. Sorry. I think I'm a little sick."

Pretending she didn't notice Ava and Ilona's odd stares, Lizzie staggered out the front door, pulling her feathered headband off. Lizzie leaned her head against the frame of the elevator. Her heart still pounded and she felt dizzy.

Hudson patted her back. "Don't listen to him. He's a jerk, Lizzie."

"Lizzie, Todd Piedmont is a waste of your time," Carina said clearly. "He doesn't deserve such a fabulous, incredible person. He doesn't."

"It needed to end," Hudson said in a soothing voice. "Let him go."

Lizzie nodded and swallowed her tears. This was so silly. Her life was going so well. It was ridiculous to let a guy get in the middle of it. She was the luckiest girl on earth, and everything — everything — was going her way. Except the one thing she cared about more than anything else had just slipped through her fingers. And she was fairly sure she'd never get it back.

chapter 26

BEEP BEEP BEEP!

Lizzie's alarm woke her with a jolt. She sat up in bed and looked at the clock. It was seven fifteen. Which meant that she had an hour to get down to the studio in SoHo for the photo shoot. As she threw off the covers, Mission Muse went into effect.

She showered, dressed in her uniform, packed her bookbag, and even ate a bowl of cereal in front of Irlene, who was engrossed in the *Today* show. Finally, she breezed through the lobby doors and out onto the street. It was another gray, chilly day. With one quick look over her shoulder at her building, she hurried down Columbus and to the downtown subway station. She'd never cut school before, and now the thrill of it was eerily liberating.

Waiting on the subway platform, she thought of Todd and their fight. She'd spent all of Sunday mulling over what he'd said, and now she felt even worse about believing Ava's story. But the way his voice had dripped with disdain, the way he'd shaken his head with disgust, the way he'd walked out on her in Ilona's house...she was only too happy to be skipping English. Of course, Mr. Barlow would be a little bent out of shape, but she could handle that.

"Lizzie! Hello!" cried Martin when she walked in, grasping her hand and kissing both her cheeks. He wore black jeans and a ripped T-shirt with an image of Iggy Pop on the front. "I'm *so* glad everything worked out. Are we ready to have a good time? And is *that* your uniform?" He bent down to touch a piece of her skirt. "That plaid is so *arcane*. I love it. Maybe I'll use it for the fall collection."

"Actually, speaking of my school, is Annalise around? I need her to call and tell them I'm sick."

Martin's eyes narrowed. For a moment she was afraid he might not approve, and then he broke into a conspiratorial smile. "No worries," he said, patting her arm. "I'll take care of it. Just get into hair and makeup. And have fun!"

Lizzie ambled over to the hair and makeup area. The studio was the size of the Chadwick gym, even bigger than the one at Chelsea Piers. A rack of clothes stood about ten feet away, and facing her was the actual set, which was already crowded with lights. The tall, lanky man in a black turtleneck fiddling with his computer, she guessed, was the photographer, Dietrich. She was in no hurry to speak to him.

Later, she was in the makeup chair, her face buried in an issue of Italian *Vogue* as the hairstylist worked on her curls, when Annalise approached with Martin's oversized appointment book in her hand.

"So everything's all set, Lizzie," she said, her eyes on Martin's book. "I just called the school and said you weren't coming in."

"Great. You said I was sick, right?"

"No. I said you were working. Was I supposed to say you were sick?"

Lizzie's stomach sank. "Um, that's okay. As long as you said that you were my mom."

"Your mom?" Annalise burst out, before clapping her hand over her mouth. "I'm not going to say I'm Katia Summers," she said, laughing.

This was just getting worse. "Fine," Lizzie said, with a tight feeling in her chest.

"Anyway, Martin wants to run some dates past you." Annalise held up the gigantic appointment book and flipped to a page. "The next shoot would be on a Tuesday afternoon next week. And then the following week, there's a store opening he'd like you to attend. In Macau."

"*Macau?* Where's that?"

Annalise seemed slightly put out. "It's an island near China. We'd fly you out there, of course. It's very important. It's going to be Martin's new flagship store in the Asian market. I can get in touch with to you about flights —"

"Actually, can I get back to you on that?"

Annalise subtly rolled her eyes. "Of course," she muttered, flipping the book closed and strutting off, visibly annoyed.

Macau? She had barely ever even heard of the place, and she was supposed to fly halfway around the world to go there? To do what, exactly? And she wondered what she was supposed to do about school next Tuesday. Martin had promised that today would be the only day he couldn't work around her schedule. And speaking of school, was she already in trouble? She cringed thinking about the word spreading to Mr. Barlow that she was gone and working. She thought of him hunting down Katia, trying to figure out where she was.

Everything's fine, she told herself. *You'll deal with all this later.*

As the makeup artist started sponging her face, she let her eyes close. For a few minutes she fell into a deep, drowsy sleep...until she heard her say, "All done."

Lizzie opened her eyes. At first, she didn't recognize herself. Heavy black liner circled her eyes, raccoon-style. Three different shades of purple shadow caked her lids. Deep purple lipstick made her look half-dead. And her hair fell in thick, crimped waves down her shoulders. She was part Goth and part eighties fashion victim. "Are you sure this is what Martin wants?" she asked hesitantly.

The hair and makeup people traded looks. "Yep," the makeup girl replied.

Lizzie took one more look at herself in the mirror. Her real face was completely hidden. Hadn't Martin wanted to work with her because of her face? So why had he put this much stuff on it?

She walked over to the dressing area. Christiane stood in front of the same lilac dress that Lizzie had ripped the week before, steaming it with fierce concentration. The other day Christiane had seemed spritely, cute, even enviably cool in her blond pageboy haircut. Now she just seemed cold. She put the steamer down without a smile.

"Okay. We had to re-cut this after we saw that you broke the zipper," she said bluntly. "Hopefully this one fits. Try it on." She slid it off the hanger and handed it to Lizzie.

"Here?"

Lizzie looked around. There was no changing room or even

a screen in sight. If she got undressed, it would be in full view of Christiane and her unsmiling face.

"Uh-huh." Christiane stifled a small yawn and then folded her arms. "What's the problem?"

"Nothing." Pretending she wasn't two feet away from another person she barely knew, Lizzie quickly shed her school uniform and pulled the dress over her head. To her relief, the silk moved easily down her arms — until it came to another abrupt stop at her shoulders.

"Oh, not again," Christiane moaned. "And this was a *six*."

Lizzie's face burned behind the silk. Of course a six didn't fit. Hadn't any of these people actually looked at her?

Christiane pulled it off of her. "All right, let's see what *does* fit around here," she sighed.

They went through each garment. One after another, each piece stopped at her shoulders or her upper thighs, refusing to budge. Each time, Lizzie clenched her jaw. *Please let me die right now*, she thought. The only piece that fit was the silk jumpsuit.

"Well, I guess it'll have to do," Christiane said with another sigh. She zipped Lizzie up the back and gave her a pair of gold stilettos to slip on. By the time she tottered out from behind the rack of clothes, Lizzie was pretty sure that three thousand English presentations with Todd Piedmont would have been more enjoyable than this.

"Oh, we're in the *jumpsuit* again," Martin said, appraising her with a forced smile.

"Nothing else fit," Christiane reported, coming to stand by his side.

Martin thought long and hard as he stared at her, chin cradled in his fist. "Lizzie, now, I hope this doesn't offend you, but I have the

241

number of a wonderful nutritionist who's really helped me. Maybe I can make you an appointment?"

Lizzie glowered at him. "Nutritionist?" she asked.

"We'll talk about it later," he said with a what's-to-be-done sigh, and patted Lizzie on the shoulder. "Dietrich! She's ready!"

She hobbled toward the photo area. The stilettos were already making her feet ache. She didn't feel glamorous, and she definitely didn't feel like herself. And when she saw Dietrich's angry, pasty-faced scowl as he turned around, she really didn't want to be here.

Dietrich pointed to the area behind the camera. "Just stand," he ordered gloomily. "No expression."

Of course not, Mr. Barrel of Laughs, she thought. If they wanted the Angsty Miserable look, they were all in luck.

Dietrich wiped away a greasy hank of hair and leaned into his camera. "Okay, we start!" he yelled.

She stood perfectly still and scowled into the camera. She missed Andrea. She missed running and jumping and kicking to Kanye West. She missed being outside, in the middle of Central Park or downtown. She missed feeling like she was doing a good job. She missed having fun. Right now she felt like a robot, being remote-controlled by some humorless dictator.

"Turn left!" Dietrich barked.

As she obeyed, her mind wandered back to school. English had probably started. Who was Todd sitting with? Did he feel bad about their fight, too? With an ache, she wished she was there.

Every time she tried to smile, Dietrich yelled, "No expression!"

242

making her jump. At last Dietrich straightened up. "Five minutes!" he yelled, and lumbered over to his assistant with his camera, muttering in guttural German.

Lizzie headed toward the catering area. She longed to go off in a corner with someone — anyone — and talk about what a stick in the mud Dietrich was, but there was nobody here for her to talk to. She stood alone at the table, scanning the soda selection and trying not to look like she was completely alone. She even missed her mom. Was this what she went through when she was her age? This weird loneliness in a crowded room? How had she done it?

She grabbed a can of Diet Coke and gulped down the fizzy drink, feeling her stomach press against the silk fabric. No wonder so many models had eating disorders, she mused. Always having to wear clothes that probably didn't fit them.

And then she heard voices near the dressing area.

"I know, but if she *really* turns out to be a disaster, we can always use Natalie. I just hope she's available."

It was Martin. Lizzie froze.

"Should I check?" Christiane asked. "Watching her up there, it doesn't look too good."

"Well, she's definitely not her mother," Martin continued. "But at least with her we'll save thousands on retouching."

"How old is Katia now?" Christiane asked. "Thirty-six, thirty-seven? I heard that last *W* shoot was a nightmare. They spent thousands just on the crow's feet."

"I'm just not even sure she *sees* it," Martin said. "But the Czech never age well. Look what happened to Paulina."

Christiane made a small mirthless laugh. "But at least she knew when to bow out."

Trembling, Lizzie put the can down on the table. A jumble of thoughts bubbled up inside her head. *I made this up*, she thought, absurdly. *I didn't just hear this. This isn't happening.*

"All right!" Dietrich yelled. "We start now! Lizzie! We start!"

Slowly she forced her mind to go quiet. With every ounce of control, she made her face go blank as she turned around.

"So we go back to before!" Dietrich yelled, stepping behind the camera. "Go!"

She hurried back to her mark. The people in the studio gathered into one large group, watching her.

"No expression!" Dietrich yelled, pressing the shutter.

She stared at the lens, fixing it with her best dead-eyed stare.

"Turn to the right!"

With a deep ache in her chest, she thought about her mom. Katia was on the plane right now, coming back from Paris, but she wanted her here now. She wanted to hug her. She wanted to smell her perfume. She wanted her to know that she wasn't old, or overdone, or worn out, and that her daughter loved her.

"I said RIGHT!" Dietrich screamed, snapping her back to the present. He stood up and pulled a hank of hair out of his furious, beady eyes. "Right, goddammit!"

Lizzie gulped. Her right leg started to shake. People were staring at her. "I'm sorry," she said. "I didn't hear you."

"Then wake up!" he yelled.

Lizzie stood there, too stunned to cry or move. *Wait a minute*, a voice inside of her said. *You don't need this. You don't need this at all.*

None of this was making her feel good about herself. It was doing just the opposite. And hadn't that been the whole point of all of this?

If this was what it meant to be someone's "muse," she thought — to be yelled at, told to lose weight, criticized, and turned into someone unrecognizable — then she didn't want any part of it anymore.

As Dietrich glared at her, waiting for her to compose herself, Lizzie looked straight ahead of her and walked off the set. Past the camera, past the astonished assistants, past the silent crowd, past Martin Meloy, who seemed too flabbergasted to speak. She headed straight for the clothing rack. In full view of everyone watching, her hand reached around to her zipper and yanked it down. This time the rip didn't faze her. She would have gladly ripped the entire thing off her body if it could have gotten her out of here any quicker.

"Lizzie!" Annalise ran over to her. "What are you doing?"

Lizzie picked up her kilt and buttoned it. The scratchy wool poly–blend skirt had never felt better. She pulled her white turtleneck over her face, not caring whether her makeup smeared. It certainly couldn't have made her look any worse.

"Lizzie," Annalise snapped. "We're in the middle of a shoot here!"

"Then fire me," she said simply as she hoisted her bookbag to her shoulder and walked out of the room.

chapter 27

Out on the streets of SoHo, the sun had come out, and there were wide swatches of blue sky in between the clouds. People brushed past her in a hurry, pushing baby strollers, drinking coffee, still starting their day. Lizzie tipped her face up to the sky and took a grateful gulp of fresh air. Standing outside the studio, she felt like she'd broken out of prison after a life sentence. There was only one place that she wanted to go, only one place that could actually make her feel better now. As crazy as it was, that place was school.

On the 6 train, clattering uptown, she stared straight ahead at a cheesy ad for a dermatologist in Queens, willing her mind to stay blank. She'd try not to think about what had just happened until she saw her friends. They would know how to help her process this. But this time, she knew that she'd done something right.

When she reached school, it was just a few minutes before lunchtime. Before she went upstairs, though, she had to wash Martin's

Night of the Living Dead makeup off her face. She sprinted through the lobby before the receptionist could see her, and ducked into the ladies' bathroom. *Yikes,* she thought when she saw her reflection. Her black eyeliner had started to run, and there were deep purple creases above her eyes. She looked like she'd just crawled up out of a grave. No wonder people had been staring at her on the street.

She scrubbed her face with hand soap and dried it with some paper towels. There was nothing she could do about her crimped hair, but she would worry about that later. She tiptoed out and climbed the stairs, listening to the familiar echo of her steps on the limestone. The air smelled warm and inviting, like an old friend. Who knew that school could be so comforting?

She opened the door to the Upper School. The halls were still. Class would be over any minute. Like a thief, she crept down the hall toward the lockers. But the sound of heavy, creaking footsteps behind her made her stop.

"Miss Summers?"

She turned around. Mr. Barlow stood in front of her, taller and skinnier and scarier than she remembered. "You're here? I thought you had somewhere else to be today," he said in a voice that sent a shiver through her.

"Not anymore," she attempted.

"That's a shame," he said, folding his long arms. "Because you're suspended."

Lizzie swallowed. "Mr. Barlow —"

"We know whoever called the school this morning wasn't your parent. Those are the rules, Miss Summers. No unexplained absences. Not even for…" His eyes drifted to her bizarre-looking crimped hair. "Jobs."

"Okay, I had a photo shoot, for Martin Meloy," she stammered. "But I walked out of it. I'm not doing it anymore. I'm done with it."

He held up a hand. "And I'm going to have to give you an F for your mythology project."

"An F?"

"You didn't show up."

"I can make it up, though. I did the work. I can just do it later —"

Mr. Barlow shook his head firmly. "No."

An F. She had never gotten an F in her life. Especially in English.

"Come on, Mr. Barlow. You know that I'm a good student. I mean, you loved my story, right?"

He let out a low, disappointed whistle and hung his head. "Not as much as I thought I would," he said.

"Why?" she asked, starting to get panicked. "What happened?"

"When I gave it back to you, I said you just needed to cut some words," he said sternly. "Instead, you wrote an entirely new story. In the first version, the daughter was awkward. She felt inadequate around her mother. Now in this one she's beautiful. And the mother is trying to imitate her. It just didn't ring true to me. At all."

"But you said I could go in another direction."

Mr. Barlow shook his head. "Another direction isn't a totally new story. The first version felt riskier, more authentic. This one…" He shrugged. "It felt like a cop-out. Like you chickened out. It didn't feel like you, Lizzie." He sighed. "They announced the finalists today," he confessed. "Yours wasn't one of them."

Her head was starting to spin. Now her story was out of the competition? "But I can change it back...can you let me change it back?"

"It's too late, Lizzie. The deadline passed. But I'd like you to read the story that *was* picked to be the ninth-grade entry."

He gestured for her to follow him into his office, where he picked up a stapled printout from his desk. "It's Mr. Piedmont's."

Now she was sure someone up there was laughing at her. She took the story, feeling her scalp start to burn with shame.

"He wasn't afraid of being vulnerable," Mr. Barlow added.

"Thanks," she said, fighting back tears.

Mr. Barlow placed a warm, steadying hand on her shoulder, as if he could sense that she was overwhelmed. His kind blue eyes looked down on her, twinkling like marbles.

"I'm sorry, Lizzie. But I hope you learned something from all this. You're a talented girl. Too talented to have gotten this distracted. You could have gotten an A on that project, and you could have been a finalist for that contest. But you lost your way a little bit here."

The bell rang. She stared at the floor as her face burned. Doors opened, releasing voices and footsteps into the halls. This confrontation was coming to an end, thank God.

"Take care of yourself," he said. "And I'll see you on Wednesday."

Still keeping her head bowed, she turned on her heels and walked out. She had gotten an F. She was suspended. Even her writing had turned bad.

This had to be the worst day of her life. But underneath the sadness, she felt a glimmer of hope. Mr. Barlow cared about her. He knew who she was, even if she had temporarily forgotten. She was Lizzie the Writer. That was her real self. Now she just needed to get back to that.

"Lizzie! You're here!"

Lizzie turned around to see Hudson and Carina running toward her. Carina stopped short, agape at her hair. "Whoa. You look like something from *Saved by the Bell.*"

"What are you doing here?" Hudson exclaimed. "What happened to the shoot?"

Lizzie pulled them toward the stairs. "Can we go to the diner, you guys? I kind of need to get off school property. Like now."

"Why?" Carina asked.

"I just got suspended," she replied.

Hudson looked stricken. "You got what?"

"Come on, you guys, let's go," she said, heading to the stairs.

They hurried down the main staircase and walked to the diner. On the way there, Lizzie attempted to fill them all in on the shoot that morning.

"I'm sorry, but if anyone made *me* wear tons of purple eyeshadow, and crimped *my* hair, and then said I needed to go see a *nutritionist*, I'd punch them right in the mouth," Carina said as a waitress put a plate of fries in front of them.

"C," Hudson said.

"I'm serious," Carina said, popping a fry into her mouth. "I mean, I get that he has a *vision* but he's still a total douche."

"Tell me about it," Lizzie quipped.

"Bottom line is, you were supposed to be his *muse,*" Hudson said. "He picked you because of who you were. Not so he could *improve* you."

"Actually, that's not really why I walked out," she confessed, taking a large bite of her buttered bagel. "I mean, all of those things were kind of annoying, yes. But the real reason is that I overheard Martin talking about my mom."

Hudson and Carina stopped eating and looked up at her. "What'd he say?" Hudson asked, her eyes wide. Lizzie could tell that she was horrified for her.

"That she was old. Over the hill. Stuff like that." Lizzie pushed her cole slaw around with her fork.

"Ugh," Hudson said.

"I know. My mom tried to warn me, too. But I was so into it and so excited and I so wanted to believe them all, that I just didn't listen to her. I guess I just really wanted to feel pretty."

As close as they were, and as many times as she had joked about her looks, she had never admitted this to her friends. But Carina and Hudson watched her, without judgment, just listening, waiting for her to go on.

"And I did, working with Andrea," she went on. "And then it all just made me feel uglier. And if *my mom's* being talked about like that, then how can anyone feel good about themselves in that world? So I think it's time I go back to the old Lizzie. Old Chia Pet Lizzie. And just accept it."

Carina leaned her elbows on the table. "Lizbutt, you *are* pretty. You're *gorgeous*. And maybe this all happened so you could finally believe that. And just remember it the rest of your life and, you know, move on."

Lizzie grabbed a fry and dragged it through Carina's ketchup. "Deep thoughts with Carina Jurgensen," she said in a mock-serious voice.

But she knew that Carina was right. She had to move on. Maybe she'd never be totally at peace with her looks. Maybe she'd always wish she looked different. But she'd never again let *other* people decide who she was — ugly, different, awkward, stunning. All that mattered was what *she* thought of herself.

"Oh, I have news," Hudson said quietly. "I think I know who gave that tabloid my number." She pointed her fork past their heads. "Exhibit A in the corner."

Lizzie craned her head around and saw, ensconced in a booth in the corner, Hillary Crumple. In a chunky orange roll-neck sweater, and an even messier ponytail, she looked even more devious than usual. She was pretending to talk with her friends but darting creepy obsessed looks at them every few seconds.

"Oh my God, you're totally right," Carina said.

"Yep, I bet you she did it," Lizzie said.

"But how?" Hudson said, trying hard not to stare. "How would they get to her?"

"They can get to anyone," Carina said ruefully. "All I know is, you're no longer nice to her. Got it, Jones?"

"Loud and clear," Hudson said, plucking a fry off Carina's plate. "And maybe your revenge obsession isn't as weird as I thought it was."

"Oh, and I almost forgot to tell you guys," Lizzie remembered. "I'm getting an F for the project, too. I'm sure Todd'll be thrilled."

Carina and Hudson exchanged a wary glance.

"What?" Lizzie asked, spearing her pickle with her fork.

Carina and Hudson looked at each other again. Something was going on.

"Spill it," Lizzie said.

Carina folded her arms on the table. "Todd's dad was arrested. For stealing money from his company. Or something."

Lizzie put down her fork. "What?"

Hudson nodded soberly. "It happened this morning. Todd left school about an hour ago. He was pretty freaked out."

Lizzie looked out the window at a young mom trying to zip up a jacket on her toddler. The art on the walls, the penthouse apartment, Todd's books...the out-of-control spending. As much as she didn't want it to, it all made sense.

"Lizzie? You okay?" Hudson asked.

"Is he all right?"

Hudson shrugged. "He didn't say anything to anyone. He just left."

"Apparently it's all over the news," Carina added. "I never thought I'd say this, but poor Todd."

She thought of Todd alone in his apartment — no father, no mother. It wasn't even a question. "I gotta go, you guys," Lizzie said, getting up. "Sorry. I'll pay you back."

"You're going to see him *now*?" Hudson asked carefully.

"Lizzie," Carina said. "The guy was a jerk to you."

"Maybe," she said, throwing on her jacket. "But he's my friend. And I have a feeling I may have been wrong about him."

"Then go," Hudson said, smiling.

Lizzie hugged her friends quickly and raced to the door. Out on the street, she pulled out her phone and called him. It rang and rang and rang, before it finally reached voicemail.

"Hey, this is Todd. Leave a message and I'll get back to you—"

She hung up. Of course he wouldn't be picking up his phone. She had to go find him, wherever that might be.

A cab with its lights on was headed up Madison. She stuck out her hand and stepped as far into the street as she could without getting hit. The cab stopped right in front of her, and she got into the backseat and slammed the door.

"Where to?" asked the driver.

Todd probably wouldn't be home — who would be there with him? He wouldn't be with his dad, wherever the police were holding him. Who else did he have to go to in a crisis? Who else besides her?

His brother. That's where Todd had been coming from, that very first day she saw him. He went to NYU. Had he mentioned the dorm? All she could remember was the corner.

"Bleecker and Thompson," she said to the driver. "As fast as you humanly can."

The driver made a sharp left toward Fifth Avenue, sending Lizzie falling against the door. Beside her on the seat, her open bookbag fell over. An avalanche of papers, pens, tissues, and books spilled out, all over the seat.

She righted herself, clipped on her seat belt, and started to shove the mess of papers back into her bag. No matter how often she cleaned it out, there was always a mess of loose papers in there — they seemed to multiply somehow.

And then the title page of Todd's story caught her eye. She turned it right side up.

ACROSS THE POND

By Todd Piedmont

She turned the page. The first line leaped out at her.

He was ten years old and eating a red velvet cupcake the night he fell in love.

With a lump in her throat that she couldn't explain and tears in her eyes, Lizzie leaned back against the warm vinyl seat and read.

chapter 28

"Looks like this is as far as I can go."

Lizzie looked up from the last page of Todd's story. They were already on Bleecker Street and she hadn't even noticed. Through the cab's windshield, she could see a pair of orange and white cones blocking the rest of the street from traffic, as a few men in hard hats and fluorescent vests worked around an open manhole.

"I can let you out here," the driver went on.

"No problem." She paid the driver, thrust Todd's story into her bag, and got out of the cab. At least she was just a few blocks away from the dorms. She pulled out her phone and called the NYU Student Directory.

"Jack Piedmont," she said. "He's a freshman. I just need his address."

The woman on the other end of the line told her to wait, and then came back on the line. "Brittany Hall. 55 East Tenth Street."

Lizzie dropped her phone in her bag and picked up her pace. She slid past a knot of tourists, jumped over a dachshund tied to a lamppost, and almost ran into a speeding taxi as she crossed the street. She had no time to waste now. Now that she knew everything she needed to know.

Todd's story had been about her. It was about a boy named Austin, who was hopelessly in love with his childhood friend from New York, "across the pond," as the English called it. The night before his family moved from New York, he kissed her as they ate red velvet cupcakes. Then, living in London, he dreamed about her. He wrote imaginary letters to her. He rode shiny bright red double-decker buses and the London Tube, thinking about her, waiting for the day he might go back to America and see her again. A girl who was so pretty it made his chest ache. A girl with long wobbly legs like a newly born horse and hair like an explosion of copper. A girl he had known all of his life, but who he was sure only considered him a friend. And once he got back to America,[1] he realized that she still did. Especially when he finally tried to kiss her, and she bolted with a flimsy explanation, and he decided to give up.

Lizzie's heart pounded as she ran. All this time, all these weeks, he'd liked her. Even as he'd dated Ava. That night at his house, when he held her hand. The night at Ava's party, when she pretended she was happy for him.

But now she'd blown it. Now he thought she was a fool. It was too late.

Maybe it was too late. She just needed to find out.

Out of breath, she reached the blue awning of Brittany Hall on the corner of Washington Square and ran inside. In the dimly lit lobby the security guard sat behind a desk, watching her try to catch her breath.

"Hi," she panted. "I'm here to see Jack Piedmont. It's an emergency."

He pointed to a phone on the wall across from him. "Directory's on the wall."

She found his number and dialed. It rang until she got a voicemail. Deflated, she put the phone back on its cradle.

"Can you please tell him that Lizzie came by looking for Todd?" she asked the guard.

The guard matter-of-factly shook his head. "I don't give messages," he said.

Great, she thought, walking out.

Still out of breath, she walked into the park. Dried brown leaves crunched underfoot. Birds twittered overhead. The morning's clouds had returned, making the sky a too-bright-to-look-at white. Wind cooled the sweat at her hairline and under her neck. Her legs ached from the running. She needed water and a place to sit down.

She sat on a bench in between the dried-up fountain and the dog run and drew her knees to her chest. Todd would probably be home tonight, if she could wait until then. Or maybe she would just hang out in front of his brother's dorm until the late afternoon. Whatever happened, she wouldn't be able to go home until she saw or spoke to him. Her heart swelled. She loved him, and he was in trouble. She prayed that he wouldn't be moving back to London.

College students strolled by in groups, laughing and chatting, and across from her a street busker played "Fire and Rain" on his guitar. Two enormous Great Danes on leashes dragged their owner into the dog run. She leaned against the wooden slats of the bench and stared ahead of her, letting the New York afternoon unfold in front of her.

And then a miracle happened. At first she wasn't quite sure it was him. His hands were thrust into his pockets and his shoulders were hunched, and he'd changed out of the Chadwick black pants and tie into a T-shirt, black wool jacket, and jeans. But there was the plastic bag from Shakespeare & Co. hanging from his wrist, and the iPod earbuds stuck in his ears, and his eyebrows were knitted together in the same way they always were when he was lost in thought. It was Todd.

She yelled out his name. "Todd!"

He kept walking. He couldn't hear her.

She slid off the bench and ran toward him. "Todd!" she yelled again, just in case.

She almost had to tackle him before he finally saw her. She grabbed his arm, almost like a mugger, and he jumped, pulling out his earbuds. "Lizzie? Jesus!"

"How are you?" she asked breathlessly.

"What are you doing down here?"

"I...I heard about your dad," she stammered. "Is everything okay?"

He took a moment to fully take in her crimped hair and the leftover raccoon eyeliner around her eyes. "I feel like I should ask you that," he said warily.

"I'm fine. I just came from school. I've been trying to call you."

He frowned. "I thought you *weren't* in school today."

"I left the shoot. That guy Martin Meloy turned out to be huge jerk and a fake. I overheard him talking smack about my mom. Saying terrible things. And I realized that this..." She touched her hair. "That *all* of this just isn't me."

She wasn't sure, but there seemed to be the faintest hint of admiration in Todd's eyes.

"And then I went up to school, and I kind of got suspended," she added quickly.

"What?" Todd asked.

"And I got an F for the English project," she went on, rambling, "which I knew was kind of coming my way, too, but that's okay. The point is, I heard about your dad. And I thought you might be with your brother so I came down here."

Todd glanced down at the pavement. She hoped that she hadn't made him feel worse. "Yeah. I knew it was coming. That's why I wasn't in school for a couple days last week." He looked up, a skeptical squint in his eyes. "Is that really why you're down here? I thought that you hated my guts."

She took a deep breath. "I don't...hate your guts. Really. I don't."

He chuckled to himself. "You could have fooled me the other night."

She swallowed and took a step forward. "I'm sorry about that," she said. "I should never have believed that story about you and Ava."

"But you did," he said. He hung his head and toed the ground with his sneaker. "I thought we were friends."

"We are."

Todd shook his head. "Really? Some of the stuff you said..."

Lizzie felt a twinge in her heart. "Please. I'm sorry. I guess I was just angry to begin with."

"Angry?"

"That you were even dating her. I didn't understand."

He peered at her, waiting for her to explain.

"I mean, she just never seemed right for you."

He shrugged. "That's why I broke up with her. Because I could never feel about her the way —" Todd caught himself, and then he glanced at his watch. "Hey, I gotta go. I told my brother I'd meet him now. We'll talk later. Cool?" He turned and began to walk away.

"Todd," she called out. "Tell Austin I said hi."

He stopped. Slowly, he turned around. A quizzical smile lit up his face.

"And tell him that I love red velvet cupcakes," she went on, her voice wavery. "And that that day I fell into his arms on the street, it wasn't really an accident."

Todd didn't move.

She walked toward him, slowly, softly, afraid her legs might give out underneath her. "And tell him that I think that he's the most beautiful writer in the world." She stood so close to him now that she could reach out and touch him. "Tell him all that stuff. Okay?"

He looked at her as if he'd fallen under some kind of spell.

"I read your story. Mr. Barlow gave it to me."

She reached out and touched his arm. His jacket was smooth

and scratchy at the same time. "I loved it," she said. "I really, *really* loved it."

She searched his eyes, still holding on to his arm. Leaves scraped along the pavement in the wind but she barely noticed them. "This whole time I've wanted to be with you," she whispered.

"But you left me that night," he said. "You bolted." Todd didn't move. He didn't smile. He just looked at her.

"I was just scared," she murmured.

Suddenly Todd reached out and brushed a curl off her forehead. His hand rested on the back of her head. They were so close now that she could smell his familiar Downy and soap scent, just like that very first day, when she had fallen into his arms. Something was about to happen, she could feel it. He was about to kiss her. And this time, she was going to let him.

He leaned down. She closed her eyes. She felt the toes of her shoes touch the toes of his sneakers. His arm fell to her waist.

"You're still here," he whispered jokingly. And then his lips were on hers.

Everything else fell away — the wind, the guitar, the people walking by. He kissed her softly at first, then more deeply, until her legs turned into stretchy Gumby legs. She was glad his arms were holding her or else she might have collapsed to the ground.

Slowly, he let her go. He kept his arms around her as she looked into his face. "So I think we need to agree on one thing," he said, his lips curling into a smile. "Let's *not* write about this."

"Yeah, good idea," she said, nodding. "Mr. Barlow doesn't have to know *everything*."

He laughed, and then leaned into her once more. She melted back into his arms.

And as he pressed his lips on hers, she knew that what was happening now, right this moment, was more wonderful than anything she could make up in her head.

chapter 29

It was almost five o'clock when she fit the key into the front door and slipped quietly into her apartment. She stood in the empty foyer, listening. Inside the kitchen, she could hear CNN on the television and her dad humming to himself. They were home from Paris. And had, she was sure, heard the news about her.

She dropped her bookbag on the floor and pushed open the swinging door, and there was her dad, making a sandwich. "Well, hello, Fuzz," he said, calmly spreading mustard over a piece of bread. "You look like you just escaped a bad sci-fi movie."

"I kind of did," she muttered, hobbling over to a stool.

From the bags of cold cuts strewn on the black marble counter, he took out some salami and cheese slices, laid them on his bread, and then slapped the sandwich together. "So you've had quite a day," he said. "Got suspended *and* failed an assignment. In English, no less." He held up his sandwich as he pretended to salute her. "A two-fer. Not many fourteen-year-olds can say that."

"Dad, I'm sorry —"

"How could you be this irresponsible, Lizzie?" he said, cutting her off. "You are a *brilliant* student."

"Dad, I know. I'm sorry." She folded her arms on the counter and hung her head. "There's been a lot going on."

"It was a mistake to let you get started on this modeling thing," he said, taking a bite. "Your mother and I thought we could trust you. Obviously, we can't."

Lizzie stared at the black marble countertop. This was worse than having to talk to Mr. Barlow. "Well, it's over now."

"I know," he said, coming to stand opposite her. "We heard from Martin Meloy."

She had almost forgotten about Martin. Of course he would also be furious with her. She looked up, swallowing with trepidation. "You did?"

"He said you walked off the shoot," he said sternly. "That you wasted hundreds of thousands of dollars of their money. That you were difficult, unprofessional. That in twenty years, he had never had a model do that." His face suddenly lifted into a smile. "And I for one couldn't be more thrilled. Of course, I didn't come out and say that to him, your mother was the one on the phone with him —"

"She was?"

Bernard walked over to her and took her hands. "I know you're a level-headed girl. At least, most of the time. So I want to know what happened there. Did the photographer do something? Tell me, Fuzz. I'd like to have as much ammunition against him as possible. They had no business letting you be there without a chaperone, either. I'd like to wring that guy's neck —"

"Where *is* Mom?" she asked, before her father got too worked up.

Bernard paused. "She went down to see Natasha. Something's come up." He turned back to the cold cuts and started zipping up the plastic bags. "She's been dropped by L'Ete."

"What?" Lizzie almost jumped off her stool. "They *dropped* her?"

Bernard nodded. "That was why they wanted her to fly back. They wanted to do it in person."

"But why? Why would they do that?"

"They wanted to go with somebody younger," he said casually, putting the food back in the fridge. "Some nineteen-year-old Brazilian model." He closed the refrigerator door and stared out the window at the city skyline. "It's a cruel business," he finally said.

"Is she okay?" Lizzie finally asked.

"She will be. But she knew this would happen eventually. That's why she started her line." He let out a bitter chuckle. "Anyway, I think this is what she was trying to protect you from. You need a thick skin to do what she does. Sometimes I don't think we give her enough credit."

Lizzie nodded. She was sure now that she didn't.

"So what happened this morning?" he asked, more firmly this time.

Lizzie bit her lip. She hadn't been hurt by what had happened, not directly, at least. But having to explain it now, in light of her dad's news, made her queasy.

"I just realized that Mom was right," she said. "I'm not ready for it. It's not who I am. And the sooner I got out of there, the better." She hopped off the stool. "Where is she right this second?"

"Oh no, no, no," her dad said. "You can go straight to your room. You're going to be grounded a very long time."

"I want to tell her I'm sorry. And, well, I could use a hug."

Bernard glanced at the clock on the microwave. "She said that she'd be stopping at a cocktail party for *Vogue*. She's probably just getting there."

"Where?"

Bernard gave a defeated sigh. "I'll call Natasha," he said.

Lizzie went to her room and changed out of her uniform into a turtleneck sweater and jeans. It wasn't the most *Vogue*-friendly outfit, but it had been the closest thing within reach. It was comfortable. And most importantly, it was her.

Before she walked out, there was one more thing that she needed to do. She went over to her desk and woke up her Mac. In the folder labeled STORIES on her desktop, she went down the list of titles until she found her original short story for the contest. She clicked on it. As soon as the first, familiar page came up on the screen, she knew she should have stuck with it from the beginning. She'd told herself that she was making the story better. Instead she'd just been afraid to expose her insecurities. And all she'd gotten for that was a big fat lost opportunity.

She left the story open on her screen. She'd work on it when she came home. And when it was done, maybe she could give Todd some serious competition for next year's contest.

She took connecting subways down to the East Village and emerged onto the Bowery forty minutes later. When Lizzie had first been born, this street had been lined with seedy tenements and drug dealers — now it was lined with trendy bars and boutique hotels. Lizzie crossed the streets toward the tall, squat concrete hotel building. A red carpet had been laid in front for the paparazzi. The few photographers still hanging around outside chatted with themselves as she walked past. Nobody recognized her. Lizzie smiled to herself. She felt like herself again.

She climbed the stairs in her banged-up Steve Madden boots and thought about her mom. The whole way downtown, she'd tried to think of what to say to her. How did it feel to be fired from a job, not because you didn't do it well, but because you didn't look as good anymore?

She reached the top step and assessed the thick crowd. It only took a second until Natasha spotted her and came marching over. "Lizzie," she said, flicking her bangs out of her sooty eyes. "I told your father that Katia's busy."

"I need to see my mom. Is she here?"

Natasha eyed her plain black turtleneck, dirty jeans, and beaten-up boots. "I'm not sure this is an appropriate venue for someone underage," she said in a clipped voice.

"Just tell me where she is," Lizzie persisted.

Natasha drew her tiny body up and relented. "Just stay away from the bar," she sniped. Apparently word had gotten out that she was some kind of rebel now. She almost laughed out loud as she followed Natasha into the crowd.

They passed stick-thin women with perfect shiny hair and bare, knobby shoulders drinking flutes of champagne. Lizzie caught some people staring at her, and heard some fervent whispering, but nobody stopped her or said anything. She wondered if everyone at the party had heard what she had done to Martin Meloy. If they hadn't yet, she was sure they would.

"There she is." Natasha pointed.

Katia stood at the far end of the room, flanked by the *Vogue* creative director and a designer known more for her celebrity bridal clientele than for her designs. She was smiling, and held a nearly full glass of champagne in her hand, but even from here Lizzie could see that her eyes were their sad color — a washed-out gray. She might have looked happy, but Katia was drowning inside.

"I think you should let her have a few minutes. She's got some important business to discuss —" Natasha began.

"No, I need to talk to her now," Lizzie said, and barged on ahead.

"Lizzie!" she heard Natasha exclaim, but she didn't stop. Natasha's advice wasn't that useful anymore.

As she neared her mother in the crowd, she still didn't have an opening line. *Mom, I heard the news? I'm sorry you got sacked?* And what if her mom wasn't happy to see her, considering everything that had happened today?

But she was Katia's daughter. Her mother loved her. No matter what Lizzie did wrong or how many times she got suspended, or how often they fought, her mother would love her, always. And today, this morning, she had learned in the stickiest way possible that she loved her mother right back. It was why she was here, after all, wading through a sea of anorexic fashionistas, trying to rescue her.

Katia didn't see her until Lizzie stood behind her. "Mom?" she asked, sidling up to her as close as she could.

Katia looked over her shoulder. In that split second, her face said everything: surprise, affection, relief. "Lizzie!" she sputtered. "What are you doing here?"

"Dad told me what happened," she whispered. "Are you okay?"

The other two women gave her hostile stares but she ignored them. She had had enough of caring what fashion people thought.

"Lizzie," Katia said, still astonished. "I'm fine."

Before she knew what she was doing, Lizzie threw her arms around her mom's neck. "I can't believe they did that," she whispered. "I hate them. I really hate them. I'm so sorry, Mom."

Hesitantly, Katia hugged her back. "Excuse me," she said to the editor and the designer. "I think we need a moment." Lizzie heard them retreat into the crowd.

"Lizzie, come with me," she said, taking her by the hand. She led her toward the back of the room, and when they reached a quiet corner, Katia turned her back to the party and faced Lizzie. "You're supposed to be grounded," she said sternly. "Didn't your father speak to you?"

"He told me what happened in Paris. With L'Ete. So I wanted to come down and make sure you were all right."

Katia put her hands on her hips, unwilling to be placated just yet. "We heard what happened today, Lizzie. At school. And at the shoot. What got into you? I thought we could trust you."

"Mom, I'm done. I'm done with the modeling stuff. You were right. It wasn't for me. And I know I didn't listen to you. But I learned. I learned in a way that I never would have if I hadn't lied and snuck around." She wondered if she had just undermined her own argument. "Does that make sense?"

"I just don't know how to get through to you anymore, Lizzie," her mom said. "For a little while there, I felt like we understood each other. And then, everything just fell apart." Katia's eyes were shiny. "Don't you know that I would never keep you from success? That I would never keep you from figuring out who you are?" She took Lizzie's hand and looked at her warmly. "I just know that you have so much that I didn't. Creative talent. Parents and teachers who love you. A good home. A good school. I didn't have any of those things. I had my looks. And they've given me a lot. But you have so much more than I did. And what you have, Lizzie, will take you as far as you want, for as long as you want."

Her mother still clung to her hand, squeezing it with every other word. Lizzie felt one hot tear start to make its way down her cheek.

"But weren't you proud of me?" she asked, swallowing a sob. "I mean, just a little?"

"Of course I was. But I was proud of you *before*. That's why I always wanted you to pose with me. That's why I always wanted you to come with me to things. Because I have always thought that you were a star. Always."

Lizzie felt another tear take the plunge down her cheek, and she wiped them away. She squeezed her mom's hand right back. "I'm proud of you, too, Mom," she said softly, starting to cry. "I know I don't show it a lot, but I am."

Katia wiped at the edge of her eye. "I love you, honey." She leaned down and hugged her tightly.

They stood like that for a moment. "Do you want to tell me what happened with Martin this morning?" she asked.

271

Lizzie paused. "I'll just say that you were right. Everyone there were jerks. He's way too fake for me."

She felt her mother nod as they hugged. Maybe Katia suspected the truth. Maybe she didn't. But Lizzie knew that she would never, ever repeat what she had heard, for as long as she lived.

"Well, I know there's someone else who isn't fake, and who's dying to work with you." Katia let her go and Lizzie could see that she was smiling. "Andrea called me last week about the Gagosian Gallery show. I think you should do it."

"You do?"

Katia ran her hand over Lizzie's hair. "She sees you for who you are. She's not going to take advantage of you. And I think she's been a good friend to you. And being a good friend back is just as important as staying true to yourself."

"Excuse me, but can we get a picture?"

In front of them, barely five feet away, stood a photographer holding his camera.

"Of course," Lizzie said.

"Oh honey, I don't know, my makeup is smearing," Katia said, dabbing at the edges of her eyes with the side of her hand.

Lizzie brushed away a tear from her mom's face. "You look beautiful, Mom."

Katia seemed surprised. "Really?"

"Yeah, you do."

Katia touched her cheek and then gave one of her dazzling supermodel smiles. She turned to the photographer. "All right then," she said, putting her arm around Lizzie's waist. "Here we go."

Lizzie leaned her head in ever so slightly. The photographer readied his camera.

"The Summers women," he said, clicking the shutter over and over. The flash was blinding, but Lizzie kept her eyes open.

"Thank you," Katia said gently, after four or five more clicks. "Thank you."

The photographer scurried off, and Lizzie reached for her phone in the back pocket of her jeans.

"I think we should probably say our goodbyes and head home now," Katia said.

"Wait one sec, Mom," Lizzie said as she opened her phone. "I'm going to text Andrea." She wrote out one word in her message. *YES*. And then sent it.

Just as a text from Carina came in. Lizzie opened it.

OMG! Come to my house ASAP!!!!

Lizzie read the text several more times. She thought of calling her back but Katia said, "Okay, honey. Let's go."

Lizzie slid her finger across the screen and tucked it back into her pocket. "Actually, is there any way I can stop at Carina's house on the way home?" she asked. "Just for a few minutes?"

Katia arched a brow and folded her arms. "Half an hour. That's all. And then you're home until further notice. And I'll be keeping time."

"No problem."

"So let's go, Lizzie." Katia stuck out her hand, and Lizzie took it.

And as the crowd watched them walk by, Lizzie was absolutely sure that she had never felt so beautiful in her life.

When Lizzie got out of the cab, she could already see Hudson pacing around inside the lobby of Carina's building. She walked toward her as Lizzie pushed her way through the revolving door.

"What's going on, H? Is there a problem?"

Hudson grabbed Lizzie's arm. Her sea foam–colored eyes were streaked with red from crying.

"She's gone, Lizzie. The doorman said the Jurg and her left twenty minutes ago."

"What?" Lizzie's voice echoed in the cold, marble-floored lobby. "That's insane. I just heard from her. *You* just heard from her. She told us to come over."

"She just left. He said they had a lot of bags. And that she was going on a 'trip.'"

"But it's a school night."

Hudson shook her head and squeezed Lizzie's arm tighter. "You don't get it. She leaked that stuff about her dad stealing money from the charities. It's online. And her dad threw a fit."

Lizzie finally grasped the full meaning of what Hudson was saying. She looked out into the night, at the cars and cabs racing down Fifth Avenue. They had just missed her.

"Where do you think he took her?"

Hudson shrugged. "Who knows? It could be anywhere. The man has a plane."

Lizzie whipped out her phone and dialed Carina's cell.

"I've already tried it," Hudson said.

Carina's voicemail started to play in Lizzie's ear. *"Hi, you've reached Carina. I'm probably surfing right now so leave a message —"*

Lizzie clicked it shut. She looked at Hudson, who seemed to be on the verge of another cry. If Carina were here, she would know what to do. But now Carina was gone, and someone had to be in charge.

"Well, we can't just stand here all night, can we? Let's get out of here."

Lizzie tugged Hudson toward the door. "Where are we going?" Hudson asked, as Lizzie raised her arm to hail a taxi.

"To find our best friend," Lizzie said as a cab pulled up in front of them.

acknowledgments

This book would never have been written without Ido Ostrowsky, who convinced me over dinner one night — loudly — that there was a series in Lizzie, Carina and Hudson. If it hadn't been for his overwhelming enthusiasm and support, the Daughters may have never made it on to the page. I also thank my agent, the fearless and talented Becka Oliver. She believed in this series from the very beginning and has taken it further than I ever expected it might go. I'm infinitely grateful for her feedback, her tenacity, and most of all, her sense of humor.

Enormous thanks go to the great Cindy Eagan and her team at Poppy. I'm still in shock that I get to write for her. I'm completely indebted to my editors, Kate Sullivan and Elizabeth Bewley, who gave me brilliant notes and suggestions, and made Lizzie's story the best it could possibly be.

My sister, JJ Philbin, read my drafts and gave me valuable and timely feedback. My friend Jill Cargerman read early pages and encouraged me to keep going. Nick Steele and Robert Castillo gave me priceless inside info about Fashion Week and music production, respectively. Rob Pearlstein and the rest of the gang in the Writers Guild lounge kept me sane through the long hours of writing.

Most of all I'd like to thank Jonny Kurzman, for sitting next to me on that plane and turning it all around. Thank you, thank you, thank you.

The sole heir to Metronome Media and the only daughter of billionaire Karl Jurgensen, spunky Carina Jurgensen has always liked to take risks.

But can fellow Daughters Lizzie Summers and Hudson Jones help their lifelong friend even after she's pulled a completely outrageous stunt?

Find out what happens next in

the daughters break the rules

JOANNA PHILBIN

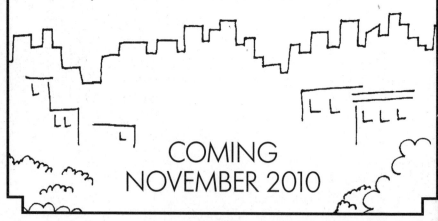

COMING NOVEMBER 2010

Welcome to Poppy.

A poppy is a beautiful blooming red flower
(like the one on the spine of this book). It is also
the name of the home of your favorite books.

Poppy takes the real world and makes it
a little funnier, a little more fabulous.

Poppy novels are wild, witty, and inspiring.
They were written just for you.

So sit back, get comfy, and pick a Poppy.

poppy

www.pickapoppy.com

gossip girl   THE CLIQUE   the daughters

ALPHAS   the it girl   POSEUR

THE A-LIST
HOLLYWOOD ROYALTY   secrets OF MY HOLLYWOOD LIFE